AND HELL FOLLOWED

DEATH'S HEAD PRESS

ISBN: 9781794239326

0000-666-0000
EY0-28OO-I8OO-697

www.deathsheadpress.com

Cover art by Don Noble

Stories compiled by Jarod Barbee and Patrick C. Harrison III

Special thanks to Kitten, Petal, Becky, and Mar

The stories in this volume are works of fiction.
For your sake and the sake of those you love,
pray it stays that way.

CONTENTS

.

And I looked, and behold a pale horse: and his name that sat on him was Death, and Hell followed with him.

Revelation 6:8
King James Version

Wild, dark times are rumbling towards us, and the prophet who wishes to write a new apocalypse will have to invent entirely new beasts, and beasts so terrible that the ancient animal symbols of St. John will seem like cooing doves and cupids in comparison.

Heinrich Heine
"Lutetia; or, Paris", Augsberg Gazette, 1842

"Lord, what fools these mortals be!"

William Shakespeare
A Midsummer Night's Dream

INTRODUCTION

Horror Authors of the Apocalypse

The Book of Revelation tells the story of the Apocalypse, the Christian God's final judgment upon mankind. For believers, this terrifying tale is as much a warning to stay free of sin, and remain loyal to God, as it is a promise of their welcome to paradise and eternal reward. For atheists like me, it is just a good horror story.

Revelation details exactly how God's imperfect creations will be punished, down to the precise number of people who will be saved (144,000) and how those deemed unworthy of paradise will be tortured and destroyed and by what. From this chapter in the Bible comes some of the most iconic imagery in horror literature, and Western culture in general. The Grim Reaper, harvesting souls with a scythe. The mark of the beast, 666. The Four Horseman of the Apocalypse. Satan taking his place in hell as mankind's accuser and punisher. Leviathan, the great dragon that will rise from the sea to wreak havoc and destruction. And many more terrible creatures that have become as familiar to us as our own friends and family.

Populated with angels, demons, dragons, devils, and talking animals, the Book of Revelation is fantasy world-building at its finest. As fantastic as anything Tolkien, George R.R. Martin, or even Clive Barker ever imagined. It is a disaster story, action adventure, and horror yarn, filled with swords and sorcery. There are six-headed dragons, sword-wielding archangels on horseback, demons, Death as an incarnate conscious being, plagues, natural disasters, and bloody wars. All are fertile soil for a good horror story. How could any writer resist playing with such rich mythology?

From classic horror movies like *The Omen* and *The Seventh Seal* to novels like *The Monk* by William H. Hallahan, and comic books like Neil Gaiman's *Sandman*, to sitcoms, and even romance novels, the Book of Revelation has left an indelible mark upon our culture, even on us non-believers. My collaboration with Maurice Broaddus, *Orgy of Souls*, featured Leviathan, tearing apart a city as it chased our two protagonists.

The sixteen stories included in this anthology take the world detailed in Revelation and warps it even further to create gruesome, and sometimes humorous, tales of madness and mayhem. Very few blasphemies were left un-blasphemed.

So, say your prayers (if that does it for you). Hold on to your bibles. Make peace with your maker (or Darwin, or Richard Dawkins). Prepare yourself to be horrified and amused. Now that you've cracked opened this anthology, hell follows.

Wrath James White
12/7/2018
Somewhere in Texas

THE WHORE OF BABYLON

Sam West

And then came one of the seven angels who had the seven vials, and talked with me, saying unto me, Come hither, I shew unto thee the judgement of the great whore that sitteth upon many waters.

–Revelation, 17:1 (King James Version)

"It will happen tonight."

The woman who had appeared next to him at the bar was a knockout. John Christian blinked, for a second there convinced that he was hallucinating. Women that looked like *her* never approached guys that looked like *him*. Upon deciding that she was, in fact, real, he looked over his shoulder to make sure that she wasn't talking to someone else. Then he decided that she must have recognised him from an author photo on the back of one of his bestselling zombie novels, which made her either a gold-digging slag or a wannabee writer.

"What's going to happen tonight?" he shouted above the dance track, daring to hope that she could be talking about shagging him.

"All will be revealed soon."

She giggled, swishing her waist-length blonde mane from one shoulder to the other. It shone in the strobe lighting, momentarily dazzling him. His gaze wandered down to her ample chest which strained against the tight fabric of her purple minidress, the neckline of which was adorned with big, garish, golden stones. In her hand she held a long-stemmed, golden goblet. John eyed it with curiosity.

"That's a strange glass. They give you that behind the bar?"

"No. It is my own."

He wrenched his gaze back up to her eyes. They were the palest blue, glittering like precious jewels in her tanned face.

"Oh. Okay," was all he could say, finding himself utterly stupefied by her beauty.

Once again, his gaze drifted helplessly down to those impossibly pert—and blatantly braless—tits, mesmerized by the firm jut of her nipples straining against the flimsy fabric. His gaze travelled lower, sweeping past the miniscule waist and all the way down the endless, tanned legs. Her purple minidress glowed in the ultraviolet light, making her seem even more otherworldly in her beauty.

"Are you an angel?" he slurred.

Okay, so he was pissed out of his tiny mind, but he felt sure that sobriety would in no way diminish her beauty.

"Yes, in a manner of speaking. I am the Whore of Babylon. And I have a message for you."

John laughed at that. So she was a funny one, and funny usually meant clever, which firmly put her in the camp of wannabe writer rather than gold-digging slag.

"The Whore of Babylon, huh? Interesting. And this is a message from God, I presume?"

She giggled girlishly—a sound he felt deep in his balls.

"Right again, *John*."

Unease permeated through the drunken fog of lust.

How the hell did she know my name?

And then he let out a shaky laugh—honestly, sometimes he could be such a *dick*. It was because she knew *who he was*, of course. And, more than likely, she thought that a five-minute conversation with him would somehow magically make him say; *dear fucking God, you are such an amazing talent, I will get onto my publisher first thing in the morning and hook you guys up so that you may sign your three-book deal immediately…*

Yet there was no denying the fact she was still a fucking knockout, and that alone was enough for him to put up with her pathetic flights of literary fancy. Especially if she thought that a blowjob might be her ticket to literary stardom.

"So, pray tell, what is this message from God?"

"Well, *John*, the apocalypse is nigh. The righteous shall ascend into the Kingdom of Heaven, and the wicked shall be tortured on Earth for all eternity. Hell is empty, and all the devils are here. *Armageddon*, John."

He frowned, that sense of unease clawing at the back of his skull. Was she taking the piss? Or did he have an actual, bone fide religious nut on his hands? He frowned. Curious and curiouser.

"And what is *the Whore of Babylon* doing in a sleazy nightclub in Broadgate? For a start, I hear the nightlife is better in Blackpool."

She didn't so much as crack a smile when she replied. "Because Broadgate is built on leylines, leylines which connect sites of ancient evil. The chasm here is wide. It is the first place the rift will occur."

Leylines? Chasms? Rifts? What was this? Fucking Ghostbusters?

"Uh huh, that's nice. And why would God wish to tell little old me about the impending apocalypse?"

"Because you are the chosen one. Because your seven novels are based on your seven visions of the end of time. Seven is the perfect number of our Divine Lord and you have served your purpose. You have shared the Lord's word with the world and you need never write another word again."

Okay, this was all getting a bit fucking much now. Yet still. The strangest feeling curdled in his guts. How the fuck did she know that each of his apocalyptic, zombie-themed novels were based on a spate of particularly gruesome—and utterly terrifying—nightmares? And that, when he had completed the seventh novel a few months back, writers' block had hit him hard?

She doesn't know about my writers' block. How could she?

Pushing aside the niggling doubts, he conceded that he had been wrong about this one, that he was dealing with some nutjob Jehovah's Witness rather than a wannabe writer.

"I'm an atheist, love."

"Yes. And a mildly-talented one at that. Of course, there are others out there with far more talent than you, but they aren't as *susceptible* as you. Your mind is as open as a funnel, ripe for God's messages to be poured into it."

Was the bitch insulting him now? His already-fragile mind decided that *yes*, she was.

"If you're the Whore of Babylon, why don't you prove it?"

"Oh, I will, in due course."

She stepped towards him, reaching out to gently rest the flat of her palm against his chest, at the same time placing her weird, golden goblet on the bar.

His heart instantly started to hammer at her touch, pumping the blood violently around his veins where it inevitably culminated in his cock. Despite his drunkenness, he felt himself harden.

In her heels, she was maybe an inch taller than him and ordinarily, if he weren't so drunk, he might've been intimidated by this fact. As it was, it only served to make her more attractive. She was a fantasy come to life, a supermodel or a movie star who had leapt straight out of his imagination and into this seedy nightclub in Broadgate.

He stared down at the slender, long-fingered hand with the bright red talons resting on his chest. Subconsciously, he flexed his pecs—not that he had anything to flex, but the instinctive reaction was as old as time itself. All too clearly, he could imagine what that hand would feel like cupping his stiff cock through his jeans and his head swam with beer and the lack of blood circulating in his brain.

"I can read your mind," she said with a sexy little smile that made his balls ache.

"Oh yeah?" he said, leering up at her.

"Yes, John, I can. I know what you're thinking. You're wondering what it would feel like if I did *this*." She cupped his stiff dick through his jeans, and he sucked in a sharp intake of breath. "And I know why you came out tonight. I know that

4

your wife left your sorry arse a month ago because of your alcohol problem and roaming eye, and that you're here tonight, all alone, desperately hoping to get laid. A sad, forty-eight-year-old alcoholic, out chasing women half his age, pathetically looking for that elusive connection with women young enough to be his daughters. You have used prostitutes in the past, but you really are just looking for that special someone, aren't you? It's really quite sad."

John was taken aback, and for a moment could think of nothing to say in reply. Partly because her hand was rubbing his crotch, and partly because she was totally on the fucking money. Her hand lifted from his cock, and with it his capacity for rational thought—albeit slightly alcohol-fogged—returned.

"Who *are* you?" he asked, the worst feeling tightening in his guts.

"I told you. I am the Whore of Babylon. Technically, I work for the Devil, but God has asked me to do his bidding. It's complicated, you see. A mortal mind could never grasp the complexities of it. Minds much brighter than yours have grappled with this for many centuries, and not one of them are still any closer to understanding it. Let me tell you something about good and evil, John, it is not as cut and dry as you might think, it is beyond *ambiguous*. It is a *war*, John, a war without end. It has always been raging and will continue to do so for all eternity. And the time of reckoning is upon us. It is time to *pick a side*. As you have fulfilled God's message to you, you can repent your sins, right here, right now. If you do so, you will be granted a place with the righteous to the Kingdom of Heaven. All you have to do is repent and *believe*."

John looked at her incredulously. "Surely you're not serious?"

"Deadly. Repent and believe. Ascend to a higher state of being or give me your *earthly* pleasures."

As she spoke, her hand curled around his still-stiff cock through his jeans. He groaned when she closed the gap between them and pressed her mouth to his. Her tongue pushed past his lips, making his brain swim with pleasure. Those big, firm tits pressed against his chest and he almost lost his shit

5

completely when she unzipped his jeans. Her fingers snaked inside his boxers where they curled around his stiff shaft.

"Fuck," he grunted when she squeezed him. "Fuck," he grunted when her hand expertly milked the orgasm from him in a matter of seconds.

Intense pleasure held him in its helpless grip, his hot semen spurting in hard jets. Only when he had finished coming did he look down at himself in shame, quickly shoving his rapidly deflating cock back into his jeans and zipping himself up again.

What the fuck just happened?

"Cheers," the woman said bringing the golden goblet to her lips. "Mmm, delicious—a wonderful thing to be drunk on the abomination and filthiness of fornication."

And then it hit him that she was to drink his still-warm semen.

"What the fuck?" he said, genuinely at a loss as he watched her chug it down.

She smiled at him, her lips coated with the stickiness of his ejaculate, and placed the goblet on the bar.

"And now it is time. You had your chance, and this is for you."

In her hand she held some kind of jar, which was the size of a small urn. He blinked. She hadn't been holding that before, and she had no bag over her shoulder… Where the fuck had it come from?

"What the fuck is *that*?" he spat.

It looked like a clumsily-thrown, untreated clay pot, complete with a plain lid. He clung to the irritation, not wanting to admit that he was secretly *scared*.

"It is the first of the seven vials that will unleash the wrath of God. The first is for the earth, the second for the sea, the third the fountains of water, the fourth the sun, the fifth the darkness, the sixth the river and the seventh, the lightning, thunder and the final earthquake that will decimate the Earth. When the trumpet sounds, it will begin."

He looked at her blankly.

"Huh?"

She smiled and placed the pot on the bar as the ominous monotone of a blaring trumpet suddenly filled the nightclub.

6

At first, John thought it was part of the dance track, but that illusion did not last long because it was way too loud. His hands flew up to protect his ears, wincing at the creepy sound.

"Where the fuck is that coming from?" he asked, but his voice was drowned out by the blaring, fog-horning of the trumpet.

After a few seconds, it stopped as if it had never been and he lowered his hands from his ears, looking around himself in dismay. Just a few seconds before, the packed-out club had been full of motion, but now everyone in the club was standing stock-still. The music was still blaring but the clubbers stood there unmoving, as if they had been hypnotised.

The sight of the small dancefloor which ran the length of the entire back wall just a few metres from where he stood at the bar was the most disconcerting, with the way the clubbers were perfectly still, standing shoulder to shoulder.

They look like zombies.

Imagery from his own books slammed into mind. Because he'd had a nightmare just like this, which had taken place in a nightclub, which had ultimately become the inspiration for his first book. In this nightmare, an invisible, unexplained force had befallen the Earth, striking the bulk of people dead, before they rose again as flesh-eating zombies. And in his nightmare, the people across the world had stood still just like this, before dropping to the ground, stone-cold dead.

And now it's happening for real…

"It is time, John," the woman said.

The Whore of Babylon said.

Smiling, she picked up the earthenware pot and lifted the lid.

A black cloud swirled from it, like the smoke of a bonfire, except thicker and impossibly dark. On and on the impossible smoke continued to pour from the pot; smoke which, by rights, should never even exist, yet alone in such *quantity*.

It quickly filled the air, and with it came an indescribable stink that made John gag. It was part rotten eggs, part over-filling binbags that had been left to spoil in the sun and part excrement.

It was the stench of death. John instinctively knew this on the basest of levels, and the smell alone was enough to curdle his thoughts to the point of madness.

And John wasn't even *in* the smoke. It completely filled the vast, high-ceilinged room, except for the small space at the bar in which he and the Whore of Babylon stood. All the while this happened the dance music continued to play, pumping out a frantic beat that matched the rhythm of his strained heart.

The Whore of Babylon calmly replaced the lid on the pot and slowly, the smoke began to clear, revealing the devastation that it had wrought.

Every last party-reveler was lying unmoving on the floor.

She came up to him in their perfectly clear, smoke-free zone and placed her hand on his chest. He cringed away from her, pushing his back up against the bar but there was nowhere to go, not unless he entered the zone of the rapidly-clearing, black smoke.

He was too scared to enter that smoke. He was too scared to end up like the clubbers on the ground.

"The trumpet will sound, and the dead will be raised imperishable, and we will be changed," she said in his ear. "Any moment now, they will awake to disgrace and everlasting contempt."

It was a good job for the bar at his back, because otherwise he felt sure that his legs would've crumpled. Especially when she drew herself up to her full height and *screamed* into his face; so loudly that he felt his bowels loosen:

"*And the first went and poured out her vial upon the earth; and there fell a noisome and grievous sore upon the men which had the mark of the beast, and upon them which worshipped his image.*"

Slowly, he began to realise that there was something wrong with her—she wasn't just standing straight, she was noticeably taller. And her mouth was *wrong*. It was too big for her face.

And *goddam* if her eyes weren't glowing red. He whimpered in terror, his vision swimming in unadulterated shock. Movement behind her caught his eye, and a hot wetness soaked the crotch of his jeans and inner thighs. Dimly, he was aware that he had pissed himself, but he was passed caring about such trivialities.

Because the people in the nightclub were shuffling towards him. And dear fucking God, they weren't right at all. They shuffled towards them, like fucking zombies straight out of a George A. Romero film…

Or straight out of his nightmares and books. As they drew closer, he saw the boils, ulcers, and weeping sores on every inch of their exposed skin. Their eyes were blank pits of despair and pain. And something else which he recognised on an instinctive level in their sorry depths: *hunger*.

The terrifying woman stepped through the approaching crowd which parted for her like the proverbial sea of biblical yore. Instantly, her too-tall figure was swallowed by the people and the tendrils of remaining black smoke. But he wasn't thinking about her anymore; he was far more concerned with the walking dead closing in around him.

Suddenly, arms wrapped around his neck from behind, snapping him violently backwards. The edge of the bar dug into his lower back, sending sparks of shooting agony through his body. The barman had him in a headlock and before he knew it, the others were upon him.

The first bite was taken out of the side of his neck by a pretty, petite brunette in a white minidress who he had noticed when he had first entered the club a few hours ago.

The pain of being bitten was extraordinary. It flared in his neck like he had been thumped there, or electrocuted, spreading like wildfire through his torso and arms.

And then the rest of them fell upon him. Ulcerated hands pawed his body. Teeth sunk into his soft skin. He bellowed in protest until teeth clamped over his jugular and *ripped* into him, severing his screams.

The pulsing beat of the dance music faded into the background, in time with his rapidly dimming vision. His entire being was awash with pain; it consumed him, pinning him helplessly in place and washing his mind clean of thought. All that burned there now was agony.

As his very life seeped away from him, he feebly lifted his head one final time. And for a split second, the heads with the snapping mouths that feasted upon him parted, and he saw his Whore of Babylon on the dancefloor. She sat atop a scarlet beast with many heads—a beast that reared up on its muscular hindlegs, pulled back its many heads, and *roared* as more trumpets blasted out.

BEHIND BLUE EYES

Chris Miller

No one knows what it's like, he thought, remembering bittersweetly her words to him, *to be the sad man.*

His eyes stung with tears as he pressed the back of his hand against his mouth. Hitching sobs escaped between every breath.

Will it always be this way? he wondered, his angst dragging him downward into an abyss of sorrow and torment. *Will the pain ever stop?*

He thought not. He didn't believe it would ever stop. Dull, perhaps, with time, but stop? No. He would carry the weight of this with him for the remainder of his days. A chunk of his heart had been ripped out, torn from his chest by a monstrous beast without care or pity. But the real hell of it was the fact it had left him with just enough of his heart to keep on beating, carrying him forward into this life, now alone, damned to keep living, even as he stood over the plot of ground where the one who had *been* his life would forever rest.

"Oh, God!" he gasped and leaned over, placing his hand atop the gravestone. He fell to his knees on the dirt, still fresh and mounded high from two days prior when it had been poured over her casket as he had stood there, watching and weeping.

All the others had gone already, several making futile attempts to get him to come along. Have something to eat. Be with friends and family who loved him. But he had denied them all with little more than a shake of his head and a dismissive wave of his arm. How could he leave her? How

11

could he walk away from his heart and soul, his life, his love, his *everything*?

It had taken the caretaker and a very empathetic cop to get him to go home that night, well after the sun had gone hell bound and the moon had resurrected the night. He'd long since quit weeping, and his face was bone white in the pale shine of the moon.

"I'll go, now," he had said. "I'm sorry."

He looked up once more to the gravestone and read the inscription, still with a sense of disbelief and horror that it was real, right here, right before his eyes.

Rachel Fletcher

How could she be gone? How could she have left him here, alone and scared? How would he ever find the strength to go on with life when his very purpose for living was six feet beneath where he knelt?

Are you the sad man, Jack? she would ask after reciting the lyrics to their special song to him. *Are you the bad man?*

"I don't even have blue eyes, baby," Jack had said to her on countless occasions such as this, wearing thin this old script. "But how could I ever be sad when I have you?"

They had laughed and embraced, their foreheads touching as they gazed into each other's eyes. His were green, however, despite her playful recital of the song, it was *hers* which were blue. A deep, oceanic blue, so crystalline that you might think you could dive right into them and forever swim there in a sea of bliss.

Behind blue eyes.

"And you make me want to be better," he had said, their faces closing in, their lips almost brushing against one another, and he finished with a whisper. "So I could never be the bad man."

He fell back onto his ass, sobbing harder than ever now as he remembered their kiss. So warm, so *intimate,* so forever gone.

Jack had no idea how long he sat there like that, sobbing and reliving countless happy memories with his beloved

Rachel, such sweet memories that now brought unimaginable pain which racked his entire body. It was the middle of the afternoon, a Thursday, and there was a chill in the air. He wasn't working on his new novel for at least the next two weeks, and he had no one expecting him. He had nowhere to go. Yet he felt if he stayed much longer, he may lose himself to madness. As much as Jack Fletcher didn't want to live without her, he knew Rachel would want him to go on, to put the pieces of his life back together the best he could, and find happiness. Not sit here on her grave, wallowing in his loss and misery.

He rose to his feet, brushing the dirt from the seat of his pants, and blew a kiss to the grave which held his dead wife, a final tear slinking down his cheek.

"I love you, Rachel," he said, straining to keep his voice even. "And I finally know what it's like to be the sad man."

He turned then and headed for the lot where his car was parked. As he went, he tried to think of something, of *anything*, other than his dead wife. First, he tried out thoughts of getting home and reading the new Ray Garton novel which had come in from Amazon earlier that day. Perhaps getting lost within a world of vampires and werewolves ravaging the countryside would bring him some solace, or at least divert his attention for a while.

Then he remembered it had been Rachel who had ordered it the day she had been killed.

"I've been waiting so long for this one!" she had said. "It's going to kick ass!"

"Always ready to dive into Garton, but can't even read one of my books?" he had replied, giggling. "*I'm* the god of the writing realm, sweetie. Garton *is* great though. Maybe one day you'll read *The Uprising*...?"

"I *fuck* the god of the realm, and I've heard so much about your book it's like I've already read it," she said with a playful gleam in her eye. "Besides, I want horror, not orcs and goblins and a giant talking cat."

"It's a cool fucking cat," Jack had pouted and then grinned.

They had laughed so hard. But he wasn't laughing now. Not the slightest chortle. He could feel new, hot tears

13

threatening his sockets with their salty, miserable presence, and he decided the book would not do. Not now. Not for a long time.

Maybe not ever.

He had made it to his car and was fumbling in his pocket for his keys when the sky darkened. It was a dramatic change in light, and it caused him to stop, keys dangling from his hand, and look up. Black clouds, ones that hadn't been there moments before, either over him or even in the distance, had gathered in a coal-like blanket in the sky. There was a rumbling sound of thunder and he heard some passersby gasp. He moved his gaze to a pair of ladies walking together on the sidewalk across the street, shopping bags in hand and a baby stroller before one of them. They had stopped, mid-stride, and were looking up to the sky as well. The baby started crying as the two women mumbled something to each other Jack couldn't make out. But he could tell whatever it was, it was laced with alarm.

That was when the first horn sounded, and agonizing pain drove Jack Fletcher to his knees, clutching his ears and wailing.

*

The deep, warbling thrum of the horn—seeming to come from the *sky*—thundered through the air. Through tear-blurred vision, Jack could see the two women across the way, their own hands clutching their ears and tormented screams ripping from their open mouths, though he could not hear them. He could not hear his own screams. The baby was almost invisible in the stroller from this angle, but he could see tiny feet and hands kicking and thrashing into the air as the poor child struggled in a torment all its own, without knowledge or reason to calm it.

Not that he had any of his own, he realized. He had no idea what the sound could be, but its incredible boom seemed to drive everyone down. Another man in the parking lot was on his knees, a look of anguish on his wrinkled face, eyes wide and confused. A man in jogging attire was sprawled on the ground, writhing in torment and what looked like pain, holding his head in his hands.

Jack fell against the side of his car, his keys now somewhere on the ground—he'd dropped them at the sounding of the horn—and pressed his palms tighter against his ears.

It did no good.

He felt as though his brain might explode. Like it may burst from his eyes and ears in sloppy gray tendrils. The sound was so intense, he could feel his skin rippling as though a heavy wind were roaring past him. And he supposed it was. He could feel a gust of air swooshing past his agonized body as the sound continued, its monotonous, thrumming roar an offense to reality itself.

His eyes fell back to the two women and the baby. The baby's legs and arms were still flailing about, and the two women were now on the ground, rolling in agony. The baby's stroller had begun to roll away, ever so slowly, down the sidewalk, but the women seemed unaware and unable to have done a thing about it.

Then he heard the baby's screams.

He'd been unable to hear anything but the thundering horn for several seconds now, but as the baby's cries cut through, he realized the sound of the horn was fading, as was the pain throughout his body. His hands began to slip down from his ears and the baby's screams became more pronounced. Jack cupped his hands about his mouth, turning towards the two women.

"The baby!" he screamed. "The stroller is rolling away!"

The two women were just getting to their knees, looks of stupefied terror on their faces. At the sound of Jack's cries, they looked at him, confusion painting their features.

"The baby!" Jack screamed again, pointing towards the stroller, now several feet away.

As their heads turned towards the stroller, a slow dawning of recognition budding on their faces, another scream erupted into the air. It was the squealing of tires, howling as they streaked across pavement.

A second later, Jack saw a large car bounce over the curb, catching a millisecond glimpse of the driver, confused and wide-eyed, gripping the wheel, their mouth open in abject terror.

Sparks sprayed as the undercarriage ripped over the curb and the bumper slammed over the two women. One of the women's head seemed to explode on impact, blood and gray matter spraying out in a jet as the car plowed into them. The other woman was lower and was sucked under the car as it roared past, her body twisting and spritzing blood as it was eviscerated beneath the car's weight and velocity.

"*No!*" Jack screamed, clawing at the air as he rose to his feet, eyes threatening to pop from his sockets.

He thought he may have heard a horrified scream from inside the cab of the car, but he couldn't be sure. It may have been in his mind, perhaps it was even his own wails, but he heard something. But wherever it had come from, it heralded the most horrific thing Jack Fletcher had ever seen.

The car careened over the women, bouncing and sparking and wobbling, and glanced off the brick side of the building abutting the sidewalk. Then it straightened and smashed headlong into the baby stroller, the infant occupant's arms and legs still failing helplessly as the stroller exploded into several pieces, all of them flipping end over end.

When the car finally stopped, the battered and unmoving remains of the baby were on the car's hood, bleeding obscenely.

The driver fell out of the door, a scream so shrill issuing from his throat that Jack almost covered his ears once again. The man picked himself up from the ground and ran into the street, only to meet a bus—which was sliding out of control—by the corner.

His body burst open and flipped under the bus like a rag doll.

Horror stole through Jack's body as he slid to his feet aside his car. His hands were trembling, his mind racing but not landing on any coherent thought. There was nothing but chaos and confusion and—

There was a terrible whining sound, as if the air itself were trying to split apart, and he looked up. A small, single engine plane was coming in towards another building about a block down the street, spinning and rolling out of control. White streaks of atmosphere followed it as the whine of the engine and the whistling of the air grew louder.

It exploded into the side of the building with a monumental *boom*.

Fire rained in all directions as tattered debris cluttered to the ground on a group of people beneath it. A man ran into the street, his body on fire, covered in flaming fuel. And he was *screaming*. The most awful sound Jack Fletcher's ears had ever heard. Utter torment and unimaginable pain.

Another flaming body fell from the building where the plane had crashed and hit with a wet *splat*, the lapping of flames almost drowned out by the cries and screams of the people down the street. A woman—an elderly one from what he could tell—was stumbling away from the wreck, coughing blood and teetering on her feet. The razor-sharp remains of a propeller jutting from her chest. She clutched at it uselessly, her blood-slimed fingers slipping off, then catching herself against the brick wall.

She collapsed, shoving the propeller through her further in a gout of blood. She moved no more.

Jack was on his feet, running towards the people. He had no thought of what he was doing. He wasn't a paramedic. He was a former forensics specialist and now a writer of fantasy novels. He had no idea what he was doing or what he might do when he got to the people, but he was running towards them all the same, his arms pumping and his breaths heaving in his laboring chest.

As he approached the street, he looked to his right. Perhaps it was instinct, perhaps years and years of ingrained discipline of *always* looking before crossing a street. Whatever the reason, it saved his life.

As he moved his eyes from the group of bloody and burning people, desperate for help and aid, he saw a pickup sliding nearly sideways on the street. He planted his foot and felt the wind gush past him as the truck careened less than a foot away from him. Its tires screamed and clouds of white smoke trailed as it slid across the street and headed for the sidewalk.

"*Look out!*" he was just able to scream, a moment too late.

The truck plowed into the survivors, bodies leaping into the air like tattered ragdolls and flipping into buildings or splashing to the pavement of the road. No one seemed to have made it.

Trembling and hitching breaths, Jack looked up and down the street, and finding it clear of any more vehicles, he staggered into the roadway towards the carnage. The driver of the truck hadn't bailed like the man in the car who'd hit the women and the baby, and he soon saw why. The man had indeed exited the vehicle, but it had been through the windshield. His head was crushed against the side of the building in a wet smear of gore.

"Oh, God!" Jack hissed as he came to a stop in the middle of the street. He was just before an intersection which led into the city, and his eyes trailed up that way to see something his mind simply could not process.

Though he tried to scream, all that came out was a hoarse growl.

*

The street before him was a littered mass of chaos and destruction. Cars were overturned and fires littered the streets. It had been less than a minute since that awful horn had sounded, but the destruction he saw before him was so catastrophic that it looked like a war-torn street in a third-world country. A fire hydrant had been mowed over by a truck and water sprayed into the sky in a geyser. Bodies were strewn about in varying degrees of dismemberment and gore, those still alive staggering around in confused terror, their eyes wide and unknowing, mouths gaping.

A woman was on her knees about forty yards from him, cradling a man's head in her arms, screaming in panicked torment for him to wake up. But even from this distance, Jack could see that would never happen. His face was a bloody pulp, one eye dangling from its socket, his left leg bent over on itself in a way it was never meant to go, the foot resting on his belly. Another woman was stumbling from her car, smashed into the side of a building and burning, screaming at the woman holding the man.

"Oh, my God!" she wailed. "I'm so sorry! I—I don't know what… what hap—"

The car behind her exploded, engulfing all three of them in flames. Jack winced and threw his hands up to ward off debris, but none reached him. He felt an intense wave of heat for a moment as the molten air blew past him, and he fell to his knees, trembling all over.

The ground began to rumble, and mounds of earth at the far end of the street—perhaps a hundred yards away—began to rise as though a gigantic mole were burrowing down the street. Screams and panicked cries burst forth from the straggling survivors, who began to run from the terrible thing, some into alleyways, others straight toward Jack at the intersection.

No one knows what it's like to feel these feelings, Rachel's voice came into his head with an insane suddenness, the silky smoothness of her voice a real and tangible thing, as though she were standing right beside him.

He had no idea how the memory had flooded to him in that moment, that terrible, unforeseen moment of total chaos and destruction, but it had. Rushed to him the way Rachel had rushed into his arms so many times after he came home from a particularly horrific crime scene before he'd retired and started writing novels.

Like the time after the massacre at the police station.

Like I do… and I blame YOU!

The words stung. Ate at his core with an exploratory pain he'd never felt before in his life. Why was he feeling this? Why were these memories coming back to him, *real* memories, though totally out of context and laced with malice? The voice was Rachel's, but the tone was not. She'd rarely cut him with her words in all their years together, but now the Rachel in his mind was turning their special song, their playful interactions of times past, into a malevolent weapon to use against him in the most perplexing and terrifying moment of his life.

He struggled to his feet just as the thing burrowing beneath the street exploded up from the earth, writhing and squirming into the overcast light. At first, Jack couldn't make sense of what he was seeing. He stared stupidly at it, his mind trying to process and find an appropriation for what it was seeing, but it eluded him for several, terrifying moments. It was a giant thing, and a pale cream color. Its body was cylindrical in shape, but was segmented every few feet, as though with seams. The skin—if you could call it skin—glistened in the gloom, a thick, mucus-like substance coating its entire body.

It rose into the air, an otherworldly roar emanating from within it somewhere, and Jack saw a mouth open at the front of it, four flaps of horrific flesh peeling back, lined with jagged fangs. There were no eyes, none Jack could see anyway, but this didn't seem to hinder the giant thing.

Screams flooded the street as the thing continued to rise, perhaps thirty feet into the air. Then the thing—a *worm* of some kind, though totally alien to his eyes—turned over toward the ground and snatched a man in its fanged mouth. There was a horrible crunching sound and the man's waist and legs fell to the ground in a shower of entrails as the thing swallowed his entire upper torso.

Then it crashed to the ground on its belly, three people crushed beneath it and spraying blood and gore as it began to writhe down the street, snatching others in its gaping maw here and there.

Jack was utterly transfixed, unable to move, hardly able to breathe. All he could do was stare at the giant worm as it worked its way down the street toward him, tearing people apart, eating some whole.

Then another horn bellowed and the pain from moments before returned. Jack was driven to his knees once more as agony racked his body. He pressed his hands to his ears again and could feel hot slime coming from them. Something similar was streaming from his nose as well, and he screamed in torment.

He forced his eyes open as the thunder of the trumpet continued and saw all the survivors on the street in similar poses. But the worm continued on, seemingly unaffected by the terrible sound, eating its way toward the intersection.

The horn ceased then, and it was as though arms tightly holding his entire body fell away all at once and relief flooded in. He fell forward to the pavement, catching himself with his hands, and retched bile onto the street. He saw his hands were coated in blood and realized it had come from his ears. His heart thrummed in his chest, panic finally boosting his adrenaline into high-gear and getting his immobile body moving.

As he rose to his feet, the overcast sky began to take on a vermillion quality, casting red and scarlet hues over all the landscape. He began to stumble backwards as the survivors, finally reaching him, rushed past him as though he weren't there. And he presumed that as far as they were concerned, he wasn't. Countless faces he didn't know sprinted past him and away from the thing—the *entirety* of whatever cosmic horror was befalling them—in terror.

Before he was able to turn and join them in their fleeing stampede, he heard a terrible series of popping sounds, replete with what sounded like splashing slime. He glanced once more at the giant worm and saw with horror that spines were bursting from the thing all down its sides. Horrific, black, barbed things spreading to either side of it, then unfolding in multiple sections. The barbed protrusions then stabbed into the ground on either side of the street and the thing stood, the legs now moving in a spider-like pattern, thrusting it forward with a speed it had not had before.

He screamed then, and began running through the vermillion mist, not going toward anything, but only away from the monster ravaging the world behind him and the other panicked people around him.

Clop-ah-dah-clop-ah-dah-clop-ah-dah.

The sound almost didn't register over the din of screams and the grumbling roar of the beast. Yet it still cut through the chaotic sounds cut like a hot dagger through ice, and Jack turned to see a new abomination coming down the intersecting street he was passing.

It was a horse. Or at least some maligned abortion of what might have *been* a horse, the closest approximation his mind could associate with it. Like with the worm-thing, it wasn't

21

really that, but only the closest thing his mind could find to make sense of what he was seeing. It had missing patches of flesh, and it shone a pale luminescence, with just a hint of green to it.

Atop the charging horse-thing was a sight which caused Jack's hammering heart to seize for moment.

It was cloaked in a coal-colored robe, the hood open and revealing a monstrous face within. Bone was visible, as well as bleeding flesh, and teeth which stood out like a gigantic, menacing grin. The hands holding the reins oozed crimson, almost black globs of what he thought must be blood. As though the thing atop the abominable horse had been stripped entirely of its skin.

But none of this was as unnerving to Jack as the thing's eyes. If you could call them eyes at all, that was. There were no pupils or corneas. No semblance of actual eyeballs in the sockets at all. But all the same, something which looked like blue fire radiated from them with a terrifying brilliance.

Jack stumbled and fell next to a car. He realized he was back in the parking lot of the cemetery where his wife lay in her coffin. The air whooshed out of him, and for a few terrifying moments he thought he would be trampled. People rushed past him, over him, never stopping, not lending aid, but merely fleeing in horror from the things coming after them. A woman tripped on his leg and he heard a sickening crack as her skull smashed into the hard ground of the parking lot. A moment later, as he struggled for breath and pulled himself under the car to get away from the stampeding people, he saw the dazed woman trying to get up, but she was stepped on and over again and again, one large man actually smashing his foot down on her head as he went, crushing her skull. Blood oozed from her eyes and ears, and Jack thought he could see what might have been brain-matter leaking onto the ground around her battered head.

"Oh, sweet Jesus!" he screamed, but it was lost in the din.

The people continued to rush past him on either side of the car. The ground rippled with the force and energy of the giant worm-thing's spidery footfalls. Each step of the thing issued a resounding *boom* and there were more screams and wet splashing sounds as it ravaged anyone it came in contact with without discrimination.

Jack stayed where he was, looking back in the direction of the horseman and saw something more horrible than any of the things he'd witnessed thus far. The horseman pulled at the reins and his damned steed halted its clopping gallop. A man was rushing past, but stopped when he came astride the horseman and gazed up at the thing. The horseman's permanent grin and blazing blue eyes—Jack could see now they really were twin flames, not eyes at all—bore into the man. The man's face and lips began to tremble. He was weeping openly.

Then the horseman pointed at him with one dripping, bloody finger.

The man began to scream, his flesh seeming to ripple like water after a rock has splashed into its shimmering surface. His eyes were wide, much wider than Jack had ever seen a person display, and his body began to jerk. The screams turned into ragged grunts as blood began to course past his lips and slime his chin.

Then the man's eyes exploded.

Like a pair of grapes smashed under a mallet, they burst from his sockets, spraying viscous ooze and blood alike. Jack's breath was caught in his throat and he realized he hadn't been breathing. He didn't know for how long, but now the air came back to him with a heaving effort, and he rasped in several long, hitching breaths.

The man with the burst eyes collapsed to his knees, and Jack saw the man's skin beginning to drip off his flesh. He realized it was actually melting, as though a barrel of acid had been poured over the man. Globs of flesh began to detach from his body, the skin turning to liquid and the meat beneath sizzling. Steam rose all about the man in the scarlet hue of the air, and still the horseman pointed his damnable finger at the man.

Moments later, there was nothing left of the man but a boiling stew of fluids and a few remnants of bone lying on the ground. Finished, the horseman worked the reins and the horse took him on into the crowd of panicked survivors.

Seeing that the stampede of people had thinned out, Jack scurried out from beneath the car on his belly and got to his feet. Insanely, he rushed to the pool of what had moments before been the man looking into the eyes of the horseman.

Behind blue eyes, Rachel's voice came to him again, once more laced with that malevolent tone.

Trembling and feeling sick, he began to stagger backwards when a new sound in the chaos caused him to look up in the direction the horseman had come from moments before.

A plethora of *things*—he could not think of them as anything else—were rushing down the street, heading toward his location. Some had the appearance of insects, though giant ones, others the rough appearance of men. But even these were deformed, horrible shapes, shambling like creatures from the blackest of nightmares toward him, their twisted features dripping with slime and blood, open wounds and fangs visible. They gurgled and growled, the snickering footfalls of the insect creatures chilling his spine in their approach.

And Hell followed with him...

The scripture came to him then, out of nowhere. He hadn't been to church in decades, and though a dusty old King James Bible was tucked into his bookshelf, he hadn't read it in years. But all the same, perhaps because of the horror he was experiencing or what he'd seen the horseman do to the puddle of a man at his feet, it roared in his mind.

This is it, he thought as he began to turn and run from the nightmare creatures lumbering after him. *This is the apocalypse.*

Before he had gotten ten strides into his flight, the horn drove him to the ground a third time.

*

His ears were bleeding. His nose was bleeding. He could even feel something leaking from his eyes and he was sure it wasn't tears. The pain was unfathomable. Every cell in his body felt as if it were being torn apart all at once, and the agony was absolute.

24

Yet, through this debilitating pain, as the thundering horn sounded on, his eye caught movement. Struggling, pressing his hands against his ears, his mouth a maw of suffering, he turned his head towards the nightmare creatures. They were undaunted by the horn blast, just as the spider-worm had been, and they were getting nearer. Only twenty yards away, and closing.

One thing, a beast with a humanoid figure but long arms and legs so short it seemed to waddle like a nightmare penguin, its face and shoulders pocked with no less than a dozen, blinking, black eyes, seemed to have focused in on Jack. What passed for its mouth opened, and two tongue-like tentacles sprouted out with small, fanged mouths on their tips. They opened in a high-pitched roar which just barely cut through the still blaring trumpet in the sky, and the thing began to increase its speed.

Using every ounce of his will and strength, Jack struggled to his feet on shaky legs and began a shambling run, his hands still pressed tightly to his ears

Will it ever fucking stop? his mind whimpered.

The things were getting closer to him, though he was moving as fast as his agonized body would move. He could hear the shrieking caws of the tongue mouths, much closer now, but he didn't dare a glance back.

He was a fit man. Not a gym freak, but fit. He should have been able to gain far more speed than he was, and under normal circumstances, he would have. But the blare of the horn and its debilitating effects were taking a toll.

Dozens of other people lay all about the parking lot and cemetery, writhing on the ground in torment. To his right, the spider-worm was devouring body after body, a thing without any outward semblance of intelligence, only raw, vile instinct.

Behind him the shambling nightmare creatures were closing in. He couldn't see the horseman anywhere now, but he suspected the thing with the fiery blue eyes was lurking somewhere near.

Jack had to move. Had to force his body to move, faster, or he would be overcome by the hellish fiends at any moment.

Please, he thought, almost in a prayer, *stop the horn! Make it stop! Oh, Jesus, PLEASE!*

As though hearing his laments, the horn stopped. At once, just as before, he felt invisible arms release him and the phantom knives of pain all over his body slip out of him, and he began stumbling from the relief. For one horrifying moment, he thought he would topple to the ground, grind an inch off his chin, and be torn to pieces from the hellish creatures.

But he managed to get his feet under him and he began pumping his legs and arms, dramatically increasing his speed. He dared a glance over his shoulder now, and saw the distance between him and creatures had been much closer than he'd thought, but now the gap was widening. The screaming tongue thing seemed to lose interest and turned on a poor soul who was just getting to their feet after being released from the horn of hell.

Jack leaped to the curb of the parking lot that bordered the cemetery and began sprinting up the grassy incline. He darted between grave stones, his breaths heaving now and sweat causing his shirt to stick to his every curve and feature. His frantic eyes both looked out for other enemies as well as watching for the stones so as not to bark his shin into one of them in a parody of error.

That was when he tripped.

He hadn't been near any of the stones, being safely between rows. As he went over, he thought perhaps a root may have snagged his foot, but even as he hit the grass with an audible grunt, he knew that wasn't the case. There were no trees within fifty yards of where he was.

A soft spot in the ground, then?

As he rolled to his back and began to sit up, he realized his foot was still caught on whatever he had tripped over. He began reaching for his foot before his eyes went there, meaning to shake it free and get going again.

But as his eyes froze on his foot, Jack Fletcher's breath caught in his throat and his bowels evacuated.

*

26

"Honey, could you run to the store for me?" Rachel had said the morning it happened.

Jack was still in his pajamas and nursing sore shoulders. He always awoke with sore shoulders these days. All part of getting older he guessed.

He stared down at his half-eaten cereal, thinking that the very last thing he wanted to do was to get dressed and go to the goddamn store. He wasn't a big fan of people in general, and the supermarket was *always* littered with hundreds of bustling souls. Just thinking about it got his anxiety going.

He sighed. "What do you need?"

"You used the last of the milk, and I was thinking about steaks for dinner. You always know better than me what cuts to get."

Another sigh from Jack.

"Can it wait?" he asked, rolling his shoulders again to work out the strain. "I'm not dressed, haven't showered, haven't even finished my breakfa—"

"Jesus, Jack," she cut him off. "I didn't mean right this second, I meant in a little while."

He mulled this over a moment before speaking the sentence that would seal his wife's doom.

"I've got to go into town tomorrow morning, can we wait until then? Do steaks tomorrow night?"

She stopped what she was doing on her phone and looked up at him, an even glare he knew all too well. She had her heart set on the steaks, but after so many years of marriage, wasn't interested in a fight. Jack knew he was just being lazy and irritable, and could tell she thought the same thing.

"I'll do it," she said, clicking off her phone and stuffing it into her pocket, a too-calm tone in her voice, masking her frustration with him only partly.

"No, no," Jack said, standing and heading for the bedroom. "I'll do it, just let me grab a shower and change clothes."

"Forget it, I'll have what I need and be back before you even get ready. I'd like a bowl of fucking cereal too, you know. You *must* know what it's like to be the *bad man*."

Her tone was sharp now. He knew when she started using their special song to hurt him, she was on the brink of full on fury.

"I'm sorry, I'm just being lazy, let me at least throw some clothes on and—"

But he stopped midsentence as she wordlessly marched through the door, slamming it on her way out.

You're gonna pay for that, Jack my man...

Still in his pajamas, clacking away on his keyboard, hard at work on his new novel, Jack lost track of the time. He hadn't even realized when an hour had come and gone and Rachel wasn't home.

That was when the two sherriff's deputies knocked on his door. As Jack opened the door on their grim faces, he knew something awful had happened.

*

Jack was aghast and hopeful all at once.

There was no root entangled about his foot, no soft spot in the graveyard. Nothing like that had tripped him. What had caused him to fall was at once the most wonderful thing he'd ever seen in all his life, and the most terrifying thing of all.

Sodden dirt coated the waxen skin of a delicate hand, the nails painted bright red. The arm attached, like the hand, had that same waxed over quality. The dress—an elegant but conservative black gown—looked moist and was wrinkled, covered in dirt.

Jack knew he shouldn't be seeing what he was seeing. He knew *nothing* that had happened in the past few minutes since the first horn blast should be possible. Had he gone mad in his grief? Had he finally snapped under the weight and guilt he carried over Rachel's death? A death, he reminded himself, that never would have occurred if he'd not been acting selfish and anti-social and just run to the damn store himself. Was that why he was witnessing all this utter chaos? Was he locked away in a padded cell somewhere, wrapped snugly in a straight-jacket, raving away to no one?

Is this all in my mind?

"Do you know what it's like to be hated, Jack, my love?" Rachel's corpse said to him.

This was not in his mind. This was real, and it was happening, and the spider-worm was real and even now chewing on the thrashing remains of a child not forty yards away. The nightmare creatures swarming the swaths of people in the streets and parking lots were real too. The horseman was real.

Rachel was real.

"R-Rach, I..." he started, but his words abandoned him. Jack Fletcher, successful fantasy and science fiction author, winner of multiple literary awards, couldn't think of a thing to say.

She began laughing then as she pulled her long legs from the earth and started toward him. Like her arms and hands, her face was waxen too, only much more so than the rest of her. The embalming and attempts at makeup to get her to look somewhat like herself for the funeral were the cause of this, he knew, but it still gave her an alien quality which left Jack horrified. Something in her eyes as well. He couldn't put his finger on it, but he knew somehow this was *not* Rachel. It may be her body, but this was not her. Something else was lurking behind her blue eyes. Something darker.

Something sinister.

"Is your conscience empty, Jack?" the Rachel-thing said in a mocking tone. "Did you put me out of your mind, relieve yourself of culpability with your fancy words? Come on, you little closet cocksucker, talk to your dearly departed wife!"

Another burst of laughter. She was almost on top of him, and something happened which freed Jack of his paralysis. As the Rachel-thing cackled maniacally before him, there was a terrible, gut-wrenching series of *cracks*, and her head slumped down and around to a horrifically unnatural angle. Jack screamed and began peddling back on his ass with his hands and feet, his heart exploding in his chest.

The mortician had braced Rachel's broken neck with some wood and screws to keep it straight in the coffin for the viewing and funeral. Jack had thought it abysmally morbid, but he had been assured this was completely routine, it wouldn't be visible, and it was better than risking an indignity of his dead wife, never mind a likely shock for everyone else.

But the brace had snapped and now Rachel's head hung in that terrible way it had when she'd been pulled from the accident. Flashes of heart-wrenching memories blazed before his eyes. Arriving at the hospital, seeing Rachel there on the gurney, the strange paleness about her which he'd never seen before. All the vitality gone.

Yet, the Rachel-thing, grabbing its hair and pulling up its head at yet an even more grotesque angle, continued to laugh at him.

"I bet you *did* purge yourself of any guilt, didn't you! Well, honey, love is fucking vengeance, and that shit ain't free!"

Jack was getting to his feet. He heard the chilling *clop-ah-dah-clop-ah-dah-clop-ah-dah* of the horseman's steed somewhere near, but he couldn't look away from the terrible thing that had been his wife. All around him, the earth was splitting and others were clawing from the ground, all in varying states of decay from as fresh as Rachel to others which were little more than bones.

And everything in between.

"How?" Jack screamed. "Why? Why is this happening?"

The questions weren't really for the Rachel-thing. They were just questions. At the brink of his sanity, and feeling himself about to tip off the edge and into the inky abyss of oblivion, Jack Fletcher continued screaming as tears fell down his cheeks. He was utterly surrounded by the dead. Or the undead. Or whatever these things were. The stench was monumental and it stung his nose.

Clop-ah-dah-clop-ah-dah-clop.

Much closer now, but still he peered at the cackling, malicious maniac that had been his wife.

"Why?" he whimpered now, his screams having faded with his sanity.

She stopped laughing, holding her head at that unnatural angle, and gave him an incredulous look, as though he were a clinical idiot who ought to know the answer to such a simple question.

"Because, *baby*-doll," she started with a venomous sarcasm, "Hell ran out of room."

He continued to cry as she resumed her laughter. He wanted to be gone from here. Wanted to be as far from all of this as he could get. Every time the Rachel-thing spoke, his heart was torn out anew with her twisted parody of he and his wife's special song. Their special little thing.

But she—*it*—was right about one thing. It *was* his fault. It was all on him, her death, and he knew it. He was selfish, he was petty, and he had pissed her off, knowing good and well what he was doing, and sent her off to her death.

He bent over and sobbed deeper, heaving, even as he felt the first hands of the dead fall on him. The spider-worm roared and charged down the street after yet more fleeing survivors, it's thundering footfalls following it. The nightmare creatures were ravaging people from all angles, tearing their flesh and bodies apart like ravenous wolves.

And the dead circled in on him.

Clop-ah-dah-clop-ah-dah-clop.

The horseman was there. Right behind him. He knew it without even turning around. The dead had released their hold on him and taken a few steps back, and Jack felt the tremors in his body hasten.

The steed blew hot breath on the back of his neck, though this did not break the chill throughout his body. Nor did it warm the cold, lonely feeling in his heart.

This was the end. The apocalypse. The end of humanity. God had finally had enough, and unleashed the hordes of Hell upon the Earth. The Rachel-thing was still laughing, the alien blue eyes dancing with delight. But Rachel wasn't here. She was somewhere else, somewhere better. Because she had been the best person he'd ever known and he *had* to believe she was safe and happy. Maybe now he could go to her. Look into her beautiful blue eyes—*behind* them, even—and come to know her even deeper than he had in all the years of their marriage. To know when to shut the fuck up and just run an errand for her and not think only of himself all the time. To know her heart in new and fantastic ways.

And to ask her forgiveness.

Yes, that was what he wanted more than anything else. And he knew that to get what he wanted, to be able to look into her beautiful eyes, he would first have to look into another pair of blue eyes.

He turned around slowly. Every muscle twitched and jerked, but he willed himself to keep going. He saw the horse, looked into its obsidian eyes a moment, and then shut his own.

"I love you Rachel!" he prayed aloud before the horseman and the dead. "I hope you'll forgive me. I'm coming home to you, now."

He opened his eyes and looked up into the blue flames dancing in the sockets of the horseman. His skinless grin was abominable, but Jack would not look away. *Could* not look away. He had discovered the path back to his dead wife, and it lay behind these blue eyes.

The horseman raised his finger slowly and pointed at Jack's face. As he did, the flames intensified, flaring inside the sockets, and Jack instantly felt pain course through his body. The sounding of the horns had been bad, but this was worse. He could feel his blood as it began to actually boil in his veins and every muscle bunched as tight as he'd ever felt them. A scream ripped from his throat, one of an agony so great, there are not sufficient words to describe it.

He was still staring into the flaming blue eyes—*beyond* them—when his own burst in a sodden mess and he saw no more. As he died, the skin melting off his flesh, he found the trail that had lain behind the eyes of the horseman, the one which he hoped—he *prayed*—would lead him home to his wife. He began to follow it, the horror of the apocalypse fading, all his memories focused on his lovely Rachel, his only reason for life, either in the past or now, whom he searched for now.

Jack Fletcher began the journey.

CENSERED

Christine Morgan

"You don't get a trumpet."

"Why the fuck not?"

Cassaiel, Angel of Temperance, winced. "Well, that, in part, for example."

She had chosen to manifest this incarnation as feminine, the better to serve as attendant and handmaiden to the Holiest of Mothers in this most difficult of times, and in hopes of exerting some calming influence on the more fire-headed of the hosts who waited with halos burning and swords of light. Her robes draped in palest rose-pink about her slender frame. Wings pure and soft as swan's down folded demurely against her back. Her hair was silk spun of silver, her eyes polished tourmaline gems, her aspect the gentlest soothing divine beauty.

All that said, Temperance or not, she rather looked as if she would've liked to smite Tabaeth upside the head when he replied, "Unfair! I call bullshit!"

There had been, in Heaven, silence for almost half an hour, a serene and peaceful silence since the Sixth Seal was opened.

A great multitude had gathered, their garments washed Lamb's white, bearing palm branches. The twelve-times-twelve-thousand had been marked as the Lord God's chosen servants. Below the high firmament, the mortal earth trembled, having been wracked by great earthquakes and volcanic eruptions, the sun cloaked in ashen sackcloth, the moon as of blood. The Riders ranged across it, bringing war, plague, death and famine upon the survivors.

But there had been, in Heaven, in this shining Hall before the very Throne Almighty, for almost a full half an hour, blissful silence. Until now.

"It's bullshit!" Tabaeth repeated. "It's fucking unfair!" He pointed at his seven brothers. "*They* all get trumpets! *They* all get to destroy shit!"

"They," said Cassaiel, visibly striving for patience, "have been proved and deemed worthy by Gabriel the Revealer."

"Just because he likes them better! He shouldn't play favorites. He's such an asshole!"

His brothers bristled. Heaven's hosts gasped. The Holy Mother Herself set delicate fingertips to Her pained alabaster brow.

Issaril, eldest of the eight, stepped forth with wings flaring and flames kindling in his gaze. "How dare you speak in such utterances of our father!"

"He's not our real father! You think he fucked any of those womb-mares? All he did was pick some duds out of the Treasury of Souls and sweet-talk his bottom bitch Lailiah into hatching them anyway like cuckoo eggs. I doubt he even *has* a dick!"

Behind Tabaeth, a throat cleared with a rumble more ominous than thunder. Cassaiel closed her eyes and drew a deep, resigned breath. Issaril squared his shoulders, folded his wings in deference, and raised his noble chin.

"Shit," said Tabaeth. He turned. He looked up. And *up*.

There, of course, stood Gabriel, none other, the towering archangel wreathed in a glorious glow. His robes were nearly blinding, and as for the corona of his halo, forget the "nearly". Mighty eagle's wings spread broad from his back. His eyes, too, were those of an eagle, sharp and far-seeing. The set of his mouth was a grim, merciless line.

"*What,*" he inquired, in another thunderous rumble, "did you call the good Angel of Conception?"

"Uhhh..." Tabaeth tried on a sheepish grin. It didn't fit.

Following Gabriel came seven of the cherubim, bearing upon velvet pillows seven long bronze trumpets with mouthpieces of bone. The smug little shits all sneered at Tabaeth's discomfort.

He cleared his own throat in an awkward mouse-squeak. His feathers rustled and the soles of his sandals shuffled on the Hall's marble floor as he shifted his weight from side to side. "Uhhh..." he said again. "Hi... Dad."

"Forgive him, Father," began Saphaeth, seventh-born of the eight, elder only to Tabaeth himself. "He—"

Gabriel lifted a hand, his eagle's gaze never moving from Tabaeth's. Saphaeth subsided, tucking his hands into the voluminous sleeves of his robe.

"You have ever," declared Gabriel, "been difficult. Impetuous of word and of deed. You alone could not be deterred from seeking out the scrolls guarded by Vulgaris, Profanis, and Obscenis—"

"I wanted to see what the big damn deal was!"

"Often have you been known to converse and confer with the fallen, and the foreign of other faiths."

"They know neat stuff," Tabaeth protested. "Cool stories. I was curious, interested, that's all!"

"And *now*," the archangel continued, raising his voice, "at this crucial moment, in this holiest of places, you disrupt the proceedings with blasphemous irreverence and vile talk."

"Well... yeah... because... because..." He looked around for help or sympathy, finding not much of either. Even Saphaeth wouldn't meet his eyes. Issaril *did*, but only to deliver a now-you're-gonna-get-it smirk. Bitter bile seethed in his gullet, anger and injustice surging again. "Because those kissasses—" here his arm swept in a gesture to encompass his brothers— "get to blow doomsday trumpets and wreck shit!"

"They will not 'wreck'... stuff," Gabriel said, and coughed.

"The hell they won't! I read the *Codex Apocalypta*, too!" He pointed at the first trumpet, which the pudgiest little fuckwit cherub held on its pillow. "*That* one makes it rain ice and fire and blood!" He pointed at the next, then the next after. "And *that* one throws a huge rock into the sea to wipe out a bunch of the ships and fish... and *that* one, that badass bastard right there, that summons Star-motherfucking-*Wormwood*—"

"Tabaeth!" roared Gabriel.

For a moment, the archangel seemed ready to wash his mouth out with brimstone-lye soap... and Cassaiel seemed ready to help.

"What? They get to wreck shit, and I don't! It's unfair, leaving me out! I know I'm the youngest, but—"

"Being the youngest has naught to do with—"

"You can't play favorites like that!" Tabaeth protested. "It's like we're in some fucked-up fairy tale, the king with eight sons, and when inheritance time comes, the youngest prince always gets reamed in the ass!"

Gabriel inhaled, appearing to swell to twice his size, his corona blazing with the brilliance of all Creation. Tabaeth gulped, suddenly and for the first time wondering if it really was possible for immortal angels to die.

Before the matter could be settled one way or the other, Cassaiel intervened. The Angel of Temperance seized Tabaeth by the scruff of his neck, hefted him one-handed off the floor, shook him like a recalcitrant kitten, and cried, "Enough! You will hush your tongue or I will hush it for you!"

Too startled even to crack smart, Tabaeth clamped his lips shut. He flushed hotly under the judgmental scrutiny of the entire Host, the Holy Court of twenty-four Elders, pretty much everyone who was anyone... except the Lord God Himself, not currently in attendance. She carried him to the front of the chamber and plunked him down—harder than was strictly necessary, in his opinion—on a stool in the corner beside the brightly burning Altar.

So unfair! Jesus cocksucking *Christ*!

He hunched over, flinching, and threw another frantic glance to make sure the Throne was still empty. It was, though half a dozen six-winged seraphim hovered expectantly nearby. Fortunately, the Lamb, seven stars forming His crown, had popped the seventh Seal upon the sacred Scroll and was frowning over it like a kid who'd studied for the wrong exam. Leaning close to His divine Mother, He murmured some sort of question.

Tabaeth, whose ears were keen, caught part of it—something to do with the Third Woe, and were they really sure it wasn't just ripping off the Egyptian thing about Ma'at and

36

Apep? At that, he almost did speak up again, risking further ire. Gabriel's umbrage about him conversing and conferring with the foreign of other faiths was not unfounded; it fascinated him how many of their ancient stories bore suspicious resemblances to what was supposedly original gospel.

Really, though, come on… all those virgin births, and resurrections? All those wicked dragons or serpents or whatever, getting a bad rap? The similarities could not be mere coincidences. He'd spoken with deities from various pantheons, the ousted and demoted and suppressed, and as far as he was concerned, the whole thing sounded sketchy as fuck.

He'd also spoken with several of the fallen, and talk about a bad rap! Talk about a setup! Even within the very Testaments, it was plain the Lord God Almighty could be a real dick.

Look at the gotcha He'd pulled in Eden, those poor suckers… if they weren't meant to eat of the Tree, why put it there in the first place and tell them so? Why not put it somewhere else and never mention it? Why the mean trick?

Not unlike the way the Olympians treated what's-her-name, Pandora. Here's this magic box, but never ever open it, oh and by the way, as a parting gift, here's a big helping of curiosity! Then they send her to marry the innocent brother of the smartass who'd pissed them off as a punishment to all humanity, who hadn't even known what the fuck was going on.

Funny how, in both, mankind ended up blaming the women, rather than the ones who'd masterminded the tricky dickery.

Or look at Job! Talk about getting fucked over for absolutely no reason. Sure, they tried to hang it on Satan for instigating, but what was the Lord God Almighty doing making wagers with the Devil to begin with? Someone have a gambling problem?

Look at Abraham and Isaac, too. What a clever pranking *that* was! Sacrifice your son… ha, ha, wait just joking, shit, the dude was actually going to do it! Look at Lot; if it was a test, what was the point?

He'd never felt very bad for Lot, or Noah, or those guys, but he felt bad for Lot's daughters, and that one of Noah's sons. Like, hey, had the daughters *wanted* to bang their drunk-ass old man? Someone from up here put the notion in their heads; there they were, city wiped out, possibly the last people on Earth, must find some way to perpetuate the species, hurr-hurr-hurr. And, hey, get a load of Mr. Build-An-Ark, wasted off his tits, rolling naked in the mud probably puking on himself; so Ham laughed, big fucking whoop, it must've been Goddamn funny! What does he get for it, though? Blammo, systemic bullshit racism for umpty-thousand years.

In front of the great Throne, Gabriel had lined up his precious seven angel-princes, while the tubby little cherubs fluttered and preened self-importantly, enjoying being the trumpet-bearers, the centers of attention. The Lamb was tracing His finger along the Scroll, lips moving as he silently mouthed his lines.

Fucking hell, they could have done a dress rehearsal at least. Didn't the apocalypse deserve a dress rehearsal? Get on with it already!

Tabaeth slouched on the stool, idly swinging his sandaled feet. Along the edges of the Altar hung rows of censers, issuing forth sweet smoke. Frankincense, but wait, there's myrrh! Wrought of gold filigree, bejeweled with diamonds, suspended upon silver chains, they resembled the kind of baubles Salome might've worn on her shimmy-shimmy belt, or gaudy blinged-up dingleballs for some hotshot's pimp-my-ride. From where he was sitting, he could almost but not quite reach the nearest with his toe. He wiggled a little, nudged it, watched the rising smoky tendrils undulate.

Wonder if he could draw one back and release it and get them all going in a clack-together Newton's cradle?

He wasn't alone in being bored and restive. The Elders dozed in their thrones, the multitudes gossiped amongst themselves. Of the four Living Creatures summoned to represent the four elements of nature, the Ox was sniff-snorting at the marble floor as if in hopes of grazing, the Lion sprawled snoozing like a cat before the hearth, the Eagle shifted restively on its perch—Tabaeth watched it closely, thinking at any moment it might flick its tail and splat forth a liquid gout of birdshit; what would happen then?—and the Man might've been waiting for a bus.

Finally, Gabriel nodded to the Lamb, and the Lamb strode to His mark. The seraphim hovering by the Throne raised their voices in heavenly chorus, singing "Holy, Holy, Holy" until the entire assembly had quieted and focused their attention.

The presentation of the trumpets began, with Saphaeth called forth first. The seventh-youngest angel looked equally divided between robe-wetting terror and total fanboy gibbering as he approached the Lamb. It was then so proclaimed that this First Trumpet's sounding would rain down ice and blood and fire upon the Earth, destroying a full one-third of all the grasses and the trees.

The multitudes gasped like this was shocking news, despite what Tabaeth had already said. Evidently, he needn't have worried about spoiler alerts. So it went likewise when the Second Trumpet was presented; its sounding yadda-yadda plunge a mighty boulder into the sea, buh-bye a third of the ships and fish. Then the Third… Star-motherfucking-*Wormwood*, poisoning—wait for it!—one third of the world's rivers, springs, and freshwaters.

He noticed some of his brothers were looking a little uneasy as they accepted these instruments of destruction. What the fuck had they expected? Toot-toot party favors? Happy Armageddon, everybody!

Next, the Fourth was given over, which would snuff by a third-portion the light of sun and moon and stars, casting a most dreadful shadow of utter darkness.

After that, things got weird.

The Fifth Trumpet's sounding was to herald the First Woe, some convoluted bullshit involving a star and a key and a bottomless pit from whence would billow smoke of the Abyss and unleash armor-plated locusts like unto scorpions with human faces and lions' teeth… maybe whoever scribed the *Codex Apocalypta* had been on drugs.

The Sixth would go for the big-budget battle extravaganza, summoning up two hundred million horsemen to slaughter thirty-three percent of the remaining people, however many might be left after the scorpion-locusts and the poisoned water and rains of ice and fire and other colossal shitstorms.

Issaril, the eldest of Gabriel's chosen, was last to receive his trumpet. After hearing what the rest would do, even he seemed apprehensive. Before the Lamb addressed him, though, there was—unbelievable!—a fucking commercial break!

Tabaeth shook his head in jaw-dropped amazement. He'd read it in the *Codex* and thought it was in there by mistake, copied from some different work. But, no, here it was, the Lamb going on about this little scroll and a dude named John was supposed to eat it, and it'd taste like honey-candy but upset his stomach as it granted him the power of prophecy.

The hell kind of commercial was it? For divine antacids? Holy Rolaids?

This was really getting fucking muddled. The Lamb mentioned an angel who'd deliver this scroll, but He didn't say who. Not Tabaeth, though; that was for Goddamn sure. Left out again, what an unfair bunch of bullshit!

The temptation to jump up in loud protest was all but overwhelming. *I object!* he'd holler, dramatic as hell. Bring the entire dumbass proceedings to a screeching halt. Yeah, it would land him in all sorts of trouble, but—the realization came to him like a warmly dawning light—what did he have to lose?

From here, he knew, the *Codex* would ramble on into a babble of indecipherable fuckery about Beasts and Harlots and Seven Bowls, which would be poured by angels… again, not *him*; Tabaeth was willing to bet his ass and wings and halo on that score! There'd be more lakes of fire and bottomless pits and New Heaven a Place on Earth like in that stupid song, and—

No! God-fucking-damn-it, no!

He sprang from the stool, as the Lamb was telling Issaril how the sounding of the Seventh Trumpet would open the Temple where the Ark of the Covenant might be seen, and the events of the Third Woe would unfold, and blah-blah-blah Seven Bowls with blood and pain and fire.

Cassaiel had drifted over to attend solicitously at the side of the Holy Mother, whose beatific aspect had become distraught, weeping for the suffering even as love for Her son filled Her heart. The Angel of Temperance's attention thus diverted, and being too far away to reach him before he interrupted anyway, Tabaeth opened his mouth to express his opinion of this fucking bullshit unfair injustice.

No words emerged. He couldn't speak. The pink-robed bitch had hushed his tongue after all, stolen his speech, silenced his voice!

Seriously, what the fuck???

He tried again.

Nothing. Not a peep, not a croak, not a murmur. He was muted! Fucking *muted*!

In a violent spate of rage and outrage, he whirled to the Altar and struck wildly at the hanging gold-filigree censers. They clanged and jangled and tangled on their silver chains, throwing crazy whorls of smoke into the air. Smoke and ash and embers scattered in all directions. Chains snapped. Censers hit the marble floor. Some split open, spilling burning chunks of frankincense and myrrh.

Oh, he had the Hall's notice now! It was pandemonium, Elders leaping from their Thrones, the seraphim screeching more like harpies or sirens than angels, the multitudes milling about in shocked confusion. A smoldering incense-coal rolled against the Lion's haunches, igniting the great creature's fur; it bolted awake and scurried to its feet and ran with its tail a banner of flame, scorching the robes of the panicked hosts. The Ox bellowed, stamped a hoof, cracked the marble. The Eagle shrieked, beating the air with its powerful wings, and yes, there was the splatter of liquid birdshit... onto Cassaiel's silver sandals! As for the Man, he sure wasn't bored anymore.

The Lamb dropped the Scroll, which unrolled in the endless way Santa's list did in cartoons. The Holy Mother pressed folded hands to Her pristine sacred bosom; if She'd worn pearls, She would've been clutching them.

Tabaeth's brothers there with long trumpets drooping in their grasps like limp dicks. Gabriel roared in a wrath more furious than the Lion's, taking flight with a whip crack-sweeping downdraft that sent the stunned, gawping cherubim spinning out of control.

He was gonna get it now.

But they had to catch him first.

Snatching up one of the censers by its chain, Tabaeth whirled it in smoke-spewing circles above his head. He thought of cowboys with lassos, David with the famous sling. It hooted a hollow bullroarer's whistle. The nearest of the Host brave enough to try to rush him fell back from the whirling blur of gold filigree and myrrh.

Gabriel landed just beyond the span's radius. There was no limp-dick about his trumpet; he smote the censer a grand slam home run blow that cracked it like an egg and sent another barrage of ash and embers showering the Hall. The silver chain sliced stinging weals in Tabaeth's palms as it was ripped from his grasp. He yelped—or tried to, still silenced—and retreated to the Altar. His heel bumped another censer, one that had sprung open on its hinges and spewed its contents but had not broken.

He grabbed it, burning his already hurt hands on the hot metal bowl. Using it as a scoop, he plowed it through the fiery bed of eternal coals packing the Altar and came away with a brimming, blazing conflagration. Sparks spun up around him in miniature tornadoes. Shimmering heat-ripples singed his wing-feathers and hair.

"Put that down this instant!" ordered Gabriel, now seeming thirty feet tall and very much a vivid reminder of how vengeful a motivated archangel could be.

And it wasn't cowboys or David in Tabaeth's mind now, but one of the foreign, a kid named Phaeton. Some hapless bastard—but literally!—of the Olympian sun-god, he'd had his own problems with neglectful asshole father figures… when he'd wheedled a promise out of his deadbeat dad to let him drive the solar chariot, the fucking horses flipped their shit and ran wild, hauling the sun on a helter-skelter path of destruction.

Had Apollo intervened, tried to help or save Phaeton? No, he'd just lounged around with nymphs feeding him grapes and olives or whatever, while that shithead Zeus—talk about asshole father figures!—zapped the poor kid into oblivion with a thunderbolt.

Gabriel gave chase around the Altar, but Tabaeth was smaller and quicker, fueled by desperation. He scooted through the milling multitudes, dodging and weaving, ducking and darting, accidentally touching off a few more fires as the censer's seething flames licked at robes and lavish biblical beards. *Stop, drop, and roll, bitches!*

A path parted before him as if old Moses had suddenly gotten in on the action, though really it was only the Host backpedaling out of his way. He found himself running directly away from the Throne, directly toward the crystalline window through which the Lord God could view his Creation. It was part magic mirror, part starship viewscreen, part gateway portal.

Until recently, the sight had been fairly scenic, a blue-green orb swirled with ever-changing patterns of cloudy white, basking in golden sunlight under the attentive care of the pale moon, surrounded by a vastness of black velvet studded with myriad diamonds and the harmonious dance of the celestial spheres.

This doomsday business had pretty much screwed things over already. The Riders were down there, wreaking havoc, spreading war and death and famine and plague. Cities burned. Armies battled. Streets ran red with blood. Continents had been jarred to their foundations, volcanoes belching forth magma and sulfur and boiling mud. The plaintive wails and prayers of the wretched reached clear to Heaven.

And that was still the pre-game show! The Seven Trumpets hadn't even been blown yet, which was when the apocalypse would really kick into high gear. His brothers were going to get to wreck shit on a seriously epic, world-ending scale... and he was, what? Supposed to sit here and watch and miss all the fun?

Yeah, fuck that. If he was going to go out, he'd go out with a bang.

"Tabaeth! Don't you dare!" cried Cassaiel.

He didn't need to look back to know Gabriel was right on his ass. Nor did he need to look back to know the Throne was finally occupied, the Lord God Almighty checking in to see how things were going. *Surprise! How's that omniscience working out?*

Just a few more paces... the censer searing unbearably in his grasp... his skin sizzling like bacon, his hair crisping away in wisps and whiffs, the trailing smolder of his wing-feathers leaving a shot-down-plane smoke trail in his wake.

Just a few more paces, and… there!

The windup, and the pitch!

What an arm this kid's got!

A crazy fireball fastball cannonball hurtling through the window-gate, hurtling through space, a flaming comet streaking down from the firmament, shattering the atmosphere with terrible lightning! Smashing straight into the abused planet!

Steeeee-rike! More bowling than baseball, but who gave a fuck at this point? Hammer-blow bullseye shit yeah! Fault lines that still hadn't settled lurched with new quakes, aftershocks jolting more mountains from their foundations. Thunder and turbulence roiled the air. Millions screamed for mercy as new agonies befell them.

There was, once again, for a minute or so, silence in Heaven. No one moved. No one spoke.

Face blistered, hair and wings singed, robes scorched, Tabaeth slowly turned.

They were all looking at him. Archangels, Elders, the Lamb and His Holy Mother, everyone. From the lowliest of the multitudes to the omnipotent, omniscient Lord God Almighty. Even the Ox regarded him with its blunt-horned head quizzically tilted. His brothers still held their limp-dick drooping trumpets. They could sure go blow themselves now, far as he was concerned.

Behind him, devastation continued wracking the tormented world. He sensed, somehow, dimly, the startled Riders asking each other what the hell had just happened; that wasn't in the script, wasn't part of the plan, was it? Someone better go back and edit the prophecies, pronto!

Tabaeth didn't bother trying to talk. Cassaiel probably wouldn't allow it anyway.

So he merely raised his curled fists to shoulder level, smiled angelically, and popped both middle fingers to flip all of Heaven a double-bird.

THE DAY AND THE HOUR

Wile E. Young

Woe! Woe! Woe to the inhabitants of the earth, because of the trumpet blasts about to be sounded by the three other angels!

I had never heard an eagle scream warning after the sea had boiled and the water had turned into poisonous sludge.

Demons still lurked about here and there; most of them had their fill of pain. Couldn't be too careful though.

I can't begin to describe the agony of that time.

I still had nightmares under the lightless night; I didn't bother turning on the solar lantern I managed to scrounge up in an abandoned academy back in Norfolk.

Maybe that bastard bird should have screamed louder.

*

Norfolk was in chaos when I left: people slicing their own throats, blood flowing through the streets when people who couldn't take it anymore plummeted from the rooftops trying to end it all.

The end didn't come for them. Death had fled the world, and the stings of scorpions had taken their place.

Five months of that and some bigwig up in the White House promised it would end—probably had read the book— but it was too late for him. Too late for most people who had taken the mark.

The air was still; it usually was out here in the boonies. I had decided to ride the rest of this out away from the cities as

45

the book had described perversions happening in them. I didn't want to be party to something like that, nor did I want to be a victim.

The sky was overcast; the limited nuclear exchanges had seen to a permanent cooling. The sand next to the sea was grey and my feet barely made an impression behind me; what little there was quickly washed away by the ocean.

I'd mostly been camping in abandoned beach houses. A lot of real estate was available these days. Disappearances... deaths... millions gone.

Just the leftovers now. Didn't pass muster I guess, didn't believe.

I believe. Sweet God in heaven, I believe...

I was still here.

Hadn't seen hide nor hair of anyone for a few days, just the corpses of beach houses, wooden docks stretching out like dying hands towards the water. I always stopped to pick the bones of any boats that were left behind. Found a few flashlights, a packet of vacuum-sealed chip bags that had fed me for a few days.

I had never found any bodies; the buzzards that seemed to make their homes in the dead, leafless trees bordering the beach went about their God-given purpose with fervor.

Those beady eyes stared at me hungrily and I warily gripped the rifle in my hand. I was down to only six shots. I didn't want to waste them, but images of savage vultures picking the eyes from my head gave me an extra sense of paranoia.

Buzzards at day, rats at night.

Hell of a life.

Charleston was the next big hub. I was going to try to bypass it through the dead woods in the interior. Couldn't risk swimming it; two rivers emptied into the sea there... No, the interior it would have to be.

I glanced at the dead trees, a thick slab of grey like gigantic thin tombstones. I'd only tried the interior once since I'd made my journey, but the things that lived in the trees now...

Let's just say I had no intention of peeling off my own skin trying to die for the next five months.

46

It was around then that the smell hit me. I knew it well; before the End Times I had filled up my car often enough to know it.

Gasoline.

There were few refineries still working in the world, and I knew that this close to the sea, it wasn't likely.

This area of the beach was obscured by dunes, and I stuck to them in case there were desperate folks watching from the woods. But I decided to trot to the top of the nearest one to my left, risking a peek to see if I could spot the cause of the smell. It didn't take me long.

It sat just off shore like a fat tick leeching blood from the water, and there was plenty of that as well. An oil tanker rested comfortably on the seabed, its dark cargo spilled out and covering the sea in a black blanket.

Wasn't an uncommon sight; the second trumpet had destroyed plenty of ships.

There was something new now: the smell of meat that had been left out in the world for too long.

I glanced down to see bodies littering the shore. Men, their faces still open in silent screams, flesh hideously peeled by knives and fingernails, flies buzzing around them as they lapped up their blood.

They had drunk the waters hoping that they would die, only to succumb to the poison after the abominations had their fill.

They weren't the only things littering the beach. Dead fish, birds, and a dolphin washed up on the high tide, covered with oil, chittering as it drowned in the thick black tar clogging in its blowhole. It sounded like a rattling car engine, and its vain flopping was so weak that I thought about putting it out of its misery.

And throughout my observation of this monument of misery I never noticed the small boy standing scant feet from me.

"Uh, hi."

I whirled around and raised the gun, my heart pounding as the kid screamed and threw himself to the ground.

My footsteps pounded in the sand and I grabbed the boy by the back of the neck. "*You came this close!*" I roared. It momentarily startled me; I hadn't heard my voice in weeks.

"*I'm sorry, Mister!*" Tears flowed freely down the kid's face. He couldn't have been more than fourteen. Must not have been a church-going sort or else he wouldn't be suffering down here with the rest of us.

There was a click, and I immediately knew that I was fucked. I'd heard rifles enough times to recognize the sound of one.

Another man, younger than me, still in his prime if a bit underfed, had me dead to rights standing at the bottom of the hill.

"Unhand my son."

I did so immediately and made sure that my gun was lowered at the ground. The man wore a plaid button-up shirt and jeans that looked like they were in need of a good wash. His eyes were clouded with storms, but not malice.

He didn't look like those back in the city, the ones who had given in and drank in the sin and perversions to take away the pain. That was one way to get through the fifth trumpet.

The man spoke again, his voice calm, solid as an anchor. "You marked?"

"I'll show you mine if you show me yours," I replied with a shit-eating grin.

The man was not amused, but his eyes softened a bit, rotating the wrist holding the grip of the rifle just enough that I could see his bare skin. He wasn't one of them, and as I showed him my bare wrists, he seemed to be relieved that neither was I.

"Dakota, come here."

The kid obeyed his father, the older man ruffling his hair as he got close, his eyes never leaving me.

"Keep going if you want, stranger. Charleston became a hellhole though, I expect you already knew that…" He seemed to eye me for a moment before lowering his rifle. "You look like you could use a hot meal and definitely a shower. Our home is open if you can find it in yourself to come."

Maybe the man could see my hesitation. He offered me his hand. "Willard Barr, and this is my son, Dakota."

Gingerly, I reached out and shook Willard's hand and hoarsely croaked out, "Virgil Cook."

Willard hefted the strap of his rifle over his shoulder and grunted with a nod of his head. "What do you say, Virgil, you coming?"

Since this had all begun, I had never trusted anyone; doubted I could here either. But a shower… clean water….

I knew better than to follow, but I went with the both of them regardless.

*

Willard had a wife, Layla. She was a pretty thing, though her gaunt face told me that the family hadn't seen much by way of food in a while. They were remarkably clean and it made my grunge all the more noticeable in the gloom of the green beach house they were squatting in.

The boy, Dakota, had managed to kill a pure crow. The wiry bird was going to be the center piece for that night's dinner and combined with the half empty bag of Doritos I had been able to provide, it was a veritable feast.

"Should we say grace?" Layla asked, her eyes darting to the curtains that shut out the world and the deadly night that had descended outside.

"Fuck yes," I said receiving a disapproving look from the two adults. Dakota repressed a giggle. "Sorry," I said meekly.

Willard gave a tense smile, one that I sensed he had struggled to maintain in recent times. "It's okay, we're all sinners here."

His wife and child seemed to agree with the sentiment. They bowed their heads and I stared around at the happy family for a moment trying to keep the tears out of my eyes. My family was gone; some taken up, and others killed in what followed. Judgment Day, trumpet sound, we're all sinners that are left.

"Kind Father, smile down upon us, give us thankful hearts—"

Dakota was halfway through the prayer when a blast split the air. The table rocked and the whole house shook hard enough that all of us were knocked out of our chairs. The whole world shook. Then as fast it came, it was gone, a tense silence returning as the four of us picked ourselves up off of the floor.

"That was it, wasn't it?" Layla's lip trembled, her face pale.

Chill bumps raced up my spine. I had read the words several times. Hell, I had been living through the last pages of God's playbook, but a trumpet blast always seemed to get me quivering even if I had managed to avoid the last five.

"What's this one, Dad?" Dakota had righted his chair but he hadn't sat, none of us had; the urge to flee was strong, to find the deepest part of the world and throw ourselves into it, beg that darkness to hide us from what was next.

"Let me go get the book," Willard said, and he moved to head to his bedroom.

"I've got one right here," I replied fishing in my bag for the book.

The Bible felt heavy in my hands, like it knew what was going on outside. I flipped to the very back of the waterlogged book that I had picked up off a dead man back in Virginia.

"So the four angels, who had been prepared for the hour and day and month and year, were released to kill a third of mankind." With each word my heart thumped a little faster and when I finished reading the verse, I could barely keep the book steady.

"Maybe... maybe they won't come."

Willard looked at me like I had lobsters crawling out of my ears. "Maybe they won't come? Are you serious?"

I shrugged, feeling desperate. Layla held Dakota tight; the boy had tears in his eyes.

My eyes glanced to the ceiling and I wondered if God was watching, if he had heard our halfhearted prayers, and if he was considering not unleashing his dogs on us.

Silence reigned as four sinners crouched in the heart of an abandoned house wondering if the wrath of God would come bursting in to slay them. Minutes passed in silence and I breathed a sigh of relief.

Layla practically collapsed into her chair and Dakota smiled broadly. It was too alien on a kid like him. A fourteen-year-old shouldn't have that many stress lines; a small man standing where a kid should have been.

"I think it would be better if we all just took our dinners separately tonight, got some sleep, maybe look to moving on tomorrow." Willard spoke sense but his eyes were on me, wondering if I would protest. I gave him a slight nod and he gestured down the hall. "Bedrooms are down there. Help yourself."

Couldn't help but notice the sweat drifting down his forehead.

*

Sleep didn't come. How can it when you're riding out the end in the darkness without stars because the sky has been rolled back like a scroll?

The sheets and the beds felt nice and God knew that I hadn't had a decent night's sleep in ages, but that feeling at the back of my head remained. *Don't fall asleep; if you go into the blackness you won't come out.*

Memories and night dreams of crowds tearing at their own skin, pining for death, and unable to find it. Knowing that the worst was yet to come.

Sighing, I got up and made my way through the dark house. It would be too easy for someone with intentions less noble than mine to come into this family's abode and prove just why it was that they had been left behind.

I eventually found myself drifting out of the house and onto the deck.

Growing used to the smell of death wasn't easy, but over it there was still the smell of the ocean. That crisp tang of saltwater, and the steady noise of waves breaking against the shore.

It took a moment for my eyes to adjust, and even then, there still wasn't much to see; the rails in front of me, the yawning dark of the house behind, but no moon and no stars. Those were gone from the black sky.

Shivering, I rummaged in my jacket pockets. The crumpled pack was right where I had left it; the small green box proclaiming SALEM was a rare treat. I still had three in the box, the original twelve having been smoked in the moments when despair had come on quick and hard. The filter felt comforting as it hung in my mouth. Maybe it would give me cancer, escape out of the world that way.

Couldn't off myself even if it was possible again. The ones who said that the Lord had issue with that were gone now, and even if I didn't know for sure I was taking everything to heart.

The lighter flicked in my hand and soon the soft nicotine high was massaging my brain. I stood on the porch alone with my thoughts, so I didn't hear his footsteps or when he slowly slid the door closed behind us.

"Spare a smoke?"

I nearly jumped out of my skin. Willard stood close behind me, his face a mask of desire as he stared at the cigarette, already halfway burned, clenched tightly between my lips.

"Yeah, just as long as you don't come creeping up on me anymore."

Willard chuckled slightly. I slipped the cigarette into his eager hand and he brought his own lighter out. Soon the smoke was swirling around the porch and Willard was staring contently out at the ocean.

"Thought about maybe coming with us when we leave tomorrow?" It was a curious question, but still just small talk.

"What is it that you really want to ask me?" I grunted, blowing a fine puff of smoke into the night.

"Are you scared?" Willard responded in kind to my blunt words.

"Hell yeah, I'm scared. Don't know if you've noticed but there can't be too many people left out there. Now a third more are going the way of the dodo according to the book..." I trailed off.

"Do you think they'll find us?" Willard asked. The question hung in the air and I inhaled a sweet hit of the cigarette. It was nearly gone, only embers burning at the end of the filter now.

"What makes you think they haven't known where we were this entire time?"

Even in the dark I could see Willard shudder, and I didn't think it was because of the cold. He coughed lightly and stared at the cigarette in his hand. I desperately wanted to light up the other one in my pocket but the urge to wait came on strong. Instead. Willard and I stood there in silence. Maybe God heard our fear; maybe he didn't.

The snap of tree branches out in the dead pinewoods stirred us from our individual reveries. The two of us were instantly alert. Big game was sparse nowadays and rats and squirrels didn't cause logs to just break.

"Go look to your family," I said gripping my rifle a little tighter. Willard nodded and disappeared quickly into the gloom. There were no other sounds from the woods, but that didn't mean jack shit. One noise was good enough. My nerves were raw and I felt the adrenaline spike as my heart pounded.

I was terrified.

From on top of the house something thumped. I swung my gun, staring into the dark sky above and trying to discern anything that stood out.

A figure stood on the roof above and the shadows seemed to cling to its form like clothing. A deep and throaty growl came from it, low and desiring of flesh.

My hands shook, and I rushed inside as the thing shrieked and dove, crashing through the deck and leaving a bright afterimage emblazoned on my eyes. My stomach churned and I felt bile rise in my throat.

The brief flash of fire had illuminated the figure for just a moment allowing me to see the sickly wings jutting from its body.

A swift beam of light lit my face and I whirled around. Willard held his hands up, Dakota and Layla standing close behind him, wicked knives clutched in their hands.

"They're here."

Willard didn't ask questions; there was no doubt who *they* were.

"We've got to run, right?" Dakota asked, his eyes darting around the interior of the house, searching for any sign of our opponents.

The kid didn't deserve to die. He should have been out in the world testing his limits, sowing wild oats, not squatting in some dim bit of nowhere. It made me angry; my knuckles ground together and I whispered to myself, "Alright…"

It's a wonderful feeling when you've made up your mind to die.

"Willard, get your family out of here, hug the beach, and avoid the cities. I don't know how long y'all have been out—"

A tapping interrupted my instructions. The four of us froze, the hairs on my arms rising as I slowly turned to stare out the window.

A figure stood on the ledge beyond, a hand like flawless alabaster tapping at the glass. Its body was flawless, no genitalia graced its pubic regions, and on its handsome face was a grin that stretched too wide. Eyes like fire burned in its sockets, charring the otherwise flawless skin. The sickly wings beat uselessly behind it, like a bird in the early stages of molting.

Its eyes locked on me, and I suddenly felt very small, the gun in my hand all but useless. Then in a voice like a landslide it whispered one word: "Sinner."

The glass shattered in front of it, the wood warping and caving in. I felt an intense blast of heat hit me, like I was standing too close to a grill. Blisters popped on my hand as my skin peeled back.

The angel crouched on all fours and skittered forward, its face warping. What I once thought was a man's face had flickered, the images of glass and fire rearranging until a wicked maw, too wide to belong to any man, sat underneath a dark tangle of hair.

A massive roar split the air; Willard had fired his rifle directly at the monstrosity clambering over the blackened wood and glass, but it didn't stop.

I raised my rifle and fired. I saw the bullet hit it, saw a wound briefly open and disappear just as quickly.

It lunged for Dakota.

A predator's smile is disconcerting; it leaves you with a feeling of unease. Maybe because they're not really smiling, they're just baring their teeth for the feast.

The angel's face, a terrible visage, was peeled in a wicked grin.

Layla stepped in front of it, throwing Dakota back. She gave a strangled cry and barely managed to nick a cut across its cheek before it had fallen on her.

I wasted another bullet, but the angel ignored me. Layla screamed in bloody agony as its fingernails raked at her stomach. I watched in horror as her face sloughed off, her rosy cheeks running from the savage heat emanating from the divine monster as her hair caught fire.

"*Get your kid and run!*" I roared at the top of my lungs. Willard didn't have to be told twice. Tears streamed down his face as he grabbed Dakota around the midsection and drug him deeper into the house. The kid's screams mixed with those of his mother.

When I was a child, I had been burning leaves after a storm and a turtle had crawled under the wet pile, no doubt looking for safety.

Layla and Dakota's cries sounded like that turtle.

I watched the pretty woman's screams fade away into a gurgle as her insides melted, the smell of cooked flesh wafting to my nose. My stomach churned; it smelled delicious and I was immediately reviled, bitter bile rising to the back of my throat as I trained my gun with trembling hands on the beast eating the blackened husk of the woman's body.

The angel stopped feasting, its fiery eyes turned to look at me with a wicked grin. "You're next," it said.

In that voice I heard a man, a woman, and a child all overlapping, and even knowing that it was beyond this world it still sent a shiver of terror racing down my spine as my mind tried to comprehend what I was seeing.

A deep scream echoed from in the house and I turned to run. The angel made no attempt to pursue me and I fled into the darkness.

I didn't have to go very far. Willard had taken Dakota and was no doubt heading for the backdoor that led into the woods.

All of us had forgotten the verse; the book had told us exactly what was going to happen, and we had forgotten.

Four angels had been prepared for the day and the hour.

Willard hung on the edge of a flaming sword. Dakota had collapsed beside him, staring at his father who stared down at the gleaming metal, his flesh cracking and oozing around the entry wound.

Its face was like a lion, warped flesh stretched out into a fanged grimace with a shaggy mane replacing its hair. Wicked talons grasped the hilt of the sword as a low roar rumbled from its throat.

It's crooked and decayed wings seemed to beat in excitement as Willard struggled to remove the sword from his guts. He couldn't speak; even his whines were pitiful groans. Smoke leaked from his lips as his eyes stared at me, begging. The sword had pierced his lungs and his insides were melting.

I grabbed Dakota from the floor. He was in shock, his eyes wide but his mind gone, lost in the sight of the death of his parents.

Another angel stepped from behind the lion-headed one, its face a warped and sickly eagle. I had never seen a bird smile but this monstrosity managed it.

"Sinner."

Again, man, woman, and child, but this time an evil screech joined them, the voice of birds adding their accusation to the cacophony.

Willard's struggle ceased, and the lion-headed angel flicked the sword upward; the man came apart in two, his body severing cleanly, charred guts spilling onto the floor.

Dakota trailed along behind me, my grip firmly on his wrist. The eagle-headed angel followed. Its compatriots took no notice of us, swept up as they were in their feasting of the boy's parents.

The heat coming from the angels had risen, the wallpaper inside the beach house beginning to peel and run up the walls like scrolls slowly rolling back.

I deftly averted falling through the hole left behind by the first angel. Dakota was blubbering something now, empty words. We took the stairs nearly two at a time. Perspiration was beginning to soak my forehead and my lungs ached. I hadn't been a young man for a long time.

We reached the bottom of the stairs, the flashlight in Dakota's hands wavering, bathing the dirty grey dunes with wisps of light.

It looked like a fog had rolled in. I nearly thanked the big man before I remembered just what it was pursuing me. The woods, dark and deep, were a long run down the beach in the open.

I whirled around and faced Dakota who stared up at me with wide eyes. I handed him the rifle. "Run, boy, and don't look back, don't stop, and make it to the end of this."

The teenager glanced at the beach and then at the woods. "Where do I go?"

I didn't have the answer for him. Instead I shoved him towards the beach. "Get a move on before—"

With the crashing waves on the beach I hadn't thought anything of it, the sound of shifting dirt, until I realized that the sounds weren't coming from the beach but from the gloom underneath the beach house deck. Directly to our right.

A figure crouched there in the shadows, a set of horns gleaming as it crawled on all fours towards us; the last angel with the face of an ox. Its horns gleamed from the heat and I shoved Dakota. "*Go!*"

The boy didn't have to be told twice. He sprinted towards the dunes, disappearing just as fast.

"Find… him…" Its voice was the deepest out of the four, its hands ending in sharp hooves. I doubted it could have stood even if it wanted to.

I knew I was going to die. I had known it ever since I had heard that blasted trumpet, even prayed for forgiveness a few times. Even if these blasphemies against nature were his, I was more terrified of the alternative.

The angel inched closer to me. I shut my eyes and defiantly stated, "Fuck you."

It gave a long and echoing roar, angry wings beating as it launched towards me. I felt the heat of the horns as they stabbed through my chest.

Searing heat, agony like I hadn't known, my skin charred and peeled, my blood boiled in my veins.

The others emerged from the house, eager to join in.

It was a long time until the darkness ended that pain.

THE OLD MAN AND THE LAMB

Patrick C. Harrison III

"Mind the curfew—11 p.m. sharp!—by order of the Church," read the passage at the bottom. It was the least significant statement on the bulletin.

If one were to view the city from above—assuming the overwhelming smog would allow such a sight—its streets would look like diseased vessels on a vast, unending body of filth. The churches and cathedrals that dotted nearly every corner (abortion clinics, which were, of course, sponsored by the Church, occupied the rest), did not offer the comfort that one might expect from places of worship. The warning at the bottom of the bulletin raised nary a question from the city's average inhabitant. For the only creatures that, after sunset, dare wander the pothole ridden roads and alleys, where garbage spewed onto the cracked sidewalks like vomit from a dying alcoholic, were whores and drug dealers and other scum of society. But, then, perhaps these *were* the city's average inhabitants.

The old man who stood looking at the bulletin, his hands stuffed into dirty gray slacks, his groin tightening with the need to urinate (fucking prostate!), wasn't a whore or a drug dealer or even a member of the scum. At least, he didn't think so. The Church and the Prophet may think differently. *And that's all that really matters, isn't it?* the old man thought.

He was a businessman in the years before the Prophet's coming, and a successful one at that. Five retail stores and two cafés had been under his ownership before the Church claimed

59

them during the Holy Reformation. But that was for the better, now, wasn't it? Or so he had been told; so they had all been told.

The bulletin meant nothing to the old man. He had seen it before. How could he not? One was likely to pass a few hundred of them on a trip to the nearest St. Michael's Grocery to buy a gallon of milk. They lined the brick and concrete walls of every structure in the city, save the churches, of course. They littered lampposts, phones booths, and collection boxes for the Holy Church Postal Service. Half a dozen of them would tumble past pedestrians with each brisk wind, and one would find sewers and ditches stuffed with them, all crumpling and torn. The instructions printed on them varied occasionally, depending on recent events, but they were all more or less the same.

The old man moved on, buttoning his tweed jacket as he passed a backstreet, a gust of polluted wind whipping odious air and crinkled bulletins past him. He hadn't been reading the bulletin, no; he had been deciding where to go next. The dusty, derelict apartment complex the old man called home lacked the enchantment of the abode on the edge of the city he and Harriet once shared. So, he walked. Taking interest in the latest bulletin while he contemplated his travels was unlikely to draw questions from the Holy Police, were they to happen upon him in the failing light of dusk.

He passed Café de Drogo, where pimple-faced adolescents prepared and served standard coffee at posh prices. They always topped their joe with an off-white froth that looked, to the old man, like some sickly lunger had hacked his sputum sample into the mug. He passed darkened, lifeless shops of old, looking like holes in the earth. He passed a retail store with a brilliantly lit sign that read, "XXX". In its windows were large-breasted mannequins in lingerie. On the door was a tattered paper sign, hung askew, reading, "Free contraceptives with every purchase!"

The old man walked on, his knees creaking as he navigated the fractured and often brittle concrete of the sidewalk. Thick clouds moved overhead and guttural thunder quaked. *It might rain*, the old man thought, and he wondered where the city's thousands of homeless scattered when the skies opened up. Did they seek shelter in the skeletal stores where they once shopped for designer jeans and handbags and sunglasses? Or did they simply huddle against the broken buildings and cover themselves with bulletins to block the rain? *Why, they take to the churches, of course*, the old man thought. How silly of him to think they would seek shelter anywhere but a church.

"I'll blow you for a fifty note," spewed a woman from the darkness, her malnourished figure unfolding from beneath an ancient wool blanket, riddled with holes and insects. The woman was young. Young, but not young. Her ghastly mouth was a toothless, rotten hole. Her bloodshot eyes told tales of insanity and addiction. Her taut skin was sheen and yellow, covered with sores that leaked purulent fluids, attracting flies and probably rats.

The old man passed her, trying unsuccessfully not to lay his eyes upon her. Battling his protesting knees, he made hast. But her claw-like hand grasped his slacks.

"Please!" she screeched, her voice like a wailing bird. "You can have my snatch, mister. I ain't tainted, believe me. Please!"

"Get away," the old man growled. He yanked his leg, but to no avail. *If she isn't tainted, then I'm the Prophet himself*, he thought.

"One denarius! You can fuck me for one denarius, mister! I ain't even got no baby box, so don't you worry. The Church took it out, God bless 'em. And God bless the Prophet."

"Let go, whore!" the old man yelled, and with a final jerk he was free of her, stumbling towards the gutter but catching himself on the leaning post of a broken street light.

Without looking back, the old man crossed the street. The gurgling sewers beneath emitted smells that made him gag. The whore cried and screamed, first pleading that he come back, then raging that she didn't want anything to do with him or his old, withered cock.

The pub was in sight now. It was called Saint Augustine's Tavern, and its neon sign (the only source of light on this side of the road, save the soft glow of the lamp outside the church on the corner) flickered strobe-like, masses of flies swarming it like an ever-evolving cloud. The old man mounted the sidewalk before its entrance, slipping clumsily on fragile concrete, and practically fell through the swinging door. A bell clanked unmusically above him as he gained his balance, the door creaking closed behind him.

"Careful now, old fella," the barkeep said in a cheerful country accent. "I don't need you taking a spill before you buy a drink."

The old man laughed but said nothing. He took a seat on the closest barstool and looked around. The walls were, predictably, covered with bulletins, both new and old. A television in the corner, its volume higher than the old man would prefer, carried on with a lengthy commercial on contraceptives—*"guaranteed to prevent those unwanted, blasphemous children of Satan!"* it claimed in a cheerful but authoritative voice. Directly behind the bar, flanked on either side by the newest bulletins, was a painting of the Prophet. He was standing in a green pasture, dressed all in black—as He usually was—with a gold crucifix around His neck, a rosary in His right hand. Seven smiling children gazed upon the Prophet with wonder and unflinching attentiveness. The old man bowed his head at the painting of the Prophet and made the sign of the cross.

"What'll it be, old fella?" the barkeep asked, leaning one sharp elbow on the bar top and smiling. He was tall and lanky, and his dark hair was slicked back in a fashion that reminded the old man of movies from his youth. His skin was smooth and tan, but his eyes showed age and heartache.

"A beer, I guess," the old man said. "Dark beer if you got it."

"Darn right I got it," said the barkeep. "Saint Augustine's has the best beer selection in the city."

The old man nodded. He saw only two beer taps and wondered if that was indeed the best selection in the city. He had not been to a pub in years so he couldn't make an educated guess on the topic, but he supposed it was possible. Most businesses—like most people—had shriveled into mere shadows of their former selves.

"Say," the barkeep said, squinting his eyes at the old man, "how you payin'? Notes or coinage?"

The old man dug in his pocket, produced a denarius and laid in gently on the bar.

"Silver! Good man!" the barkeep exclaimed, smiling wide, showing absurdly white teeth that were most certainly fake. "I apologize for asking, old fella. It's just that my usual customers at this hour are men of the cloth. Being so close to dark, you know?"

The old man waved his hand. "No need to apologize."

The barkeep turned around, grabbed a porcelain stein from the counter. On one side was a beautifully painted blue cross, and on the other, written in elaborate calligraphy was, "Praise the Prophet. Praise the Church. And praise God." The barkeep held the stein under the tap, then paused and placed it back on the counter. He grabbed a glass beer mug and quickly began filling it.

The steins are for men of the cloth, the old man thought. *He temporarily forgot who he was serving: an underling of the Church; a petty follower.*

"There you are," the barkeep said, spinning around and setting the frothy mug in front of him. The liquid beneath the head was a dark, cloudy brown, and suds dripped over the edge of the glass like they often do in refreshing beer commercials.

The old man nodded his thanks and tilted the mug to his lips, taking a long swig. The beer was almost painfully cold, and there was a reason for this: it tasted like shit. The ale had an uncanny flavor that was simultaneously sour and bland. The sourness, the old man guessed, was from an unintentional infusion of bacteria during the brewing process. The reason for blandness was simple enough. Barley and hops were at a premium these days, and a desperate brewer was likely to use whatever was in arm's reach to create his bubbly—corn, rice, or even hay. But it was cold and wet, so the old man forced it down.

"Good stuff, ain't it?" the barkeep said. "God bless the Prophet and God bless the monks who bring us our brews."

"God bless," the old man said dutifully, lifting the mug to the painting of the Prophet and taking another gentle sip. "You got a latrine? I gotta take a leak."

"You bet, old fella. Down the hall on the right." After snatching the denarius and dropping it in his pocket, he thumbed towards a dingy corridor past the bar, barely illuminated by a bulb that appeared to be on its last spark.

The old man set the beer down and dismounted the barstool, his knees complaining with every movement. He wondered if the barkeep could hear them creak. The bathroom door opened with a creak not much different than the old man's knees, and his blindly searching hand found the light switch, flooding the small room in blinding white. Stepping from the hallway to the restroom was liking walking from dusk into high noon in the desert.

The restroom had, at some point in the recent past, endured a volcanic eruption of liquid shit. And as bad as the sewer smell in the street had been, it was even worse here. A thin, grimy brown film covered everything, including the toilet seat, sink and mirror. *Thank the Prophet I don't have to take a squat*, the old man thought. He briefly wondered if what he saw was caused by an explosive occurrence from an unfortunate soul's bowels, or from the rickety pipes and cesspits below the city. He decided he was better off not knowing.

The only thing not blemished by the crusty remnants of diarrheal devastation, was the new bulletin posted behind the toilet seat. As he undid his fly, the old man concluded he would prefer reading the bulletin to scanning the walls of filth.

"Faithful Followers," it read, "the subsequent orders were drafted and agreed upon by the Prophet, the Cardinal Senate, and God. Failure to abide by these laws will result in detainment and prosecution by the Holy Police.

"(1) All children under the age of 3 must be registered with the Church and subjected to yearly examination by the Holy Church Medical Core. Any child not registered and examined within one month of birth will be permanently removed from parental custody.

"(2) Within one week following a child's third birthday, they must be enlisted in God's Youth and enrolled in

Confraternity of Christian Doctrine weekly classes. Failure to enlist and enroll any child will result in their permanent removal from parental custody.

"(3) All adults, 16 years-of-age and older, with viable reproductive organs, are required to attend monthly educational programs on the topic of Satan's threat to our children and the impending birth of the false prophet. Documentation of attendance must be accessible at all times.

"(4) All adults, 16 years-of-age and older, with viable reproductive organs, must attend yearly well-being seminars with representatives from the HCMC, with the focus being on the health and spiritual benefits of sterilization. Documentation of attendance must be accessible at all times.

"(5) The subjects of the Church are not to take the name of the Prophet, the Church, or the Lord in vain. At no time can a person—adult or child—speak ill of those aforementioned without being in direct violation of Church Law. It is the duty of all Church subjects to report such violations to the Holy Police.

"(6) It is the duty of all Church subjects to appropriate goods, moneys, and assets—including properties and corporations—to the Church under determinate circumstances to assist with land expansion under the Kingdom of God, economic empowerment for less fortunate subjects, and wars against the armies of Satan.

"(7) All small arms, cutlery not intended for culinary or trade use, and other potential weapons of war must be relinquished at the nearest office of God's Holy Army to assist with preparation for wars against the armies of Satan and the coming of the false prophet.

"Submitting thyself to the Prophet and the Church and God, and adhering to these Laws and God's Ten Commandments (as rewritten and approved by the Prophet and Cardinal Senate) ensure thyself an eternity in Heaven alongside the Lord our God."

Then, almost as an afterthought, was the passage declaring one must abide by the curfew.

The old man shook off the last few dribbles his prostate would allow, then zipped his fly. Carefully balancing on one foot, he triggered the commode with the other. It flushed and, unbelievably, the stench was momentarily made worse.

Exiting the restroom, the old man closed the door in hopes that the odor wouldn't shadow him back to the bar. Leaning over the counter and looking at the latest issue of the Saint de Sale Journal, the barkeep, in a quiet, out-of-tune voice, was singing "Pleasure Thy," the latest hit single from the Future Saints. "Satan's got to die! The falsehood's got to fry! So, stay out of other's eyes! Ignore that beckoning cry! And...*pleasure thy!*" The old man wasn't a fan of God Metal, but this song—promoting masturbation over the dangerous act of intercourse, which could inadvertently result in the birth of the false prophet—was hard to avoid these days.

Returning to his seat, he took a long drink of beer, swallowing fast to avoid, as best he could, having to taste it. Again, he made the sign of the cross at the painting of the Prophet. The barkeep, noticing this gesture, looked up from his magazine, nodded at the old man, and smiled. *Better safe than sorry*, the old man thought, not knowing if the barkeep was a hardliner when it came to etiquette. *Better safe than sorry, and spending the night being questioned by the Holy Police about why I don't love and respect the Prophet and the Lord our savior.*

On the television, an overzealous salesman was declaring that the Doomsday Warehouse was the ideal shopping destination for anyone hoping to survive the End Times. Thunder cracked outside, but rain, for the moment, held fast. With the commercial over, two news anchors—the male outfitted in typical priest attire and the woman in her nun's garments—appeared. The barkeep turned to watch.

"Tensions are growing in Persia and the Orient," the priest was saying, *"as the armies of Satan stand together in defiance against of the one true Prophet and the Kingdom of God. Not since the Battle of Jericho has the threat of total war been greater. But our blessed Prophet, along with the Cardinal Senate and God's Holy Army, guarantee safety and prosperity for all those within the walls of God's Kingdom, and destruction will be brought to all who defy the word of the Prophet and the will of God. God bless the Prophet!"*

With that, the priest turned and looked uneasily at the nun. *"Yes, God bless the Prophet, for He will lead us to victory!"* she said. Then, *"In other news, 342 unregistered children were detained over the weekend as the search continues for the coming of the false prophet. Church officials say—"*

"I reckon the Church will be seizing more farms," the barkeep said.

The old man barely heard this statement and didn't even realize that the barkeep had turned to face him again. He had been watching the report and wondering what would happen to those 342 children. Would they end up in an orphanage where the Church would oversee their upbringing? Would they be placed with a holier, more God-fearing family? Or would they cease to exist? Would they be swatted into nothingness like an annoying fly on one's arm? The old man had heard the rumors (most of these rumors, valid or not, were uttered by those druggers and drunks that littered the streets like crumpled bulletins) that the children that were seized by the church were rarely, if ever, seen again. "What's that?" he said.

"I said, I guess the Church will be taking more farms. Ya know, with the threat of war on the horizon. That's what I used to do. Farm."

"Oh," the old man nodded. He wondered if the barkeep and former farmer secretly despised the Church and the Prophet and everything they stood for. Did he hate what the world had become and long for the days of old, when the sun shone on the soul as well as the land? Did the barkeep wonder, as he did, that it's possible—just possible!—that the Prophet Himself may be the false prophet? That it is He who is leading this world, this Kingdom of God, down the path to Hell? What would this former farmer do if the Prophet stood alone before him in this bar? Would he genuflect and perform the sign of the cross, or would he offer a far less obedient gesture? "Yes, I suppose they will," the old man said.

The barkeep winced at this, however minutely, and his face seemed to grow older almost instantly.

"I, uh, I used to own several businesses before the Holy Reformation." The old man said this timidly, but purposely showing the hurt in his eyes. Then, opting for safety, he added,

"Sacrificing for the good of the Church can be... difficult. But it is our duty." This last bit was stated with no conviction.

"Yes," the barkeep said, staring blankly at the bar top. "For the good of the Church, of course." He looked up, his eyes seeming to brighten a little. "Say, old fella, can I trust you? Could I show you something?"

"Certainly," the old man said, curious and flattered.

"As I said, I used to be a farmer. I relinquished my land and livestock to the Prophet himself when His band of warriors, priests and monks brought revolution to the western provinces. But I couldn't give up everythin'. Perhaps it was a sin and perhaps I will burn in Hell for not surrendering every last thing under my ownership, but it just seemed too spectacular to let loose of."

The old man's interest was presently peaked. He finished off his beer and set it gently on the cracked, stained wood of the old bar. "Barkeep," he said, "you seem a good and passionate man. Whatever you have to show, I will look upon with wondering eyes and sealed lips."

The barkeep appeared to mull this over for a moment, then, with a chortle, he nodded. "Fair enough, old fella. Follow me."

The old man, beyond intrigued, ignoring his creaking knees as he once more left his barstool, followed the barkeep into the dank hallway, holding his breath as he passed the revolting restroom, his mind suddenly conjuring up images of mutated miniature monsters climbing from the toilet, spraying shit from their gullets like mythical dragons breathe fire. God and Prophet, his imagination really got going once it got going. *At least the Church can't take that from me*, he thought, and then: *Prophet, forgive me for all these blasphemous conceptions*.

The barkeep came to an old door of near rotten wood. Dozens of flies had collected on the door, and the old man was reminded how when, after revolution and reformation, people had committed suicide by the thousands, their decomposing bodies attracting swarms of flies to congregate on their doors and windows, just waiting to be let in. Was there a dead body beyond this door? Surely not. At eye level was a sign that identified the room beyond as a utility closet.

Producing a key from his pocket, the barkeep looked over his shoulder at the old man, seeming not to notice the flies that briefly buzzed around his head, and said, "This is really somethin'." He turned the lock and then the knob.

The smell that emanated from the passage—it clearly wasn't a closet—was almost as bad as the restroom. It was a different stench, like fermenting vegetation with an overwhelming sour must. He followed the barkeep into the darkness of a descending stone stairwell, and the old man noted how warm and humid the corridor was. It was like he was walking straight through that awful smell. Remembering his sour beer, the old man thought he wouldn't be surprised if there was a makeshift, and completely unsanitary—not that anything was really sanitary these days—brewery housed in this hideous dungeon of disgust.

The stairwell ended in a dimly lit basement which, surprisingly, *did* have some utility items, like mops and brooms and water bucket. But that wasn't what the barkeep had brought him down here to see. Like the curfew notice on the bulletin, the rarely used mops and brooms were only an afterthought of the basement.

Standing amongst several damp tufts of hay and dry balls of dung, was what the old man first recognized—deformed though it was—as a small goat, little larger than a terrier, tittering on its legs as if drunk. The old man's eyes widened with simultaneous fascination and disgust. The thing's wobbly stance likely wasn't caused by drunkenness, as if it had been sipping from a trough of sour beer. Instead, the multiple cloudy, bloodshot eyes, dripping with puss and lined with crust, that dotted its face and snout probably, the old man guessed, made it difficult for the goat to gain its feet or avoid trotting into a brick wall.

The old man counted them. Two eyes were on either side of the head where eyes were supposed to be. Another one bulged from the end of its snout between its nostrils, appearing to look straight at the men. Two more on its forehead were askew and stared at opposing corners of the room. An eye, dripping with long strands of discolored, putrid gunk, swelled from the left side of its snout, then sunk inward, almost

69

disappearing before swelling again. The old man realized that this eye was being sucked in and pushed out with the goat's breathing. And yet another eye gazed unblinking from the right side of its head, into the things ear. *Seven eyes!* the old man marveled.

Twisted horns sprouted from its head like a crown of gnarled wood. Some long and some short, they curled around its ears and head, and two hung over its face in the style of a greasy-haired teenager. And one horn at the top of its misshapen head spiraled skyward several inches, ending in a broken tip. And how many were there? *Seven! Seven horns, too!*

"Jesus Christ," the old man muttered, unbelieving, completely forgetting the barkeep standing next to him.

The barkeep snickered, covering his mouth with his hand. "Don't worry, old fella. Your use of the Lord's name in vain is safe with me. We're keepers of each other's secret's, alright partner?"

The old man, his eyes like saucers, nodded agreement. He turned his attention back to the goat. *No,* he thought, *not goat; lamb. The Lamb! The Lamb of God!* The goat—Lamb— seeming to acknowledge the old man's inner thoughts, cocked its head to the side, focusing most of its seven eyes on him, its canker-ridden tongue lulling out of its mouth, dropping a glob of discolored spittle on the floor.

"I told you it was somethin'," the barkeep said. "I raised all types of sheep and goats and such, you see. I can't be sure what oddity in the herd birthed this crazy buzzard. He was just kinda there one day. I seen him trottin' along with the rest, running into every-damn-thing. You see that broken horn? He done that running into the wall last week when I came to feed him." He pointed to a blemished spot on the mortar next to the stairwell.

"You're right, barkeep," the old man said, "it's really something." And in his head, he was thinking, trying to remember the role of the Lamb in the Bible. *Wasn't it in Revelation?* he thought. *Seven eyes and seven horns and everything, I believe it was.*

Just then, the strangely music-less bell rang from upstairs. The barkeep gasped, his gaze whipping around to the flight of stairs.

"Stay here, old fella," he said quietly. "Can you do that? I ain't supposed to be giving nonmembers of the cloth private tours. The place is owned by the Church, you understand?"

The old man nodded. "Yes, go. I will stay and keep quiet."

With that, the barkeep bounded up the stairs and closed the door at their peak. Though the sound was muffled, the old man heard the barkeep greeting his patrons as *Father* and "*your Eminence*. A priest and a cardinal, they were. The old man had only ever seen a cardinal once, and thought how he may wish to meet a man of such power and influence in the Church. He was, of course, a writer and passer of laws and Church doctrine. But then his focus was on the Lamb again.

It stared at him with what eyes it could, perhaps hoping the old man would produce some treat from his pocket—a piece of fruit mayhap—and offer it to him. Or, on the other hand, maybe this Lamb—the Lamb of God—had been waiting for him for much longer. Maybe this Lamb and been waiting for the old man its entire life. A treat was nothing to this mutated piece of livestock meat. But the old man himself, that's what the Lamb wanted.

"Ridiculous," the old man muttered. "It's just a testament to the strangeness of nature. Nothing more." But his mind searched its inner archives, its teachings of the Church and the Bible, grasping for memories before the coming of the Prophet, before the Bible was changed to suit those in power, before Harriet was crucified with hundreds of others in the Valley of Nonbelievers.

The old man's eyes glazed over with tears at the thought of his lost beloved. He remembered that last night, when they huddled together in the dark of their once brightly lit home, waiting for the sound of bootsteps and the cries of the Prophet's warriors. "Heretic!" they would say. "Sinner!" they would cry. "Nonbeliever!" they would accuse. The old man— a young man then—weeping, tried to convince Harriet to sign the document of belief. To commit to being a faithful follower of the Prophet and the Church. He had done as much himself, but Harriet would have none of it.

"This is the end, don't you see?" she had whimpered, grasping his hand in hers. "The End Times, Walter. I will not bow to this man who calls himself the Prophet. Not for anything in the world. Runaway with me, my love! We'll go beyond the borders of what they're calling the Kingdom of God, and, together, we'll wait for the true God. Please, Walter! Please!"

But then the searchlights were in the windows and boots thudded around them. "Heretic! Sinner! Nonbeliever!" they screamed. And then she was taken from him forever. He cowered, afraid, wanting to be flung from this new world, where faith and obedience trumped all. He wished it all a dream. Indeed, in that moment, he *prayed* it to be a dream. But the Prophet's warriors and the Holy Police were not to be wished or prayed away. And in the end, Harriet was nailed to a cross like the rest.

Walter, the old man, had gazed upon the gruesome Valley of Nonbelievers—where crucified men, women, and children littered the earth to the horizon and beyond—from a distant hilltop, not knowing which of the "damned souls" was his wife. He had cried and cursed and vowed vengeance.

"In time," a woman said, startling Walter from his ravings on the hilltop, the bloody sun setting on the horizon.

"What?" he said, looking over at the woman, her face hidden by the blue cloth that draped around it.

"In time, the Lamb of God will bring destruction, and an end to your pain."

"Destruction?" he had sneered. "Lady, the God has already brought plenty of that. As for my pain, it has no end. So, go fuck yourself!"

But the woman was gone. *Or had she ever been there?* he wondered.

And now, in the basement of a dingy bar in a rotten city, the old man looked upon the Lamb of God, with its seven eyes and seven horns. Of this, the old man had no doubt. And he knew what he must do: Sacrifice.

The Lamb looked at him dumbly, strands of saliva dripping from its lumpy tongue and strands of yellow mucus oozing from the eye on the side of its snout. The old man searched his pockets and his belt for the knife he knew wasn't there. It, of course, had been claimed by God's Holy Army in preparation for war. He looked at his thin, feeble hands, wondering what they were capable of without the assistance of a weapon. Could they do the job, even to something as defenseless as this Lamb appeared to be? He had to try.

"Lamb," the old man said, his voice quiet but stern, "I sacrifice thee to the one God Almighty."

Sinking to one knee, his old bones creaking, he seized the Lamb by the neck. It jerked back, more powerfully than the old man would have guessed, nearly escaping his grasp. But his arthritic hands held true, clamping down on the beast's neck. The Lamb screeched, the sound not unlike that of wailing child. "Harriet, after all these years, forgive me," the old man said.

The beast thrashed its head and screamed again, its seven eyes bulging like miniature balloons, trails of snot and drool slinging through the air. The Lamb's hind legs jumped and its head lurched skyward, causing the broken horn to rip the old man's chin open. Blood poured and the old man lost his grip, the Lamb stumbling from him and falling over a mound of decaying hay and shit.

The old man cursed, wiping his chin and inspecting the blood left in his hand. Then, gritting his teeth and growling like an angry dog, he went after the Lamb on hands and knees. It screeched, seeing its peril in one or more eyes, flailing its head back and forth, catching the old man's left palm and tearing it open. But his hands closed around it once more, this time grabbing the head. The Lamb bit into his right hand, its jagged teeth easily puncturing his elderly flesh. The old man howled with pain, but did not let go.

His thumbs and fingers searched for the thing's eyes and pressed on them. Warm jelly burst over the thumb that griped the beast's snout. Two more eyes burst on its forehead, splattering gelatinous goo on the old man's fingers. His pained hands squeezed on the Lamb's face, blood and eye jelly and mucus and dribble dripping over his wrinkled skin like water from a damp rag. The Lamb screamed and the old man screamed with it. His fingers dug into its eye sockets, wriggling through goo and blood and the lateral muscles that once held the eyes, and finally puncturing through the rear and gnawing at its brain. At last, the Lamb went limp and fell from the old man's gore-streaked hands.

"*What have you done?*" the barkeep shrieked from the base of the stairs, a look of horror on his face. Trailing behind him was the priest and cardinal, looking saintly in his red cloth.

The old man turned to face them, blood dripping from his chin, hands, and clothes. Then: "It's the Lamb of God. The sacrificial Lamb of—"

"Shut-up, you old fuck! Get out of my way!" The barkeep rushed forward, pushing the old man aside.

The priest and cardinal stood like statues, bewildered.

"I… I had to," the old man said, looking at his hands and then at the puddled blood on the floor.

"What the hell?" the barkeep said, backing up now.

"Dear Prophet, help us," said the cardinal.

The priest made the sign of the cross.

The old man followed their gaze to the Lamb. It was slowly rising off the floor, its fur dirtied with blood and clinging hay, as if being lifted by an invisible hand. Everyone took a simultaneous step backwards, their eyes never leaving the Lamb. Once it reached about eye level, it stopped, hanging like a lighter-than-air feather. It was clearly lifeless, its sickly tongue still hanging from its mouth with dripping gore. Two dead eyes that had escaped the old man's prodding fingers, stared at nothing.

The barkeep made as if to touch it, but then it was curling into itself. The Lamb's head and limbs and nub of a tail all curled inward, towards its belly. The old man heard bones snap as the legs and head and horns all converged. Its flesh split along its back and sides, spilling fresh blood and mushed organs. The horns that hung over its face stabbed though its abdomen and punctured the flesh around its broken spine. The Lamb had curled into a gory ball, hanging on air. And then, as quickly as a snap of the fingers, what had once been the mutated Lamb of God imploded in a single burst of blood and was gone. Gone. Only a few stray hairs remained, floating down like falling leaves.

"What the hell just happened?" the barkeep said, whirling to face the men of the cloth. They looked terrified and clueless, offering no opinion.

"It was the Lamb of God," the old man said, a smile emerging on his face.

"You're crazy! Shut your mouth before I—"

A sound of immense power blared all around them, like the sound of a giant horn, shaking the building and the foundation, causing cracks to emerge in the walls of the basement. The men covered their ears. But as quickly as the blare had begun, it was gone. It was replaced by screams from the streets and thunder from the skies. The barkeep, priest and cardinal fled up the stairs. The old man followed.

The bar's television showed the Prophet—the false prophet—pumping his fist and roaring that he had declared war on the armies of Satan. In the streets beyond the pub's windows, people fought, clawing and biting at each other. The old man saw the whore who had propositioned him, yanking off a fallen man's trousers. She mounted his lower body and ripped off his genitals with her mouth. Thunder cracked and a hard, blood rain commenced.

"*What is going on?*" screamed the barkeep, his fingers shaking as he uselessly locked the bar's door.

"The Lamb," the old man said. "Only the Lamb of God is worthy to open the scroll and break its seals. The apocalypse has begun, barkeep."

APOCALYPSE… MEH

John Wayne Comunale

The end of the world wasn't the fantastic spectacle of death and destruction it had been hyped as in that book everyone used to read. In fact, the actual Apocalypse wasn't like anything from any book people read, religious or otherwise. It was a complete blindside.

The Four Horsemen weren't pain and pestilence manifested as giants who rode skeletal stallions from the sky, but instead were roadies for Metallica, Slayer, Megadeath, and Anthrax from the original *Big Four of Thrash* Tour. They rode into town on four old, beat-to-shit golf carts covered in stickers for metal bands, most of which were unreadable.

They drove their battered, electric-powered steeds directly to the discount liquor mart and stole several handles of bottom shelf whiskey. As the rode away at eleven miles per hour the Horseman drank deeply from the bottles while giving the finger to the clerk who shook his fist as they disappeared on the horizon. The four drove around town getting drunk while offering backstage passes to people on the street in exchange for weed or blow.

From dirty fingers they dangled brightly colored, laminated rectangles of cardboard attached to black lanyards and held them up as they drove by like some twisted form of peacocking. There were no takers, but they did draw a small crowd when some people thought they were a performance art troop. It took twenty minutes to realize they were just drunk, and the gathering quickly dispersed. These so-called "four horsemen" weren't the least bit scary or destructive, and at most were mildly annoying.

There was no god-type person who appeared in the sky to open seven seals, or a seven-headed beast with ten horns, or any of the other stuff the Bible said would happen. The moon didn't turn to blood, but the sky did take on a distinctive red hue that wasn't altogether unpleasant and reduced UV light by eighty percent.

The dead didn't rise from their graves, which would have been totally awesome, but Main Street split open up the center creating a deep chasm in the center of downtown. Fog belched out onto the street from the opening, but no one really cared until they noticed the smell. It was mix of body odor, cigarette butts, and the inside of a heavily used portable toilet, but surprisingly not the slightest hint of sulfur.

On the heels of that smell someone, or something, started shambling up and out of the hole, only it wasn't devious minions led by the ferocious Cerberus who finally allowed the dead to escape the pit. It was people. Just people. They looked normal but shared something oddly specific in common. Each and every person rising from the depths donned the garb of a metalhead.

They wore black t-shirts with unreadable band names, or pictures of the kind of beasts you would expect to populate a Hellscape. Denim vests with back patches, and leather motorcycle jackets seemed to come standard with each head-banging hoodlum, and long, stringy, greasy hair and sunglasses were equally as prevalent among these new arrivals. Every so often at least one out of twenty metalheads had some slight mutation like extra limbs, giant eyes like a fly that took up their whole face, and some even donned slick, veiny bat-like wings, although none of them took to the air.

God-fearing, lifelong Christians fell to their knees and shrieked at the sky for their Lord to take them home, but these prayers remained unanswered. They fled to their churches, locked themselves in, and pleaded for their Creator to intervene.

One of the first things the roving metalheads did was set fire to every church in town, which was pretty "on brand". The people inside had trapped themselves, and since the Apocalypse meant no one could die anymore, they just burned with the building until enough of the structure fell away for them to escape. They would aimlessly walk the streets as shriveled chunks of sizzling, over-cooked meat clinging to char-burned bone, wondering why their God had forsaken them, some realizing they had wasted their lives on the fool's errand of religion.

Other changes happened gradually over time until they became the new normal, with one exception that took us all a while to figure out. Suddenly everyone on the planet had become badass musicians. People who had never looked at a guitar in their lives could now shred with the lightning speed precision of Yngwie Malmsteen. Arthritic grandmas who could hardly move found themselves able to play drums like prodigious clones of Neil Peart, and toddlers plucked out thunderous bass licks while stumbling around on wobbly legs after three whiskeys and half a pack of smokes.

This newfound ability came with a catch: the only kind of music anyone could play was metal. Even those who already had the ability to play music in any capacity regardless of their chosen practiced genre. It wasn't as if they sat down to play jazz and metal came out, they just played metal because it was all they wanted to play now. All previous musical knowledge was abandoned and replaced with iterations of metal, including near infinite sub-genres. Thrash, Industrial, Black, Death, Doom, Crust, Grind, Glam, Sludge, Drone, Power, Post, Nu, Prog, and everything in between. Except for Folk Metal. There was no Folk Metal.

Of course, this was just fine by me because I'd already been playing in metal bands for most of my life. My name's Tad, and I play drums. It would be more accurate to say I used to play drums, and now I play drums a hundred times better.

While everyone now had the ability to play, most people didn't know the first thing about actually starting a band or playing with other people. I on the other hand grabbed a couple of guys who used the same rehearsal space I did, and started a band called Scrottooth. Our logo was a ball sack with fangs and the two Ts were upside down crosses. It was pretty badass.

The world changed in other ways as more and more metalheads came out of the Main Street chasm. Industry changed when the newcomers opened businesses or took over existing ones, turning them all into bars, record shops, or instrument stores. Every business had a stage setup and held regular nightly shows. At first, I thought it was great having so many places to play, but things became competitive very quickly, and just because there were shows every night didn't mean people were going to them. There were a handful of popular places and the most popular bands played them regularly, making it extremely difficult for other bands to get their foot in the door. Bands like mine for instance.

Once Satan and Judas got here it became damn near impossible to play the same club as their bands. Satan wasn't some giant, red, horned beast either. He was just a regular guy with shoulder length, black hair teased and pulled in a Nikki Sixx kind of way. He was thin, but not heroin skinny, and his complexion was pale and vampiric. He wore a black buttoned up shirt, black leather pants, and black motorcycle boots. There was nothing particularly sinister or threatening about him in the least.

Satan fronted a Glam/Power Metal band called Satan's Dick in which he sang and played guitar with a Van Halen meets C.C. Deville type of flair. They became instant legends, and Satan's Dick was given a nightly spot at the best bar in town, Diane's Pussy. It was owned by one of the metal heads from the pit named Diane who was wide as she was tall, and had a penchant for the ladies.

Judas was a different story. He was just as pale as Satan, but actually had some muscle attached to his slim frame. He wore a black t-shirt with the sleeves cut off, black jeans, and black boots similar to Satan's. His jet-black hair fell to the center of his back, and around his neck he wore a noose. The rope was black and frayed where it had been cut and hung just above his waist like a morbid necktie. Wearing the noose you were hanged with was the most metal thing I had ever seen.

Judas also played guitar and sang in his band called Judas, and they played the most brutal Death/Thrash I'd ever heard. Judas's riffs were flawless and crushing, and his rhythm section played with the destructive force of demolition explosives. The band became instantly popular as well but attracted a much different crowd than Satan's Dick.

Judas was given a nightly spot at a bar on the east side of town called Burn the Bishop, which exclusively showcased bands who played the same brutality charged music as Judas. A head-banger from below named Ghost ran Burn the Bishop, and he'd cultivated an environment as violent and vicious as the music played there.

We were all untied in our new post-apocalyptic existence under the umbrella of metal, but it didn't take long for the many subgenres to divide everyone again just like old times. There were those who preferred the flashy, Glam-ish style of Satan's Dick, and they all hung out at the bars on the north side of town with Diane's Pussy being the crown jewel of the scene.

My band, Scrottooth, consisted of me on drums, a guy named Lincoln on guitar and vocals, and a large, bearish man who wore nothing but a leather thong and a dog collar named Gentle Ben, but we called him Ben for short. It didn't take long for us to jive with each other, and we started gigging after a month of rehearsals in smaller, less popular bars.

Once we played in the corner of a magic shop run by a man who claimed he was Lazarus. He said being raised from the dead was his greatest illusion but "that Jesus punk" took all the credit. Lazarus was slightly stooped with a small hump in the top center of his back, and wore a filthy, tattered tuxedo complete with topless top hat. He was always wet too, and I don't mean sweaty. Lazarus was covered in a slimy sheen that would stay with you for hours after shaking his hand. We played there a couple times but stopped because no one ever came, which left you alone with Lazarus leering while licking his drippy lips.

The gigs were shit, but I wasn't discouraged because I knew we'd get there, and we were really starting to tighten up as a band. The music we made fell into a Thrash meets New Wave of American Heavy Metal, and we sunk our teeth in full bore.

One night, Lincoln showed up late for practice, recounted how he'd just come from seeing Satan's Dick for the first time and had some new song ideas. While I didn't agree with Lincoln and his appreciation of all things Satan's Dick, I could relate to his experience. When I left rehearsal that day, I walked down Main past the pit, hung a left, and headed east toward Burn the Bishop. When I got there the place was packed wall to wall with leather and denim-clad patrons awash in a sea of greasy, tangled hair and body odor.

The door closed behind me, and feedback swelled from the far left corner of the bar. The lights went out, and the audience shrieked as Judas took the stage. The band launched into the first song with a kinetic ferocity that exploded from the stage, instantly affecting everyone in the room, myself included.

The riffs were choppy and precise while the rhythm section mercilessly pummeled the crowd with sub-sonic licks that hit like a boulder to the chest. The audience churned and kicked and wailed as if under some evil spell, and I had to admit I was beginning to fall under it as well. Before I knew it I was in the center of a swirling pit of bodies heeding the siren's call, and taking out a lifetime of pent up aggression in one thirty-five minute set.

When I emerged from Burn the Bishop bloody and beaten, I had been forever changed. I didn't want to play in Scrottooth anymore, but I didn't want to start a band like Judas either. I wanted to be in Judas.

I decided I would continue to play with Scrottooth for now so I could use the rehearsal space to work on my chops. I didn't know who the drummer in Judas was, but his ability was insane. I was great too, but not like him; I was going to have to practice to get to his level.

The next night at rehearsal Lincoln wanted to wrap up early so he could catch Satan's Dick's set, which gave me the perfect opportunity to practice by myself. When Lincoln and Ben took off I went around the corner and bought a twelve pack.

When I got back, I pulled out the Judas record I'd bought at the show from the backpack I left behind my drum kit. I carefully removed the vinyl disc from a black sleeve with the word Judas printed somehow in darker black and placed it on the turntable. I plugged in the extra-long chord for the headphones so they would reach the drums, chugged a beer, dropped the needle, chugged another beer, and set to work.

For the next seven hours I listened to the record on repeat while doing my best to keep up. By morning I was better than I'd been when I started, but still had a way to go. I removed the record from the turntable, put it back into my backpack, and crashed in the corner behind my kick drum. I didn't wake up when the other guys got there until Ben not-so-gently nudged my ribs with his boot.

"Whoa dude," said Lincoln. "Did you sleep here last night or something?"

"Yeah I guess so," I said yawning. I noticed the top of the Judas record poking out of my backpack, and I feigned stretching to reach out and cover it back up. "I decided to stay and practice the... changes to the songs you made Lincoln. I guess I kind of fell asleep."

Ben and Lincoln exchanged confused looks while I held my breath and hoped they bought it. Lincoln approached me as I pulled myself from the floor, put his hand on my shoulder, looked me in the eyes, and shook his head.

"This is the kind of dedication we all should be putting into this if we're gonna land a gig opening for Satan's Dick," Lincoln said, flashing an un-ironic smile. "Thanks for the kick in the ass we needed, man. Tonight we all stay and practice until we pass out!"

I was not expecting this from Lincoln, and while I wanted to protest, what could I say? *Sorry man, if we do that I can't practice for the other band I want to quit this one to be in.* I looked past Lincoln at Ben hoping to get some push back from him on the idea, but he just shrugged and tuned his bass.

"Okay," said Lincoln finally removing his hand from my shoulder, "let's get to it. Tad, show us what an all-night practice session can do."

When Lincoln turned to walk away I noticed something different about his hair. He had teased out large chunks similarly to the hairstyle Satan stole from Nkki Sixx. This was worse than I thought, and rehearsing the new lame version of Scrottooth all night would take away the time to practice my

Judas licks. I needed to change Lincoln's mind, and I knew just the thing.

"Oh dude," I called to Lincoln from behind the drums, "I got an alert on my phone sometime in the middle of the night while I was practicing. It said tonight at the end of their usual set Satan's Dick is going to play a brand new song."

"*What?*" Lincoln's face went paler as he fumbled to pull his phone from his back pocket. "I don't remember getting an alert. Where was it posted? Who said this?"

"I'm not sure man. It was late and shit like that auto-deletes on my phone after I see it."

Lincoln continued staring at his phone as his pallor changed to pink then quickly to red as his thumbs flew furiously across his screen. He glanced up and stared at the ceiling as if in deep thought, but I knew he had typed a message out to someone asking about what I had said, possibly Diane or even Satan himself, and was trying to work up the courage to send it.

"You know what?" Lincoln slipped his phone into his back pocket. "Let's start the all-night rehearsals tomorrow. We'll work on the new stuff I wrote tonight, and tomorrow we'll hit it hard on with a whole new set. Sound good?"

I nodded, Ben grunted, and Lincoln tuned his guitar before stepping up to the mic.

*

Lincoln fell for the trick, which gave me extra time to work on my Judas licks, but I couldn't stay in the rehearsal space all night again. I wasn't as good at playing the songs on the Judas record as I would have liked, but I was going to have to make my move tonight. My phone vibrated in my pocket as I left the rehearsal space, but I didn't bother checking it since I knew it was Lincoln. He'd been calling and texting for the last few hours, and I chuckled at the thought of him walking around Diane's Pussy asking the other lame Satan's Dick fans if they knew about the new song. He'd probably managed to start a rumor by now.

I walked in the direction of Burn the Bishop, unsure of what I was going to do when I got there. It was still a while before Judas took the stage, and I brainstormed methods to get to the band without doing something to result in my being bounced from the club. I weighed the options of bribing a bartender to get me into the green room versus trying to sneak my way back there somehow.

I was less than a block from the club and still deliberating, so I walked down the side of the building to mull over the options. When I ducked into the alley I could hear voices coming from the behind the bar. I stepped carefully down the narrow space between buildings and peered around the corner.

I couldn't believe my luck. The voices I'd heard belonged to Judas and the rest of his band. Each of them held a beer, and a cigarette dangled from the corner of every mouth. Now that I was only ten feet away, I very quickly deduced the band was having a full-blown argument.

"Because man," Judas growled, "I'm sick of your shit. We all are!"

I couldn't tell who he was directing his statement toward, so I crouched to get a better view and still not be seen. I could see the bass player, and the second guitarist flanking Judas while the man on the other end of the ear-beating was hidden by the shadow of the building. By process of elimination I determined it was the drummer who was being chastised, and my heart fluttered. Could I actually be witnessing the firing of Judas's drummer?

"My shit?" came a voice from the shadows. "I just want to mix it up some, add some more groove to our songs. What the hell is wrong with that?"

"We don't fucking *groove*," Judas said through clenched teeth. "We fucking brutalize. If you want to groove so bad take your ass down to Diane's Pussy and groove away with Satan and his band of losers."

The drummer stepped forward into the light, and I had to cover my mouth to stifle an audible gasp. The man wasn't a man at all. He had large, round, red eyes, a flat nose, and a mandible full of sharp teeth that moved in an unnatural way when he spoke. More surprising though, the drummer had four additional arms growing out of his back. It was no wonder the guy could play so fast and precise with six arms, and since I'm usually being crushed in the pit during Judas' shows I never noticed the extra limbs.

"You know what?" The drummer stepped right up into Judas's face now. "I think I'll do just that."

He lingered in Judas's face as if he expected a rebuttal, or maybe even a goodbye kiss, but all he got was a lungful of smoke in his face.

"Fuck this! I'm outta here!"

The drummer coughed as he pushed past Judas who wheeled around and flicked his cigarette at his now ex-drummer. It struck him in the back between his extra arms and exploded into a shower of orange and yellow sparks that quickly became ashy, white dust in the wind.

The mutated musician turned and took an aggressive step back toward Judas but had no intention of confronting him. Judas stood stock still clenching and unclenching his hands into fists, the noose around his neck swaying slowly in the cool evening breeze. He was the very embodiment of not giving a fuck, which is probably why it was so easy for him to betray Christ.

The drummer rounded the corner into the alley before I had time to get out of his way, and the six-armed monster-man ran right into me. I froze, expecting the worst as two sets of his hands clamped around my arms to hold me in place, but all he did was snarl and throw me down hard against the gravely concrete. The impact knocked the wind out of me, and I struggled to gulp down air for almost a minute when I realized three faces were staring down at me, a frayed noose hung inches from my face.

I was caught completely off guard and feigned trying to catch my breath for a few extra seconds so I could think. I'd heard of Serendipity, but I thought she was a dancer who worked the early shift at The Fat Wet Hole Gentlemen's Club on Tuesdays until now. I reached my hand out for one of them to help me up but no one accepted, so I rolled over and got up on my own.

"I'm Tad," I said throwing out my hand. "I'm your new drummer."

I had no idea why I said that, but I opened my mouth and out it came. My hand remained suspended in front of me, and my stomach twisted with each second it hung empty until a cold, firm hand clamped down like an industrial press.

The hand belonged to Judas.

Judas unlatched his hand from mine, took a pack of cigarettes from his back pocket, and screwed one into the corner of his mouth.

"You better be good," he said as the bass player held a flame to Judas's cigarette.

I didn't know what to say so I just blurted out, "I'm the best."

"I hope so," Judas said exhaling silvery smoke through his nostrils like a mythical, evil beast, "because if you're not we're gonna' rip you apart on stage."

*

Judas made me wait out back alone until it was time to play while he and the rest of the band went inside to drink the massive amount of booze in their green room. I was glad they went in because the second they did I puked my guts out as reality set in, and I realized there was no way I was better than a six-armed drummer. I puked again when I thought about being pulled apart.

I bent with my hands on my knees to catch my breath. Maybe it was the lightheadedness from puking, but I experienced a moment of clarity wherein I saw a vision of myself being able to do it. I was a drummer back before this so-called Apocalypse gave everyone musical ability, so I had an advantage. I wasn't as good as a six-armed drummer; I was better.

I pulled sticks from my back pocket and started to warm up by playing against the wall and the trashcan lids. In my mind I heard the songs from the Judas record, and I played along with perfect form and spot-on timing. My phone went off again, and I paused to view the latest message from Lincoln.

What are you doing? Are you coming to hear the new song or what? Satan's Dick is about to go on!

I decided I'd answer him this time to let him know plans had changed.

There's no new song dumbass! Fuck you nerd, I quit! I'm playing with Judas now.

I added a picture of the back door to Burn the Bishop, and myself giving the finger. I hit send and tossed my phone into one of the trashcans, uninterested in what Lincoln had to say ever again. Just as it clattered to the bottom of the can the door flew open and smacked against the wall with a crack like a gunshot. Judas was standing in the open doorway.

"Let's go."

His voice had taken on a deeper, darker quality. It was hypnotic and terrifying at the same time. I stepped in and Judas yanked me down the low-lit, narrow hall, talking fast as we went.

"The set list is on the snare. Frank and Murray do this feedback loop thing before we start the first song. When Frank gives you the cue count off while I take the stage."

Frank and Murray? The guitarist and bassist in Judas were named Frank and Murray?

"Got it," I said as we came within feet of the stage. "Which one is Frank again?"

Judas shoved me out onto the stage so hard I stumbled into the back of Frank, or it might have been Murray. He gave me a not-so-gentle shoulder check that sent me in the direction of the drums. I regained my balance, stopped to compose myself, and sat behind the kit.

The set was huge, much bigger than what I was used to playing on, but I wasn't intimidated. I reached out to adjust the closest ride cymbal, raised the height of my hi-hat, and I was ready to go. I checked the set list and saw the opener was "Stone the Fetus", a classic and personal favorite of mine.

I determined the bass player was Frank, because from the corner of my eye I could see him frantically nodding in my direction cueing me to count off the song. I nodded back, clicked my sticks together four times, and as the first note sounded Judas appeared from the darkness at center stage. Thunderous chaos erupted from the crowd at the very sight of him. Judas laid the lead lick down over the churning rhythm leading up to the verse, but something didn't sound right.

The churning rhythm wasn't really churning, and was instead an indecipherable, syncopated, pile of ear-garbage like we were all playing a different song. All of a sudden I realized why it sounded like such shit. It was because of me! I don't know why I ever thought I could play like or better than a six-armed drummer, but I clearly could not. I plowed on, trying to nail the complicated fills, and was so focused I didn't realize the others had stopped playing. Feedback was the only thing accompanying my out-of-sync, off-time, ugly, ugly drumming.

Judas stood in front of the drum riser with Frank and Murray glaring from either side of him. The audience was still and silent unsure if this was part of the show or reality gone horribly wrong. I slowed to a stop awkwardly, holding my sticks while looking from Judas to Frank to Judas to Murray, and back again.

I didn't feel it and barely saw Frank or Murray even move, but a second later the two of them had turned around to the audience using some kind of rubber tube to spray fake blood onto them. Blood poured across the kit in front of me as well, and I was hit with the sensation of my body rapidly depressurizing.

Frank crossed from one side of the stage the other, and I saw a drumstick dangling from the tube he was shooting blood out of. It was my drumstick in my hand attached to my arm, which was no longer attached to me. Murray had my other arm and poured blood on his face before bringing it to his crotch where he mimed humping the bloody stump. The audience response was deafening.

On either side of me arcs of shimmery, wet crimson exited my body in spurts from where my arms had been only seconds earlier. I looked up and caught of glimpse of Judas before my perspective suddenly changed. Now I was looking down at the drums, then at the ceiling, and then at Judas's chest before I spun around to face the gore fountain that was my armless, headless torso. Judas had ripped my head off with his bare hands, and briefly showed me the horror show that was my body.

Judas turned to show the crowd, opened his mouth, and let the blood from my severed brainstem flow down his throat. The frenzy of the crowd shifted into high gear at the sight of Judas drinking my blood, and letting it pour on his face and chest. Bloodlust swept across the entire bar and they writhed in agony begging to be satiated. They were then appeased as I watched my right arm being thrown out to them immediately followed by my left.

Suddenly the scene whirled past my field of vision so fast I couldn't see a thing until the spinning stopped, and I had a fantastic view of the stage. My perspective changed in an instant to the floor, someone's hands, the ceiling and then the floor again. Judas had thrown my head out into the crowd where it was being tossed around like a beach ball at a summer music festival.

I caught a glimpse of the rest of my body being tossed off the stage to gleeful audience members who wasted no time tearing chunks of me into smaller and smaller bits. When they stopped volleying my head and began to tear it apart as well it became difficult to determine what was happening.

Everything went black. I could still feel a buzzing vibration running through whatever was left of me, possibly just my consciousness, but then it stopped it too stopped. Everything was quiet, and I was gone.

I don't know how much time had passed, but my awareness returned to me suddenly. I opened my eyes and was staring up into the faces of Judas, Frank, and Murray. We were still in the club, but all the lights were on, which was oddly disorienting. Every single bit of my body inside and out ached with an extraordinary pain accompanied by heat and pressure. It felt like I was being cooked from the inside out.

"Wha... wha—"

I tried and failed to make words.

"What happened," barked Judas, "was that you were awful."

"So we tore you apart on stage," followed Frank.

"Just like we said we would," chimed Murray.

I remembered now. I *had* been awful and I *had* been torn apart.

"Come one," said Judas extending a hand, "get up."

I struggled to lift my arm high enough to accept the help but I couldn't quite make it, so Judas bent down, grabbed my hand, and yanked me to my feet. Electrifying waves of pain bounced through my raw, hot insides like a sadistic game of Pong. The pain was blinding, and I reeled at what Judas, Frank, and Murray said they had in store for me next.

*

It turned out taking that chance and falling flat on my face was the best thing I could've done because after all the pain I went through I landed a spot in Judas after all. I wasn't the new drummer; in fact I wasn't playing an instrument at all, but I was still technically in the band.

Judas and the guys told me they'd never seen a crowd go so bat-shit insane, and it was all because they ripped me apart on stage. Judas liked the reaction so much he said he wanted to be able to invoke it every night, and the next thing I know I'm in the band. Technically, like I said.

So that's what I do now. I come out toward the end of the set and the band descends upon me ripping pieces off and tossing them into the crowd while drinking my blood and feasting on my gore. You'd think it would get old, but they keep coming back for it night after night.

Judas ended up getting their six-armed drummer back, and I came to find he was fired or quit every two or three days but was always taken back. I haven't seen Lincoln or Ben since I don't ever really leave Burn the Bishop, but I'm sure they got a new drummer, and I'm sure they suck worse than ever. I can't complain though. I'd much rather be ripped to pieces on a daily basis than play that glammed-out bullshit Lincoln was writing. There's nothing brutal about that at all.

FALLEN

James Watts

The old hardwood floor creaked as Roman went over to the window, puffs of dust creating tiny clouds around his feet. A large rat scuttled across his path and he kicked it indiscriminately to the other side of the room. He had chosen the one-time corner store as it had reminded him of his life before his original death. So many years had passed since that day that he had forgotten when it was. His service above had eaten up so much of his memory that he had lost so much—until his fall. Now his memories were returning, and with them, the pain of all that was no more.

Adding to his dismal mood was that it was raining again. It seemed like all it did was rain these days. That or it would be unbearably hot. Somewhere around sixty years had passed since a real winter had shown its face anywhere near the Southern United States and Roman believed another sixty years would pass before one did. The Horsemen had worked the world over right and proper as they descended the Heavens and rode across the globe. And what was left some 175 years later was a dysfunctional climate, thousands of ruined cities and towns, and a scant few human survivors sparsely dotting the continents in dirty shanty communes or dwelling in what remained of the cities. The world had fallen in the course of one day.

In that twenty-four-hour period, fires had engulfed forests and plains, plagues had dined on the living, and demons and other Hell Spawns had risen to claim the spoils in the wake of the Horsemen's ride. Many had perished of starvation, while others had endured by ingesting the flesh of their neighbors. Having witnessed all of this, having been a part of it, Roman had taken the first steps in what would lead to losing his wings.

A clanking, rattling noise interrupted his thoughts, overwhelming the heavy thumps of rain against glass. Roman stepped away from the window and listened for a few seconds. There was something else mixed with the rattles and clanks. This new sound was more distinct, one Roman remembered, and one that many had come to fear. The clip-clopping of horse's hooves on pavement was what he was hearing, and from the minute squeaks and groans accompanying them, he knew they were pulling something, most likely a homemade wagon, or cart.

What fool would be out in this weather? He thought. *Only the insane or the desperate would dare travel in such conditions.*

Whoever it was, they were passing through on the street running parallel to the west side of the building. Roman hurried as quietly as he could to that side, barely missing the rat he had kicked earlier as it limped out of his way. He thought this town to be deserted; he had searched the remains of every building and home when he had first arrived a few days earlier. Rodents, insects, and arachnids were the only occupants he had discovered. Then again, as remote a spot as this town was, it would be the ideal route for the most deviant of souls.

Approaching the big picture window, Roman pushed a housekeeping cart aside and slid up against the wall, risking a peek outside. Two black horses were pulling a wagon with a poorly constructed cage atop it. Inside the cage were three people: a man, woman, and young boy. All three were dirty, and all three wore the hand-sewn clothes that were so common these days since tailors and mass-produced clothing manufacturers no longer existed. The cage was uncovered and all three were drenched from the rain and huddling together for warmth. To the man's credit, he *was* trying to use his jacket as a makeshift umbrella for the woman and child.

An old man in a mud-spattered blue suit led the horses along, neither of the nags showing any signs of disobeying the old timer's commands. The old coot did not seem to be in too much of a hurry despite the current weather conditions, yet he would turn to the horses every few feet and bark out orders for them to move faster. Roman observed this peculiar behavior in silent discord until the wagon went around the corner of the defunct service station at the end of the street. In this case, out of sight was not out of mind and Roman could not help but feel pity for the family locked in the cage. The old man was either a slave trader or a cannibal; neither of those things hinted at a promising end for his prisoners.

Appalling an idea as it was, and as much as he dreaded to do so, Roman walked over to the counter for his long coat and hat. Old habits sometimes refused to die. A few minutes later, he stepped out into the rain.

*

Two hours had passed since Roman had first started trailing the old man and his captives. Several times he had considered rushing in under the cover of the heavy rains to attempt a rescue, only to have his efforts deterred by the presence of something monstrous. In the dense brush alongside the road opposite of Roman, another had taken an interest in the travelers. Stalking them with hunger in its eyes, it waited for its prey to be at their weakest before pouncing and devouring them. Any moves made by Roman before that time was apt to cause an early strike by the beast.

Forest Behemoths, also known to children as Terror Bears, were composed of various animals: bears, mountain lions, and wolves, and preyed on anyone that wandered into their territory. The behemoths and Trots, a virus that led to a person excreting their liquefied internal organs in its final stage, was the legacy of Death's ride. Roman had hoped never to be anywhere near either. However, punished to live an extended mortal life, he had been closer than he was comfortable with on many occasions.

I could just let the creature have them. After all, look what defending the human race has already cost me. I have been reduced to nothing less than a wandering hermit.

It was true that he could just walk away, let the grizzly course of events unfold as they would. The old man, as determined as he seemed to be about reaching his destination, was still much too frail to fend off the beast. The trio of prisoners, trapped as they were, would fare no better. Their poor excuse for a cell would offer only meager protection from the behemoth's size and strength. And Roman, as much as he wished to deny the truth, still cared a great deal about the innocent souls condemned to survive the hellish wastes of this long since fruitful world.

Roman pushed deeper into the woods, praying that only one behemoth roamed the area. A plan had yet to form in his mind and the only viable option at this point, or so he believed, was to outdistance the old man. In the years since being cast out, what little remained of his abilities had faded to such diminutive levels that Roman dared not use them unless faced with the direst of situations. Although, as dire as his present predicament was, he doubted any of what he had left would be enough against even the smallest of these monsters. Lucky for him, however, he had one small advantage. It was still raining.

Simple as it was the rain actually dampened the creature's senses to a degree. If he could somehow play against its weakened senses, maybe lead it astray without confrontation, he could prevent the loss of life. But, was he swift enough to successfully pull off such a maneuver? Despite their large size and weight, Forest Behemoths were by no means sluggish brutes. They were quick, strong, and relentless. Whatever distraction Roman came up with, he would have to carry it out with precision.

"Whoa!" The old man suddenly shouted in a deep baritone voice. "Whoa, now!"

The horses and wagon came to a slow, steady stop. The hasty halt by the travelers caused Roman to turn and venture to the edge of the road, being careful not to expose himself by ducking behind the overgrowth alongside it. There were no structures, manmade or natural, that could serve as a shelter, and he was curious as to why the old man would make such a strange call. Of course, after near continuous travel in this heavy downpour, everything Roman knew about the old man, which was very little, was strange. The fact that he, his nags, or his prisoners were not sick from the constant exposure to the elements was even stranger still. The lining in Roman's long-coat and hat was similar to that found in industrial raincoats, keeping him dry for the most part. He imagined the clothing worn by the four travelers did not have the same feature.

Then what is keeping them in such good health?

Distressed neighs issued from the horses. They also sensed the presence of the behemoth and were spooked. The old man turned and shushed them with a few harsh commands, although the horses continued to fidget and show their unease. Ignoring their hysterics, he passed them by without a glance and approached the makeshift cell. The woman and boy scooted away from the bars as far as they could while the man slid in front of them protectively. Even though the old coot's back was to him, Roman somehow knew there was a huge smirk on his face.

Words passed between the man and the old man and Roman strained to hear what they were saying, but the wailing wind distorted the bulk of their short conversation. There was a brief, sharp cry of pain from the man and a raucous laugh from his captor. Leaning forward, pushing the boy behind her, the woman began screaming obscenities at the elderly monster tormenting her family. A monster was just how Roman thought of him, too. What he was doing to those people went beyond inhumane. It was an act born of evil.

Across the road, just a few feet ahead of where the horses continued to protest being easy targets, there was movement in the weeds. Too centered to be the wind, Roman knew the behemoth was done being patient. It was preparing to pounce.

As much as he would like the beast to rip the heartless old timer to shreds, he did not wish the same fate for the innocents in his possession. With no solid plan in mind, Roman rushed forward and onto the road, the crumbling asphalt proving to be slicker than he had anticipated, and slid to an unsteady stop. All he could do now was hope the beast focused on him and pray he could outrun the fiendish amalgam before it tore him apart. It was a feat that Roman was unsure himself capable of, but one he felt should at least be attempted.

"What's all this, now?" The old man was both startled and furious. "Say, boy!"

Roman caught a glimpse of the old man's face. Scarred and twisted with a nose like the dorsal fin of a shark and a thin layer of stringy white hair sodden from the rain, it was a repulsive visage. Roman found it nauseating just looking at him.

His eyes are wrong. Something is...

Capturing Roman's full attention and silencing his thoughts, the Behemoth charged from hiding with a cavernous roar. Although it appeared to be a cub, no bigger than an adult black bear, it was still dangerous. This variation in particular was highly aggressive.

For a few moments, there was a standoff between man and beast; nothing barring one from the other but rain and opportunity. Ravenous growls escaped from the behemoth's wolf-like head, muscles stretched and tightened along its bear-like body, and its feline tail swished in anxious jerks. Without any consideration of the outcome, Roman bolted to the left to where the road fell away into a twisting hill. The slope in itself was not too steep, but he was relying on the current slickness of the fragmented blacktop to aide in his ill-conceived decision. Behind him, the behemoth roared once more before giving chase.

Roman hit the treacherous incline in a full sprint, descending with long strides and struggling not to spill forward while laboring to avoid the slipperiest sections of deteriorating asphalt. So far, he was fortunate enough to have retained a fraction of his god-like speed and reflexes, but it was not much, and as hindered as the behemoth was from the rain it was closing the gap between them with alarming momentum. Worse yet, it seemed as if the road grew even more slippery the further down he went. Soon, Roman figured it would be like trying to run on a sheet of ice.

What in the hell is making it so slick? And, how on Earth does the old timer think he can even navigate such an unsafe path?

There was a hard tug as the behemoth seized a mouthful of Roman's coat and shirt. Wrenching its head to the side, the beast succeeded in hauling him off his feet. The world spiraled for the briefest of instances and then the behemoth slammed him to the ground. Pain shot up his legs and back as he fought to catch his breath, as lost a cause as that was. Then with a muffled growl; it lifted Roman into the air once more. He sensed his shirt rip and it felt like his skeleton was going to buckle as the behemoth raised him over its head and brought him back down with enough force to dislocate his shoulder. It was at this point that Roman realized, although hazy and disoriented as he was, that both he and the behemoth were sliding.

In all the years he had had the long-coat, this would be the first time its durability was a con and not a pro. He knew it was military grade, having pillaged it from an abandoned military base, but knew nothing of the material used to make it. Whatever it was, it was more resilient than he had imagined, not giving in the slightest no matter how much the behemoth shook him. This left Roman with no other choice, regardless of his fondness for the coat. Relaxing his body and stretching so that his arms rose above his head, he slipped free, spinning out of control and away from the monster pursuing him. The behemoth discarded the long-coat, bellowing in fury as desperation hijacked its primitive mind. In spite of it being beyond hopeless, the beast peddled its feet in a frantic attempt to gain ground and retrieve its prey. Once upon a time, the sight of it would have been rather amusing.

This was no time for humor, however, as the road curved sharply at the bottom of the hill. If Roman skidded past the curve, he would no doubt tumble down the rocky hillside on the other side of it, most likely breaking every bone in his body in the process. Spinning wild as he was, the outcome seemed grim, as he could not think of any way to keep from going over the edge. With a silent prayer, Roman mentally prepared for what was to come, even though surviving the upcoming fall seemed doubtful.

Refusing to give up, Roman made frantic attempts at grabbing hold of objects alongside the road as he slid past them in hopes that one would hold his weight and save him from his dilemma, a fist full of weeds the only reward for his efforts. He was too dizzy and moving too fast to have much success. Then Roman's hands clamped around something rough and sturdy as he slipped past the curve. A million knives stabbed at his dislocated shoulder and his body jerked from the sudden stop, his feet hanging over the side of the steep, jagged slope. Raising his head, he saw that he had managed to grab a hold of a young oak tree.

More than a little relieved, Roman eased his legs back on solid ground. He was still lightheaded from his ordeal, and his right shoulder was on fire, but he was alive. Seconds later the behemoth, yelping like a wounded puppy, collided with him and they both went over the edge.

*

"Pa? Where are you, Pa? I'm lost again. I can't find my way home. Pa?"

Roman's words echoed through the deserted streets.

"I'm cold, Pa. I'm cold and all by myself. Where are you? Where are all the people?"

October 17, 1948. Today was his tenth birthday. Today he was supposed to meet his Pa at the corner drugstore. They were going to go to the Jericho Hills Fall Carnival. His Pa had promised ice cream, cotton candy, and cold sodas. It was going to be just the two of them, no big brothers or sisters tagging along, just him and his Pa. But where was his Pa? There was no sign of him, and it was three o'clock on the dot, the time his Pa said to meet him. He was not lost anymore. It was his Pa and the people in the town that were lost. They could not find their way home, not him.

That did not change the fact that he was cold and alone and that the clouds had come and hidden away the sun. That did not change the fact that he was scared. It did not change anything about his current situation at all. A frigid wind whipped and whined through the town, creating eddies of dust along the dirt track streets, and Roman felt even more abandoned. He was not ready to be all by himself. He was used to having all of his brothers and sisters around, and his Ma and Pa.

Movement spied from the corner of his eye gave Roman a start and his eyes went from staring at the tops of his mud-caked shoes to a man across the road from him wearing a navy blue pinstriped zoot suit with a matching fedora atop his head. The man wore the hat with its brim pulled down just above his brow, obscuring most of his face. Roman could not remember ever seeing anyone like him in Jericho Hills. A snazzy dressed good-time Charlie was what his Ma would call the man if she were here, one of those men that his Pa said liked to chase loose women, drink beer, and smoke cigarettes. He did not know what a loose woman was, but they were the devil's harlots his Pa had told him, and that he should always steer clear of them. This was no better an explanation, as Roman did not know what a harlot was either.

On the other side of the street, Charlie, which was how Roman now thought of him, began to cackle and snort, the wind picking up speed and ruffling his suit. The eddying dust was now miniature dust devils and there were two eerie green orbs glowing from beneath the shadows hiding the man's face. Roman backed up until his back pressed against the front window of the corner store, his heart beating in rapid thumps. Nausea swept through him, his insides feeling as if being churned around with a big, knotted stick. Chill bumps raced along his skin and the hair on his neck rose to attention. The man cackled again and took a step forward. Roman eased away from the building, his legs shaking so hard his teeth were rattling.

"What a sight you are, boy." Charlie shouted. His voice was gruff and condescending. "A pitiful waste, that's what

99

you are. I bet you tryin' your damnedest not to piss and shit yourself."

Roman could find no words and swallowed hard. His Pa should be here. If his Pa were here, Charlie would not be talking to him like that. His Pa would whoop up on him and teach him some manners.

"Is that so?" Charlie asked and started walking toward him. "I think not. And my name is not Charlie, you little mongrel."

Unable to stop it, Roman peed himself, the warm urine soaking through his trousers and streaming down his leg. Embarrassed by this and more afraid then he had ever been in his young life; he stepped away from the corner store and broke into a run, away from the mean, terrifying stranger. He had to find his parents. He had to go to where it was safe. Overhead, the skies darkened further and the man laughed hysterically.

"Where you goin', boy!" The man called after him. "Don't you want to know my name?"

No! Roman's mind blared, tears spilling over his cheeks as he ran. All he wanted was to be away from the wicked man and his hateful words. He did not give one lick what the man's name was. The stranger was a bad man and that was all Roman needed to know.

Using every ounce of strength he could draw upon, Roman pushed his small frame to its limits. Muscles aching and burning, he reached the first of the small town's four intersections, the jeering laughter of the stranger rising above the shrill wind as the man continued to bark out threats and belittling remarks. It was here that Roman witnessed the world around him morph into a dark parody of itself, his hometown twisting into a nightmarish caricature.

The buildings along Main Street were no longer places he knew, replaced with dark stone structures with wooden shingles, and the ground at his feet had turned to coal. In some of the windows, dim candlelight escaped in lackluster shafts, while other windows were nothing more than dark, unknown orifices. The few street signs in Jericho Hills were splintered planks of wood nailed to leaning, rotting posts.

Roman did not recognize any of the names on the signs, and as he crossed the intersection, forcing his body to move faster, he caught glimpses of some of the street signs as well as the larger signs on the buildings. They were all foreign words that he could not read, and a handful of them were random letters, numbers, shapes, and symbols.

After passing through the last intersection, Roman arrived at what appeared to be the end of town, mocking laughter emanating from the darkened buildings to either side of him. The road ended at a dense patch of woods, another post, and sign centered before it. Shivering from both the cold and fear, Roman tried to make out what it said, but it was more gibberish. The only words he could read were "death", "church", "anguish", and "guile". On top of the sign perched a large crow, canting its head and giving him a quizzical stare. It cried out in a series of loud, high-pitched caws. The bird's sudden outburst startled Roman and he backed up a few steps.

It's a warning, Roman thought. *But a warning of what?*

"I wouldn't wander off in there, boy," the stranger cautioned, closing the distance between them. "Some places are best not ventured into."

Roman turned to face the approaching man, the length of a rail car all that separated them.

"You go in there, boy, and the devil gets to devour your soul." Charlie's mouth spread into an abnormal grin. "And I get to dine on your flesh and wear your bones."

Roman cried harder, his heart triple tapping in his chest. He was trembling with such intensity, waves of sharp, jerky spasms pinballing through his body, that it appeared as if his legs had betrayed him. He did not want to die. Not like this. Not so some evil man could eat him. But he was shaking too hard to run away. If he tried, Roman was quite sure his legs would buckle and he would fall down. That is when the stranger would pounce, ripping him to pieces with his dirty, broken teeth.

"What's it goin' to be, boy?" Thick strings of drool hung from the corners of his mouth and Charlie smiled wider; wide enough that one would think the dubious grin was splitting open his face. "You goin' to chance the darkness or... I'll make it painless child. It'll be like gettin' rocked to sleep, like when you were a baby."

Choices were sometimes very difficult for Roman: what trail to explore when going down to the creek, whether or not he should tell his friends he had a crush on Susan Willis from school, or what bait to use when his Pa took him fishing. This was one of those times when the choice was in no way difficult to make. In spite of his leg's refusal to budge, Roman took enough control to turn and run into the unwelcoming darkness of the woods. Charlie shouted curses after him and the crow took to the darkening skies, cawing warnings as it flew away.

*

Roman was not familiar with his surroundings; these were not the woods around Jericho Hills he so enjoyed playing in. This was an abysmal place. Full of shadows and warped, gnarled trees that grew at odd angles, some curly-cued, others entwined with other trees, and some so mangled he could not force his mind to perceive them as trees. The scant light in this eerie wood was pale and surreal, with no source that Roman could find.

I bet there are witches here, Roman thought, remembering the scary stories his older sister was fond of telling him on late nights before bed.

"Only makes it worse to run, boy!" Charlie sounded angry.

Roman dared a peek behind him. He could not see the man, but he could hear someone or something thrashing through the brush. He had to keep going. He had to find his Pa. Roman wiped fresh tears from his eyes with the back of his hand and started up a narrow dirt path to his right. It was scarier and the trees along the path were even more deformed, but his resolve on this decision was firm. He was nearing exhaustion and he wanted to get as far away from the crazy man chasing him as he could manage.

102

The path was darker than the way in which he had come with waxing and waning patches of hazy moonlight every few feet or so. The murky woodland surrounding Roman grew increasingly more vibrant as he moved, with the calls and cries of several unidentifiable animals echoing around him. Some sounded big, some sounded small, but to Roman, they all sounded hungry. Hungry enough, he imagined, to eat a scared, defenseless little boy should he be unfortunate enough to happen upon them.

Unsure that his decision to venture into the depths of this lurid world was the wisest of acts, he prayed that he would live to see his mother's face, to feel comfortable in her arms. Even as a large rat the size of his German Shepherd Molly scuttled across in front of him, disappearing into the dense thicket of brush to his right, all Roman could think of was rejoining his family and putting this horrendous place behind him forever.

Perched on the branch of a rather sickly-looking oak Roman was passing was an even sicklier looking two-headed owl. It made a strange, strangled hooting noise and locked onto Roman with an all-knowing stare. Prophecy shone in all four of the owl's eyes, a foretelling of events beyond speculation for any logical outcome. With a little more vigor, Roman moved on, the weird owl continuing to hoot as if desperate for him to understand and heed whatever message it was trying to convey.

"You ain't doin' nothin' but buyin' time, boy!" Charlie shouted from somewhere back along the trail, his shrill, scornful voice cutting through the darkness.

Roman began to run, the salty taste of his tears on his tongue, Charlie's mad ravings in his ears, and his chest feeling as if it were about to collapse and crush his lungs at any second. Something screeched as Roman trampled over it and a mangy gray cat hissed at him, swiping its claws across his ankle. The wound burned fiercely, the cat's claws having buried deep enough to bring blood, but stopping to attend to it was out of the question. Emerging from the obsidian wall of night ahead of Roman was the first true sign of hope he had witnessed since his entrapment in this farce of a reality.

Spilling from a door-sized archway was a light far more illuminate and inviting than the ebbing moonlight currently enshrouding him. The corners of his face curved into a smile, followed by uncontrollable, joyful laughter. No longer was Roman agonizing over the bleakness of his immediate future. He would finally be with his family and safe from harm.

Warmth like that of a summer day greeted Roman as he passed through the archway, the pristine white light that had been so appealing bordering him from all sides. It was a comforting light, as tender as a loving embrace, and he was reluctant to leave it. Roman wanted nothing more than to bask in its radiance, to take pleasure in this virtuous light forever. The sensations he was now feeling were so intense, so complete. In his young mind, this was what he knew Heaven must feel like.

Childish snickers invaded Roman's newly discovered sanctum, tearing him away from his reverie. To either side of him stood other children close to his age, all of them looking rather battered and lost, and all of them dressed in clothing usually associated with the poor. Every single one of the children was waving him along, big, ugly grins on their faces as they did so. It was weird, Roman thought, how out-of-place those smiles were compared to the angelic light showing down on them. Why was there a presence of malevolence invading such a sacred place? What Roman considered as a holy place?

Startling Roman even more the children began to sing:

It's raining; you're bleeding.
The old beast is feeding.
He swung his ax down on top of your head.
You won't see the morning because now you're dead.

They sang their little song over-and-over, each time with a lunatic's passion. There was a frenzied glare in their eyes and thick strings of saliva slowly dripped from their chins. An icy chill smothered the blessed warmth and darkness sprang forth to cloak the light. The children became shadows, their singing dropping to a whisper. Roman fought to make sense of what was happening and longed for the sanctity of the light to come back. His anxiety was returning and muddling his thoughts. It was a tease, a false hope, and now he had become lost again. A frigid breeze rustled his clothes and soughed through the trees.

"Don't make this harder than it has to be, boy!" Charlie's raspy voice had returned. "I'm just tryin' to help you along, is all!"

Help me into your belly is more like it, Roman thought as he finally cleared the woods. The path continued upward and came to an end at the steps of a small white church with soft candlelight pouring from its windows. The mere sight of the old church elated Roman. He would find his family there. He would find the peace his exhausted body yearned for. Euphoria took his hand and led him up the path, the dead grass and burned-out husks that may or may not have been trees in some past era irrelevant in his passing. Only one thing mattered to him now.

"Home," Roman whispered. "I'm going home."

Several crows flew away from the church as Roman reached it and climbed the steps, their disapproving caws going unheard. Crossing the small porch to the open doors, Roman could see his family standing near the pulpit, waiting for him. His Pa, his Ma, and all his brothers and sisters, they were motioning for him to come to them. A big grin on his face, Roman tried to step through the doors but could not enter. Something kept pushing him back.

"Pa!" Roman shouted. "Come and let me in, Pa. It's cold out here and a crazy man wants to eat me, Pa. Please come let me in." Tears streaked over his cheeks as his pleas fell on deaf ears. The family on the other side of the doors, his family, faded away as the creepy children had.

"I told you there was no use in runnin', boy," Charlie said, his fingers like icicles as they clamped onto Roman's shoulder. "Ain't no one can outrun that horse."

Roman closed his eyes.

*

The first thing Roman noticed upon waking was that the rain had stopped. The second was that a dislocated shoulder was the least of his worries. Pain flared from every part of his body and he was having trouble moving his arms and legs. It was hot, too, and sunny. Roman squinted his eyes and was able to roll his head a little to the right. Thanks to the behemoth, he was no doubt an easy entree for the local wildlife. This, however, would be one meal the behemoth went without, as it lay on its side only a few feet away from Roman with a broken neck, its head twisted at an odd angle and its mouth hanging open. A swarm of flies was buzzing around its bloody muzzle.

"Shame ain't it." It was a familiar voice. "Those sons of bitches usually don't kick out so easy."

It took more of an effort than expected, but Roman managed to roll his head to the left. Sitting on a rock next to him was the old man, his horse-drawn prison wagon about ten feet behind him. The makeshift prison was empty.

"What did you do to them?" Roman croaked.

"Ain't nothin' I could do to or for them, boy. I'm just the middleman, ya see. My job is merely transportin' and droppin' off."

Roman cleared his throat and spit out a wad of bloody phlegm. "You are a slaver then," he said. "A despicable trade for a despicable old man."

The old man laughed. "How was it, boy? Reliving the day you died? Or should I say reliving what happened after you died."

"It was just a dream," Roman spat. It was all he could think of for an answer to such an off-the-wall question.

And how does he even know what I was dreaming about? It was so horrid, that macabre vision that was more hallucination than a dream. But how was this elderly devil remotely close to knowing what had transpired in Roman's unconscious mind?

"I guess it would come off like that, seein' as how you are a grown man and all." The old timer pulled from his breast pocket a tarnished, silver flask with the image of a dolphin crudely engraved on it, twisted off the cap, and offered it to Roman. Roman shook his head and the old man shrugged and took a swig before screwing the cap on and returning the flask to his pocket. "I imagine that shit would taste better if I could actually *taste* it. Old habits, boy."

"You are a peculiar one," Roman said, confused on rather the man was a little off in the head or purposely messing with him.

"You were never supposed to see that place," the old man went on as if oblivious to Roman's words. "I was runnin' late, boy, and your death was... untidy."

"I am not—"

"Cody Blackhall. The Ballpark Butcher. Or that was the name the press penned for him. It's where the bodies of all the children were found, in the dugouts of the Jericho Hills public ballpark."

What insanity is he babbling about? Roman wondered.

"Like the other children, you was strung up like a deer and gutted alive. Your heart, liver, testicles, it all joined the meat skinned from your chest and ribs in a stewpot. Cody was a quick bugger, too. No way I was going to make it before..."

"You speak nonsense." Roman hesitated.

"A wee bit unsure of that, are we?" The old man leaned forward, hands on his knees. "I never did tell you my name. You just called me Ch—"

"Charlie."

"Yep. A name you made up for me. My real name is Joseph."

"I was just a little kid afraid of strangers. And you came after me."

"I tried reachin' you boy, before you wandered in too deep."

"You were going to eat me and wear my bones. I had to run. I had to get away. I had to find my Pa. I did not want to die."

Joseph shook his head. "That is where your memory is little wonky. You was already dead, see, and your spirit had already been sucked into a dark patch on the edge of the wanderin' plains. I was too slow to keep it from happenin'. Most of what you heard, what you thought I was sayin', you confused it with what ol' Cody had said to you after snatching you from that street corner."

Roman used his arms to push himself into a sitting position against a large rock similar to the one Joseph was sitting on. It was pure agony to do so. "What are you? Not human, that is obvious. Demon?"

This caused an unexpected, pleasant chuckle from Joseph. "Far from it, boy. I round up lost souls, just like the three you saw earlier. I help those doomed to spend eternity suffering from one torment or the other to find peace. And you were special. You had a purpose above. A purpose you served without hesitation. Well, up until you defied His will. When the seals broke and the riders were free to do as they pleased, you interfered. Lost your wings for it."

"So I imagine you are waiting on me to die to get my soul."

"Son, you are nowhere near death. Banged up pretty good, but you'll live."

"Then why are you still here? Your business is complete and I am quite sure you're not sticking around to catch up on old times."

Although Joseph's face was mangled and hard to read, Roman noticed the solemn expression that was there now and the fleeting flash of crimson in his eyes. "Lots of holes in your memory, both before your death and before your fall. You have enemies, boy. Some ancient and powerful ones, at that. Terror Bears and Brood Worm slicked roads are the least of your troubles. I'm just keepin' watch until you heal enough to get along on your own."

Enemies? The old man is delusional. I have no enemies.

"But you do, boy." Joseph tapped a crooked finger to the side of his head. "Hard to hide your thoughts from me."

"Then you knew I was trailing you the entire time. Yet you never gave any indication of this. With these enemies you claim I have, would it not have been wise to alert me then and avoided all of this?"

Joseph nodded and said, "That I did. I knew someone was followin' me, just not who. Then when the behemoth caught your scent, I was a little curious to how that was goin' to end up."

Roman gritted his teeth and grunted in pain as he tried to stand. As much as he loathed violence, he wanted nothing more right now than to break Joseph's jaw. All he managed to accomplish was stumbling forward with a sharp cry of pain. Joseph caught him as he fell and eased him back against the rock. The old timer was quicker than he looked. "Best not try doin' that just yet, boy. Got a busted leg, broken ribs, and no telling what else."

Roman tried to get back up, regardless of his leg, but Joseph pushed him back down and placed his palm on Roman's forehead. "No more of that, hear? Rest is what your body is clamoring for."

The next three weeks were a combination of fever dreams, chills, sweat, and dry heaves. Roman had no clear recollection of everything that happened during that time, other than waking a few times to vomit up the greasy stew Joseph constantly force fed him while saying things like, "Swallow it down, boy, or you ain't goin' to get any better," or "You best eat if you want to see the sun again." But that was still better than suffering through dream after dream full of jumbled memories. His Ma and Pa and brothers and sisters, his time above, and his time up until now, all of it merged into a series of incomprehensible slideshows of his life, each image a grim reminder of what was and what came to be.

It was not until the last day of the third week that Roman's fever broke for the last time. He woke weak and hungry and puzzled on his surroundings. It was a small cabin or shack with only two windows that Roman could see. Animal furs and other hunting trophies adorned the walls; the prize of the collection he assumed was the head of a large twelve-point buck mounted above a moderately sized fireplace. In a far corner was an old wood burning stove. The bed he was in was the only piece of furniture in the room.

"Good to see you up, boy."

Roman sat up and shook off the light-headedness that followed. Once his vision cleared enough to bring the room back into focus, he saw Joseph standing next to the door. "Got somewhere to be?" he asked.

"Yep," Joseph replied. "I done took too long as it is. Need to get movin' on before the wrong ones notice that I'm gone. I left somethin' for you out on the porch. I figured you would need it."

Several years had gone by since that last time Roman had shed any tears, but he was on the verge of doing just that. He had thought Joseph to be this monster, some horrible demon that got his kicks from hurting others. And here he had tended to Roman's wounds and nursed him to health. Roman was not even sure how much time had passed.

"A good three weeks," Joseph replied to Roman's thoughts. "And no worries about the other, boy. I ain't holdin' any grudges."

"What of these enemies you spoke of?" Roman asked as Joseph opened the door. "Is that the truth?"

"I couldn't tell a lie if I wanted to." Joseph stood in the doorway, that solemn look returning to his face. "When you leave here, boy, search out the House of the Wolf and the Order of the Dolphin. You find them; you find everythin' you've lost. In the time in between, keep low and quiet. The apocalypse was only the first round."

Saying no more, Joseph stepped out of the shack and shut the door behind him. Roman replayed the old man's words over in his mind for a few minutes before getting up from the bed. Weak and wobbly at first, Roman slowly crossed the room and opened the door. Hanging from the porch railing was his long-coat and hat. The apocalypse was only the first round, Joseph had said. Roman looked out over the dusty, treeless yard, the heat from the midday sun introducing itself to his skin, and a deep frown wrinkled his face.

GODLESS WORLD

Michelle Garza and Melissa Lason

When the four horsemen symbolically rode through, no one recognized what was taking place; there were no otherworldly entities astride spectral horses coming down from the cavernous sky, but their appearance in the form of endless wars, then famine and sickness, heralded the end of the world and left the earth a graveyard planet. Those who did survive could do nothing else but look up and wonder why they had been abandoned by the multitude of gods worshipped over the centuries of man's reign. The most confused and vulnerable were the orphaned children, those who watched their caretakers die and their nightmares became reality as Hell opened its maw and sent forth its hungry denizens to claim them.

*

The screen flashed in bold red letters *END HIM*. Trina victoriously slapped the buttons and punched the joystick to the right. Her character, Razor Beast, leapt onto his opponent and sliced into his skin with the jagged blades embedded in the mutant's forearms. Joley and Sally cheered and slapped hands.

"Three more and you reach Gorgorus, the final boss!" Sally said.

"I've been waiting for this!" Trina said.

A high-pitched shrieking shook the tinted window panes lining the front of the dark arcade, causing the three girls to hesitate and clutch one another.

111

"Billy said to stay in here, that everything would be okay…" Sally whispered.

Trina put her finger to her lip to quiet the younger girl. A silence fell on the city beyond the locked doors, but they knew what the cries signified. Trina also remembered the promise she made and intended to keep it.

"Let's keep going," she said. "They won't come in here; they won't fit."

The arcade was one of few places where the electricity still worked, but that was only because Billy got the generator in the back room running before going out the back exit with the remainder of its gasoline. Trina was left in charge since she was the oldest at fifteen while Joley had only reached the age of twelve and her sister Sally only nine. Trina loved the arcade on Twelfth Avenue; it was the only thing that brought her memories of her life before the world ended. Her dad used to bring her there and let her watch him play Godless World, the game she was embroiled in beating. She hadn't played it since the world ended, and the resemblance between the city around her and the blasted wastelands of each level made her stomach turn, and the creatures she fought: those were far too familiar now that Hell had opened up.

The sisters stood behind her, their breath held each time she entered a new match. Billy had opened the machine and rigged it to not require tokens anymore before squeezing Trina's shoulders, looking her in the eyes and saying, "Do not leave this building. Take care of each other. I'll be back soon… you remember our pact?"

Trina nodded to herself and the memory of Billy who smiled in return, but the teenager could recall seeing no happiness in it. Once Billy was gone, she gripped the joystick of her favorite game and called her adopted sisters over to her, drawing their attention to its flashing screen. The arcade was a place of wonderful memories for Trina, but just as it did with her father when he divorced her mother, she knew it was just a diversion for a shit storm going on beyond its walls.

*

Trina readied herself to fight Hurricane, a character who could wield wind, rain and lightning. Her hands were tired from hitting buttons and gripping the joystick, but she refused to lose. She had to defeat Gorgorus; it was a matter of honor.

"Trina, you said your daddy used to bring you here?" Sally asked.

"Quiet, I'm about to start!" Trina growled.

She glanced over her shoulder at Sally's dirty face and her momentary anger faded.

"Yeah, he brought me here all the time on the weekends when I went to stay with him."

"Did he teach you how to play?" Joley asked.

"He sure did. He was the best at this game."

"Did he ever beat Gorgorus?"

"No." Trina answered and fell silent, concentrating on the battle before her.

Her character was a pixilated mutant; her opponent was a ninja dressed in blue and black, his hands glowed with bright azure light each time he prepared to launch his tempest attack. Razor Beast was agile and fast; his attacks were brutal and easily executed. The ease of operating him was one of the reasons her father taught her to use him as her character, plus his finishing move, the slasher, was one of the bloodiest of the entire game.

Trina fell in the first match. Her character was left encased in a block of ice before Hurricane sent a bolt of lightning directly into Razor's head, leaving it a poorly animated mist of blood.

"Damn!"

"You can do it. Billy fixed it so you can keep continuing," Sally said.

She knew it was a mistake to talk after Trina suffered a defeat and received a sidelong glare.

"Do you think Billy will come back for the last match?" Joley asked.

"I hope so. Billy would be proud!" Trina answered and tried to hide the pangs of fear in her gut before they revealed themselves on her slender face.

The next bout began and the three girls became fixated once more on the action on the screen, but on the peripheral of Trina's mind she wondered about what Billy was up to.

*

Billy could smell them before their ugly faces ever peeked around the corner of the building. Three of them in all, wearing ragged robes and the filth of months without a bath. They were hunters; Billy knew their type too well, and they were looking for fresh meat to not only feed their selves but to appease *them*.

"Why don't you stop your stupid game and come on out!" Billy announced.

"You don't sound very friendly!" one of the men answered.

His voice made Billy's skin crawl.

"I never said we'd be friends,F" she replied.

"So that's how it's gonna be?' He said and stepped from the shadows.

The sun had already begun to set, the grey light spilled over his wrinkled face displaying what Billy already felt, a depraved soul beneath his ragged flesh. Most of the survivors were exactly that: the rotten leftovers of society after the plagues came and fires fell from the sky and the citizens of Earth were devoured by things that crawled from fissures in the ground.

"I heard about you." The man said as he approached, his companions in tow.

Billy lit a hand rolled cigarette with a zippo lighter, a hand-me-down from her father, and waited patiently for them to get closer.

"You're that lezbo who shaves her head and keeps little girls as pets."

"You got the first part right, old man. The second part not so much... I'm their protector."

"Protector?" the haggard hunter laughed, the sound of a hungry jackal.

"What are you protecting them sweet little things from?" one of the men behind him asked.

114

Billy could feel this conversation growing dangerous, a cat and mouse game that only lit her fuse.

"From walking pieces of shit like you." Billy answered and dropped her cigarette on the ground.

A line of gasoline she prepared while they remained hidden from her around the side of the building went up in an instant and sent a line of fire racing towards the three men. They scattered, cursing and threatening to skin her alive. She remained vigilant for the beasts that would surely come to the heat of the fire and the ruckus she and the hunters were sure to make. The creatures, those who wailed beneath the sun in cries of dominance over their new territory, they were what truly scared her. She had already heard the crying of one nearby and knew it wouldn't be long before she caught a whiff of the nasty bastard. They were constantly hungry, like towering wendigos birthed from the cracks in the blacktop, their appetites never quelled no matter how many offerings of flesh and blood were placed at their clawed feet.

"Couldn't smell my surprise over your own stink!" she hollered.

The alleyways on each side of the small one-way street behind the arcade were crowded with cast aside charred debris, plenty of hiding places. Trash and piles of ash were everywhere after the end, survivors rummaged through it already, taking the useful things and leaving the rest behind. Only garbage and scattered bones of those who succumbed to the raining flame and insidious sicknesses plaguing the forsaken world remained. Men like the three she was tangled with wallowed in the filth around them and did as they pleased without the fear of consequences, like ravenous rats in a junkyard. Hell had opened up and claimed Earth as an extension of itself, creating a land of nightmares and pain. The men before her reveled in it. The freedom of no longer being held to a moral code and the absence of any kind of law made it a playground for sickos. Their only masters were things far worse than themselves, the monsters from literal Hell, who prompted the hunters to make sacrifices to them in the form of gut piles. The beasts delighted in the fact they hunted children, so long as the men left a mass of flesh and bones behind in tribute, and those who refused to leave the delicate child meat behind were doomed to be devoured.

Billy was no stranger to their kind and had already put a few down. She was old enough to remember what life was like before everything went to shit, before the man upstairs turned a blind eye to his children left to fight for their survival among the creatures of the world he created and those who invaded it from below. The cities were burned-out ghost towns, asylums ran by whatever lunatics who crawled from the wreckage alive, like parasites hungry to devour the last of the purity on the face of the Earth. She quickly learned that the good guys were dead, and to trust no one.

The hunters dashed back out into the street, as she knew they would, and came for her. It wasn't the first time she had to choose between living and killing. Her hands already carried the blood of four men; three more didn't matter much, for God had abandoned her to kill without consequence in the land of death. The girls in the arcade were the only thing she cared about and made her fight to keep living anymore.

They'd been surviving together for a little more than a year in a world that God had forsaken. She picked up the sisters after finding them living in their boarded-up house, surrounded by the remains of their family members. Trina she found hiding in the back of a burnt out grocery store searching for food that hadn't spoiled yet. It took some work, but they became like blood sisters; they trusted her with their lives. They ventured to the city together in order to scavenge supplies; it was safer than leaving them alone in an abandoned house on the outskirts where they could be found by man or beast. When she caught wind of the men stalking them as they scavenged, she made a hasty plan in her mind. Trina was overjoyed when Billy finally agreed to let them visit the arcade; it would give her closure over her father and provide Billy some time to do what she had to do. She had to kill the hunters.

"Hand them over and we'll let you go."

"Forget it." Billy answered.

She knew damn well what happened to little girls in the new world. It made her sick to her stomach to recall the number of tiny mutilated corpses she had discovered, all pieced out like

116

lambs after the slaughter, small mounds of innards left on sidewalks for the nightmare beasts to gorge on.

"Fine, have it your way." The leader of the three answered as they dodged the last of the flaming line of fluid.

"I can smell them already, real tender meat, but before we roast 'em you know we're gonna poke 'em." The third man smirked; his teeth were crooked and black. She could smell the rot on his breath from five feet away. He rubbed his grimy hands together and licked his cracked lips. Billy sneered. She could feel their hostility growing. The leader pulled a knife, a long serrated one. It reminded her of something her father used to gut trout with.

"You probably won't taste very good, but I'm sure you could use the touch of a man, or three, or nine!"

"There are a few things my father taught me before he died," she began.

"Oh, yeah? Did he teach you about peckers?" the old man asked lewdly squeezing the crotch of his pants.

A deafening screech echoed down the alleyway, and the hunters' faces dropped. Their game of dominance had ended and the apex predator was about to claim their prey. Amidst the smell of refuse and filth a familiar scent turned Billy's gut. She didn't want to betray the fear quaking through her extremities, so she straightened her back and accepted whatever fate had in store for her before speaking.

"He was a good man, my dad, not a pig like the three of you. He spent most of his life on the wrong side of the law, but he taught me a few things before he died… he taught me about killing."

*

Trina's fingers ached' her palms were clammy. She rubbed them down the front of her jeans and resumed her stance at the machine.

"I smell something. Fire!" Joley worried.

"Billy told us not to leave this building." Trina answered, knowing something was going down outside.

Trina had blood staining her hands and scars on her heart from meeting men like the hunters Billy was dealing with; she was lucky to have survived. When she first encountered Billy, Trina hid and armed herself with a broken bottle. It wasn't until the stranger spoke that Trina realized she was a woman. It took weeks for her to fully trust Billy, but now she did completely. When they entered the city, she begged Billy to see the arcade and when Billy unexpectedly agreed Trina was ecstatic, but then the scent of sulfur filled her nose and the shadows of strangers passed among the alleys. She could see Billy plotting as they made their way to the back door. The pact was made in haste; it twisted her heart, but Trina understood it.

If one day I don't come back, you need to be strong, and you need to take care of your sisters. Promise me, Trina.

"Is she going to be alright out there?" Sally asked.

"There's one of *them* outside, right? Is Billy okay?" Joley asked frantically.

"I told you, they're too big to get in here, so just do what Billy said, stay put!"

"But, what would we do without her?"

"That's not gonna happen." Trina said. She shook as her voice rose.

Joley and Sally fell silent, but their faces remained frozen in masks of concern and fear.

"Hush. The final round is starting." Trina snipped, trying to draw the attention of the other girls.

Gorgorus was nearly twice the size of Razor Beast, Trina's character, the warrior who had carried her to the final bout. She no longer prayed anymore, but in her heart she hoped whomever watching over her would help her defeat the final boss and that Billy returned from the battle she was sure to be caught in. Trina owed it to her father to beat the game, and she owed it to Billy to keep the other two girls hypnotized by her gameplay long enough not to see the carnage beyond the arcade.

Trina's father had no gravestone over his body, no obituary in the papers to pay tribute to him; she knew if Billy died it would be the same, the snuffing of a candle, a darkness that would consume her. Trina wanted to pay homage to them both in the only way she knew how anymore: by defeating the final boss.

Her mind flashed back to seeing her father for the last time. The blood in his charred lungs kept him in a coma for weeks while the hospital became a tomb and not a single doctor or nurse survived. Trina found him all by herself after her mother and stepfather died, when she was forced to survive all alone in the savage world. Her heart ached and she banished the memory of his emaciated corpse from her mind. She wanted to remember him as he lived, and the arcade on Twelfth Avenue accomplished that. She could imagine him standing over by the counter, ordering her a slice of pizza, wearing his denim jacket covered in patches from the punk rock bands he played in.

She admired him so much; not only did she love him because he was her father, but she just thought he was the coolest person she had ever known. His name was James, a child at heart always and forever, but also the kindest, most understanding man she had ever met. His temperament was much like Billy's: calm and patient and yet could turn to a stone cold badass when he had to. That was why Trina thought she grew to love Billy so much and to trust her so completely. They shared those memories about those who had already left the forsaken world behind, the ones they hoped awaited them in death. Billy told Trina about her own father, how he was a bastard sometimes, but he was always there to protect her, right up until the end of his life.

A wailing bellowed outside and rattled Trina's insides. The cries of the creatures were unmistakable and nearly sent Trina cowering beneath a dusty table like she did when she roamed alone, but she stayed glued to the arcade game, it was what Billy would have done too. Billy was out there and there wasn't a damn thing she could do to help her; it would mean breaking her promise, and Trina knew she couldn't do that without risking the lives of the girls huddled around her. While she fought imaginary monsters in a fictional world, Billy fought real ones hunting just beyond the walls of where they stood.

The screen lit up with the introduction scene for the final boss, Gorgorus. She tensed. There was too much riding on whether or not she was victorious; to her it meant the world. The two girls behind her held one another, not daring to speak another word.

"Come on, Razor!" Trina said. It became her mantra as the bell rang, signaling the beginning of the fight. In her mind she pictured Billy squaring off against a gargantuan beast, an end boss in the flesh, just outside, only she didn't have the luxury of unlimited continues.

*

The old man came for Billy, his knife out before him. He was like a desperate animal, a starving dog taking any chance it had to just to snap the meat out of some larger animal's mouth before they could claim it. She took one step back then sidestepped as he came at her slashing the air; her father's fighting lessons were ingrained in her muscle memory. In her mind she could see him, in the evening light, a knife in his hand, and even as the sickness took him, he still looked proud and strong.

"Show them the same amount of mercy they'd show you: not a fuckin' ounce." His voice was hoarse from coughing up blood.

"You've taught me this before, Dad." Her own voice echoed in her memory.

"Well, one of these days I might not come back, and you gotta promise me you'll take care of yourself," he said and faced her, and in the dim light she watched the hollowing of his cheekbones and the grey hue his lips were becoming.

"I promise." Billy said, knowing her father was readying himself to die.

He had disappeared more than a few times in her life, mostly when he was sent to jail, and though it hurt her and she cussed him out over the phone, when he finally called to check in on her she always welcomed him home with open arms. This time there would be no reunion, not in life anyway; it would be for the last time.

*

120

Billy grabbed the hunter's wrist as his blade sailed by her. She twisted his arm behind his back and yanked it upward. There was a snap and a garbled cry of pain mixed with the foul curses he spat at her. He fell forward to his knees as his companions came running past him, seeking to get a hold of her before she could run. Their hands were nearly on her when the scent of death overpowered them, and a great screeching prompted them to abandon not only Billy but their leader as well. They pushed by her, the smell of their unwashed bodies and old blood overpowered by the breath of the supreme creature dragging itself down the crowded alleyway. It was giant and spider-like, only its many legs were fleshy and tipped with clawed hands, its head like the boney skull of a dead goat whose flesh rotted beneath the sun, only it had massive fangs. Billy had seen a few in her time but never this close up. They were all different in ways, and once Trina whispered to her it was because they were created from nightmares, so they took the shape of the darkest things children might dream of. The explanation always sent a chill up her spine when she thought of it because it seemed to be a correct assumption.

This beast was by far the largest Billy had even seen. It dragged a bulbous fleshy sack of a rear end behind it while its black eyes hungrily focused on her. She had heard they could paralyze people with their emotionless eyes; she wasn't sure if it was some unearthly power or just from the sheer dread they instilled in their prey, ut she felt as if she couldn't move her legs. She couldn't even scream when looking upon the massive thing crawling its way towards her. Billy cursed herself for daring enter the city, for putting the girls in such danger, and for possibly leaving them to fend for themselves in such an unforgiving world. A single tear wound its way down her cheek as the hot breath of the monster crawled over her. It was moving closer, a living nightmare which dragged itself right from the belly of hell.

The ragged hunter kneeling at her feet half turned and gasped as it drew near. Those who fed the creatures feared them too; they held no loyalty to humans, even those who left out scraps of corpses to feast upon. Billy's trance was broken by a metallic clattering at her feet. Her eyes found the hunter's knife. His useless hand had relinquished it while he struggled to stand.

The beast halted. Its black eyes held the void within them as it focused on the humans before it. The stench wafting off of its body was of pure sulfur and ash, of something birthed in the foul netherworld sewers where tarnished souls were sent to languish. Billy had often wondered if the cities surrounding the fissures were haunted by escaped souls of the damned and it kept her from lingering long among the ruins after dark. They were already plagued by beasts and men, but the thoughts of those hungry ghosts screaming as they freed themselves from eternal torture made her skin crawl.

The creature hissed and spoke a line of something in the devil's tongue, a broken language which translated itself in terror and agony within the soul. Billy wasn't sure if the hunter understood the language of the beast being its thrall and servant, but it prompted him to struggle harder. He tumbled to his side, his twisted arm unable to break his fall. He fell hard on the appendage and howled in pain. For a moment he looked like a possessed break dancer as his feet pumped and propelled him in a half circle while his sickening screams tore through Billy's gut. If she could have had it her way she would have put him out of his misery right then, but the monster eyed her, licked its gaping maw and slid-scurried forward. It snatched the injured man up in one of its massive hands and held him out in the air. It seemed to relish in his torment as it lifted another one of its spider-like limbs to grip his legs within the deformed hand at its tip. Billy swallowed the bile in her throat as it tore him in two, his innards spilling out on the ground of the filthy alleyway. She used the moment of distraction to retrieve the knife at her feet. Her eyes scanned the narrow passageway between her and the creature; just behind it was the graffiti covered door leading into the back of the arcade. Billy screamed internally for Trina to remember the promise she had made before holding the knife aloft.

*

Gorgorus was a massive foe, comprised of the shredded corpses of its enemies all pieced together in a mosaic of pain. The final level, its lair, was a black cave engulfed in the fires of the inferno. The imagery sent a chill up her spine, but she gripped the joystick and positioned her hand over the red and yellow buttons. Trina mouthed a silent prayer, one she knew would be ignored but it was something from her past life she still hadn't let die. A flashing countdown in the center of the screen put her on edge, and when the announcer ordered her to fight, she went in with all she could remember, everything James had taught her. Razor Beast's health bar was only half as long as his opponents, but Trina knew a way to beat the system so to speak, a trick her father had passed on to her one night while they walked home from the arcade defeated only after James ran out of quarters.

"It doesn't matter how big your opponent is. If you know his weakness you can bring him down."

Her father's advice was for more than just the video games they had spent hours playing; it was meant to stretch into real life as well, but that night all she could focus on was losing again.

"How do I beat something so powerful?" Trina asked, her young mind fixated on losing to Storm Witch.

"Next time I'll show you. She's powerful but takes too long to cast her spells, so you gotta roll in and hit her in the stomach with your razors. I heard that's how to kill the main boss too, Gorgorus."

Trina nodded. She could picture it; her father was right. She stood behind an older boy and watched him make it all the way to the final boss but died within minutes of facing Gorgorus, only because he hesitated, afraid of the powerful fireballs the enemy was casting. If he had done as her father said, he might have had a chance. It eased her frustration and allowed her to calm down enough to agree to trying again when she was allowed to come back, but that chance never came.

Gorgorus roared as the match began. Trina waited for the moment to strike, avoiding his flailing arms until he paused and his entire body lit up orange as if he was being immolated. Quickly, she slapped the buttons and made Razor Beast roll forward. She then instantly started slashing the stomach of the massive beast. Gorgorus howled and fell back, his life bar shrank, and Trina grinned in determination. She rolled Razor Beast away as it prepared to lash out with its lanky appendages, and then rolled back again as Gorgorus prepared to light her on fire.

"Die, motherfucker!"

"You can do it!" Sally cheered.

"Kill him!" Joley chanted.

Trina never broke the sequence and watched as the final boss fell, its body bursting in flames. The three girls cried out victoriously as the end credits rolled and the coveted screen appeared which prompted her to leave her name in the list of those who had beaten the entire game and became a true champion of Godless World. Trina thumbed the joystick and selected the letters J, B, T, S, J and entered it there. Her triumph was cut short when she remembered no one would ever see it, but her homage was paid and she hoped her father was proud.

"What do those mean?" Sally asked.

"This victory was for all of us. Those are the first letters of our names and my dad's name and of course Billy's name," Trina said and morbidly added, "Now when we die we'll at least have this, kinda like our tombstone."

"You're the coolest." Joley spoke and put her arms around Trina.

"I wish Billy could have seen that." Sally said softly.

"She will." Trina spoke and looked to the door leading to the back of the arcade.

*

Billy felt her heart stutter as the beast devoured the last of the hunter's remains, his blood painting its grotesque body. She held the knife ready, remembering her father's face, his voice, and welcomed the thoughts of reuniting with him for a moment. That's when she heard a banging and knew Trina hadn't kept her promise.

It turned to look back at the little girl banging trashcan lids together. She smelled like fresh blood, and the hunger in the

124

creature's gut howled with the anticipation of feeling her meat churning in its belly. It screeched and attempted to turn back around, but its bloated rear end got caught up in the debris cluttering the tight alley.

"*Trina! No!*" Billy screamed.

The monster was awkwardly turning itself around when the girl answered: "Run for the front door!"

Billy spun around and headed for the end of the alleyway; the angry cries of the hell beast as it realized she was escaping shook her from behind. Billy didn't look back; instead she willed her feet to move with every ounce of speed she could manage as she zigzagged between piles of refuse and old bones. The angry creature wouldn't be fooled so easily. Instead it abandoned the tender morsel of a girl as she ducked back into the painted door behind the creature and slid the lock in place with a loud clamor. It returned its attention to its original prey as it frantically attempted to escape.

Billy rounded the side of the building as she exited the alley and headed for the front door of the arcade. Great openings in the concrete and blacktop belched noxious smoke in her face and burned her lungs as she hurried to where Trina was already waiting; like poisonous mouths waiting to swallow her, she skirted around them. Her heart pounded in her chest, battering against her ribs like a startled bird in a cage of bone. A shrieking shot through her as a second beast came lurching out of hiding within one of the deepest crags, like a trapdoor spider waiting to spring out on a desperate insect. Billy felt the last tendril of hope she held onto slipping from her grasp. It was dragging itself free when she scurried past it and breathlessly made her way in the direction of Trina, who held the door open. Pain erupted in her leg and she tumbled forward. Billy looked back to see a spiny leg was thrust through her left calf muscle. The new beast had impaled her on one of its spindly, bony limbs and was ready to drag her back to its waiting mouth. Billy was still gripping the serrated knife in one trembling hand. She could hear Trina screaming her name; it gave her the strength to stab the creature in the same leg it used to pin her down with. Her feeble attempts didn't harm her attacker; its body was covered in armor as thick as stone, but the piercing cry of the first monster rattled every bone in her body. It came to challenge the second spidery beast who was now attempting to steal its meal. Billy was released as the beasts met head to head.

She covered the ground between her and Trina in agonizing slow motion. The girl caught her as she fell through the arcade door, her blood pumping out in a hot river down onto the stained carpet of a place that once held excitement and joy for all who entered. Trina threw the door closed and laid over Billy, repeating to her how much she needed her and loved her. It was in those moments Billy thought she knew how her father felt those times when he returned from jail after leaving the most important thing in the world to him alone in the cruel world to fend for itself. She felt like a fool for leaving them and she felt unworthy of such loyalty... but she was overjoyed to have it.

"You didn't keep your promise." Billy spoke.

"Yes, I did. You said if the day came you didn't return, and here you are..." Trina answered as she wrapped Billy's leg in an old towel.

"Did you beat the game?"

Trina nodded. "Left our initials immortalized. We'll live forever in Godless World."

HAM AND PUDGE

K. Trap Jones

"Is that guy fucking a corpse?" Ham said, trying to free his foot from the entanglement of severed human limbs.

"I don't know. When I squint, all I see is his gyrating bare ass," I said, not paying much attention. "I guess we'll find out when we make it over there."

"Imagine that; you survive the apocalypse, the scourge of Satan, the wrath of Jesus, and your first order of business is to bust a nut."

"I'm not surprised. Humans were never good at prioritizing," I replied, poking a hollowed-out skull with my foot.

"They sure categorized their sins, though. I mean, fuck. These assholes ruined the planet quick, didn't they Pudge? I probably would've bet against the planet anyways, but I sure as shit wouldn't have thought it would go so fast."

"Shit, this one's alive. What were we supposed to with live ones?" Ham said, widening the eyelids of a random woman with his fingers. As he raised her head, half of the skull separated, falling from its position. A small moan leaked from her mouth as the eyes rolled back into position. Her blonde hair was completely saturated with blood. She was offering us her severed arm. I guess she wanted us to stitch her back together.

I unleashed my machete from the casing on my back and jumped to a large man's chest in order to get a better view. The humans were huge compared to us. We only stood about a foot and a half in height, created by Jesus to comb through the remains and gather anything of value. Not too sure why he chose to equip us with a machete; the damn blade was about as tall as both of us and heavy as all fuck.

"He said there would be no survivors," I replied, scratching my elongated beard.

"I mean, there's this one and that horny bastard over there," Ham answered, trying to put the skull back together. "You see, that's the problem with planetary ruling; there's no quality control."

"We are the quality control. The only other alternative is to tell Boss he missed one," I offered with a smirk of denial.

"Fuck that!" Ham said, letting the skull split apart again. "I'm not highlighting his mistakes. He'll turn us into fish and eat us as tacos. Although, I am adding Quality Control Manager to my resume. Shit sounds important."

"Alright, let's set some ground rules up front," I explained, slipping down the barren, bloody chest of a man. "Whoever comes across a live one, it's on them to fix it."

"Deal, but this first one shouldn't count, right?" Ham announced, trying to pick specks of rust from his machete. "Plus, I'm not sure how to go about killing and all."

The field was littered with human carcasses spanning the entire horizon. The gore infested battleground was the bloody aftermath of the recent duel between Satan and Jesus. The earth still tremored in fear, rattling the limbs and entangling them more into the labyrinth of decaying meat. The once lush field of wheat was contorted into a feasting ground for the hordes of vultures. We'd scare them away, but they didn't give a shit as they just flew to another pile of flesh. The fat bastards were gorging themselves, causing them to barely be able to fly. Some were belly up, slumbering in a food coma.

Ham tilted back the head to expose the neck. She kept whimpering, but sympathy was not a trait gifted to us.

"So, you think this one was a believer?" Ham said, taking the arm and tossing it aside.

"Depends."

"On what?"

"Did she shit her pants?" I said, trying to see through the interwoven limbs.

"Ha, true. I would've loved to have seen the faces of the nonbelievers when they first witnessed either of the bad boys rising. I'd probably have shit my entire internal organs. Just fucking turning me inside out."

"Couldn't have been too pleasant for the other side either. I mean, they thought he was their savior, thinking he would actually… save. Doomed either way. To live is to brutally be slaughtered and die a miserable death."

"Still, I bet the nonbelievers had it rough; reflecting on their past life and shit. At least the believers were both right and wrong; the others were just plain wrong."

"How in the hell are we supposed to cover this much ground anyways?" I said, twisting around looking at the field. Standing atop a cresting man's shoulders, it was like standing on a boulder in the middle of large dead lake.

"Do I stab or slice?" Ham said, turning to look back at me.

We weren't given much in order to complete the task. A couple of machetes, a pair of satchels and a donkey pulling a rotted, wooden wagon. To make matters worse, the fucking donkey was absolutely useless; dumb ass kept getting distracted by the vultures. The wagon was a rickety piece of shit with two nearly broken wheels which wobbled, dropping already collected shit. To top it all off, we were molded after the rodent species, which made no since to us at all. A demented cocktail somewhere between a rat and a prairie dog. Not sure why I was named Pudge; Ham certainly drew the wrong end of the weight stick, but who were we to question our creator?

"Never really done this type of thing before," Ham said, rotating the blade in different angles.

Me neither," I said, shrugging my shoulders. "I suppose the goal is to drain the blood."

"What about stabbing the brain? I mean, it's right there," he said, hovering the blade over the cerebrum. "Seems like it would be quicker."

"Not sure whether Boss wants to save the organs or not. He mentioned something about creating a new race, but I don't know whether he is starting from scratch or reusing these assholes."

The woman's pupils sporadically shifted causing her head to follow suit. A loud screech of the donkey caught our attention as we both stretched our necks to peer over the makeshift vines of legs and arms.

"He's alright. Looks like he's still hitched to the wagon," Ham said.

"He's such a fucking dumb ass," I replied, thinking bad thoughts. "Of all the capable donkeys in the world, what are the odds we get stuck with an easily frightened one who can't even pull a wagon forward?"

"Shit, he's eating the flesh again."

"I fucking swear," I said, making my way over to the donkey.

"You think he's immortal?" Ham said, wobbling the woman's head as if asking the question to her.

"Who? The donkey?" I replied, looking over my shoulder.

"Yeah. You think he's immortal? Not like these shitheads," he said, pulling back the moaning head again.

"Only one way to find out, I guess," I said, jumping before the donkey. His head lifted up with his teeth dripping with blood. He tilted his head in confusion while pinning his ears back. A tiny morsel of sympathy infested my thoughts as I loosened my grip on the machete handle. He couldn't let it go, though. He pushed me to the edge when he flapped his disgusting ass lips, showing the bloody, decaying teeth as he laughed. My eyes turned red with anger. I swung the weapon so hard that my body was lifted from the ground, following the rotation. The blade sunk deep into the neck of the animal, abruptly stopping only when it met resistance with the spine.

Slipping from the bloody handle, my body kept going from the momentum. The gurgling laughter from the donkey blended perfectly with the wind as I bounced from different corpses, finally coming to a stop within the crotch of a large man who was upside down. His nutsack struck my forehead as I slid down the belly. Reaching up, I grasped upon his limp dick in order to stop my descent. With muffled ears and blurred vision, all I was able to make out was the sound of a ringing bell and the continued faint laughter from the donkey. Trying to pull myself up, I used the organ to climb.

"What the fuck are you doing?" I heard Ham say, but didn't know from where.

"I... I—" I tried to explain, but mainly focused on ascending over the belly.

"I leave you alone for one minute and you're killing ass and stroking dick," Ham laughed.

"Is he dead?" I said, standing in the crotch, using the ass crack to stabilize my footing.

"Who? The man you just gave a hand job?" Ham replied with a smirk.

"The fucking donkey."

"Yeah, he's dead. You decapitated him."

"Good."

"Not really. Who's going to pull the damn wagon?"

It pissed me off knowing that the donkey was probably laughing at us in the afterlife. The wagon was older than dirt and appeared to be constructed by a blind man with one arm.

"We're cursed to fail, you know that, right?" "I stated, making my way back over to Ham. "These tools; the tools provided are pointless. We're given bodies the size of horse turds, dull rusty blades and a shit show for a wagon pulled by the stupidest animal in the world, and to carry what? Trinkets? Relics? What the fuck does the creator of the planet need with nuggets of gold when he can just create whatever the fuck he wants?"

"Maybe you're right, but it still doesn't change the fact that we have a task to do."

"I bet Satan would've given us better equipment. A fucking sharp ass sickle or even a reaper's scythe. And definitely a better, cooperative animal like a goat or something. Maybe the hounds of hell."

"I wouldn't mind a goat. Did you know that they can remember how to perform tasks, even months later? That's pretty fucking sweet, if you ask me."

There was a brief moment of silence as we stood amongst the vast sea of the dead overlooking the task at hand. Neither of us wanted to continue digging through the garbage meat landfill.

"Well, boss did give us the gift of noses without smell," Ham said, trying to sniff the air. "I can't smell anything."

"Now that you mention it, I can't smell anything either," I replied, leaning down to catch a whiff of a disemboweled body. The extracted large intestines were completely out of the split torso and wrapped around the neck of a nearby carcass. My whiskers worked overtime, trying to gather any small amount of aroma.

"Alright, let's get back to work. I'm going for the neck," Ham said, still holding the moaning head of the woman. A puss induced stream of drool connected her dangling tongue to one of her exposed breasts. Dragging the blade across the entire outstretched neck, Ham easily cut deep through the already bruised esophagus. The stomach convulsed as her abdomen restricted, forcing a wave of vomit to spurt from the opened pipe. Releasing his grip, the head dangled backwards against the shoulder blades. The vacant eyes stared at me from upside down. The acid and bloody puke spewed like a fountain, painting the face with a darkened, brown hue. The bubbling bile continued as her body involuntarily stirred at an increasingly rapid pace.

"Think she's going to blow," I said, taking a step back.

Ham barely made it away as the chest split apart. The high-pitched crackling sound of the ribcage separating was mind numbing, forcing me to take a few more steps back.

Watching the events unfold, Ham and I were perched on some dude's bent over ass. We each stabbed our blades deep into the butt cheek we were standing on in case we needed to hold onto something. The splintering bones gave way to an escaping, shivering soul. We stood there watching the soul desperately trying to make sense of death as it flapped around like a wounded bird, confused by seeing its own body.

The wind intensified, picking up anything not wedged tightly in the mass of bodies. Forcing the sporadic soul, the wind current sucked the entity further into the field where it eventually faded. That's about when I heard it; a specific heckling laughter. We both turned around to the wagon where we viewed the donkey's body shifting about. It was lying on its back and all four hooves were kicking in the air, trying to get upright. The detached head was a few feet away and neighing hysterically.

"I guess he's immortal," Ham stated, patting me on the back.

"Alright, let's put him back together," I responded, making my way over to him.

"At least we don't have to pull the wagon. Not like we were physically capable to doing it anyways."

"Grab the head. I'll get the body," I said before I was brutally donkey-kicked by the hind hooves. The force blinded my eyes as I flew through the fog infested air. The flight was somehow peaceful. The dampened fog cooled my busted nose until I landed snout deep within a large wound of a person.

Trying to extract my face, I could open breathe through the smallest of cracks on the sides of my mouth. Wheezing, I was able to open my eyes to survey the situation. I looked up over a belly where two nipples served as lighthouses. Using both arms and propping up my feet for leverage, I wiggled my snout in order to loosen it. With one final push, I landed within the armpit of another body. Spitting to help my tongue from tasting, I peered deep into the torn cave-like vagina. The buckled legs were rotated against the knees and bent towards the head. The torso was ripped, leaving behind a gaping hole, tripling the size of the cavity.

"Fuck, he's biting me!" Ham screamed as I scurried upwards, using a rigid arm for support.

Ham was running around with the head of the donkey attached to him. His arm wasn't visible. The donkey's lips were flapping against the shoulder as the tongue flickered against Ham's face. He was trying to cut the animal, but the blade was too long to get a meaningful swing. Tumbling down the small hills of dead bodies, Ham was going ballistic; flailing like a fish out of water. I grabbed both of the donkey's ears and leaned back.

"Wait, wait! His teeth. He's dug in deep," Ham said.

"Hold on, I have an idea," I announced. Squatting, I looked up through the open wound.

"What are you doing, man?" Ham said in a panic.

"I'm going to reach inside him; try to control him like a puppet," I replied.

"Like a what?"

"You know, like a puppet," I answered, holding up my hand like it was talking.

"Ah fuck, he's going to gnaw my arm off; I'm losing a limb. I can't go through life with one arm. I mean, fuck, I'm already a hideous rodent with no game," he said, sniffling. "I'll be a wobbly, off-balanced dipshit who lost his arm to an ass. And not even the good type of ass.

"Are you crying?"

"No, no, I have sweat in my eyes," he explained as the donkey's tongue kept licking his face.

"Hold still," I said, inserting my hand up through the severed neck. The inside was warm and moist as my fingers inched upwards through the neck. The donkey's laughter subsided as he swallowed excessively, causing the throat to shudder and tighten around my forearm. I was shoulder deep when I finally reached the back of the tongue. He gulped as I flipped the tongue backwards, holding it tightly while I retracted my arm. The ears pinned back in defiance as he breathed through the nose. Ham shielded himself from flying snot bubbles as the tongue ripped at the base, forcing the mouth to open and the teeth to release their grip. Ham was free and he very pissed; hacking and slashing the head with his blade.

"Relax, mother fucker," I said, spinning around. "My arm is still in."

The laughter started back up as I threw the head into the wagon. The breeze of death filtered through the rotting landscape, whistling as it funneled between piles of broken bones and extracted spines. We sat for a while, covered in blood, vomit and a crap ton of stomach acid, which was causing an irritable rash. We both sighed at once as the sound of flapping skin echoed. Looking behind us, the horny man was still pounding away, trying to reach climax.

"What do you suppose he's banging?" Ham said, scratching his rash.

"Could be anything, really," I said, picking a scrap of flesh from my ear. "I'm thinking he's old school missionary."

134

"No, no. This one's a freak. He's fucking the busted-out arm pit of an old lady."

"Alright, I'll change my answer then," I replied, scratching my head. "He's using the small intestine as sort of a pump; small, tight."

"I'll take that bet. Whoever's the furthest away from the point of entry pulls the wagon first."

We shook on it and made our way over to the man. It was hard to make out at first due to the mass of mangled bodies. The penetration zone was difficult to discover, but he sure was having a grand old time. His back was tattooed with all kinds of gaping cuts and bruises. The skin of his lower back was peeled off and he was missing an entire butt cheek, but he was in no pain as evident from the look of ecstasy plastered on his face. The arms were pinned beneath, holding onto something. It wasn't until we moved towards the front that we discovered what it was.

"Now that's messed up," Ham said.

He was fucking the half-beaten skull of another man through the canal of a missing ear. When he shifted backwards, his penis was being shredded by the rigid, cracked bones of the skull. The skin was completely peeled off and resting on a rim of the crevice, but yet he didn't stop. The spliced veins spurted blood, self-lubricating against the friction. His member was nothing more than a small pillar of cartilage. We weren't sure he was actually feeling anything, but he kept going.

"Should let him finish, right? I mean, that's the right thing to do," I said, trying to look away, but couldn't.

"If he does finish. At the rate he's going and by the looks of his distorted shaft, we could be here for quite some time."

The constant motion of being ear fucked caused both of the eyeballs to be dislodged. Ham had enough and stood on the man's back using his mullet to lift the face. A heavy stream of blood spilled down as agony wheezed from the fresh wound.

"Kind of looks like a fountain of wine," he said, proud of his accomplishment.

With life draining, he still performed pelvic thrusts, but at a slower, more pathetic rate until eventually stopping. Heading back to the wagon, we determined that neither of us were able to pull the damn thing so we opted on putting the donkey back together. The fucker was pissed, trying to buck and kick the living hell out of us, but we tied him up pretty good. His head was a little tilted to the left only because he kept trying to bite us while the immortality trait was working to rejoin. Afterwards, he wasn't the same and seemed to have lost function of his right eye; not sure where he was looking at most of the time. His anger spiked whenever we neared him. He made it known that he hated us and wanted to eat us at any given chance.

We stayed in the field searching through most of the terrain until late one night we noticed a fire on a nearby hilltop overlooking the battleground. Sneaking up the embankment, we came across two individuals huddled around a fire pit.

"What the fuck is this?" Ham announced.

Satan and Jesus were sitting on a log surrounded by wine barrels. Swaying, the red liquor sloshed within their golden goblets as they laughed. Wearing a black pinstriped suit and top hat, Satan was a thin, lanky man with a long, braided beard separated into three sections. A pitchfork tattoo decorated his neck which was a prong entering both ears and up his chin. Jesus, on the other hand, was a larger, muscular man with long brown hair in a ponytail. His beard was long enough to almost conceal the massive tribal crucifix tattoo, dividing his chest into four quadrants.

"You have got to be kidding me." I said, stabbing my machete into the ground.

"There they are," Jesus said, lighting up a joint. "These are the little bastards I was telling you about."

"Well, look at that. You weren't lying. They are tiny little parasites," Satan replied, leaning towards the fire to relight a cigar.

"What the hell is going on?" I said with a sigh.

"Been there, done that," Satan replied, causing Jesus to spit out wine with laughter.

"The apocalypse? You were battling to the death?" Ham stated.

"The entire human race has been wiped out," I added.

"Pretty sweet, huh?" Jesus said with a grin. "Did you have a good seat?"

"But, you're mortal enemies; good versus evil and all that bullshit," Ham said.

"It's all an act for our father; he loves a good battle," Satan explained while accepting the joint from Jesus. "Plus, it allows the big guy to start over. Kind of wipes the slate clean; gets rid of all the grime in the cracks."

"He's always fucking up," Jesus said, tapping another wine barrel. "It's our responsibility to keep him in check as to how the humans are mutilating his beloved planet."

"When civilization gets flushed down the shitter, my brother and I rise up; the second coming. Of course, when that happens, it's too fucking late. Shit just got real," Satan continued. "I'm starting to get the munchies."

"Why task us to collect all the trinkets and crap?" Ham said.

"It's for the big guy. What can I say, he's old school. He still believes in tithing and all that other religious stuff," Satan said.

"So, what now?" I said, sitting by the fire.

"We drink, we smoke…" Jesus said.

"We eat, we sleep…" Satan continued.

"Then we go home. Until we have to wipe the planet's ass again," Jesus said, toasting the goblet with his brother's.

"Is that a donkey?" Satan said, peering down the hill. "Never cared for them. Next time, give them a goat; much more trustworthy."

"Unfortunately. He's a bit of an ass," I stated, shaking my head.

A brief moment of silence filled the air as Jesus and Satan took another turn hitting the joint.

"We're going to need a bigger fire. I'll get more wood," Jesus said, standing up.

"I'll build a rotisserie," Satan added, setting down his goblet.

Ham and I looked to each other with a grin.

"We'll bring the meat," we said in unison before sprinting down the hill to retrieve the donkey.

HORSE

Wrath James White

When the lamb opened the second seal, I heard the second living creature say, "Come!" Then another, a fiery red horse of bloodshed, came out; and its rider was empowered to take peace from the earth, so that men would slaughter one another, and a great sword of war and violent death was given to him.

– Revelation 6:4

"Yo, why do they call it horse when it ain't even white? Is this shit even real heroin? Why the fuck is it red?" The kid asked.

Dicky was just shy of his twenty-third birthday, so "kid" was an entirely subjective description. But the kid still lived in the same house he grew up in, same bedroom he'd had since he was a toddler. The walls were covered in hip-hop posters, video game, horror and sci-fi movie posters, and centerfolds. Action figures, well-worn comic books, old sports memorabilia and used equipment cluttered the shelves, and soiled clothes littered the floors. According to his birth certificate, he may have been twenty-two years old, but Dicky's emotional and mental maturity had been arrested the day he'd smoked his first joint at thirteen. That joint had been followed quickly by crack, heroin, and meth. Now, he seemed to bounce indecisively between the three.

I'm not suggesting that weed was some sort of gateway drug and Dicky would have been some regular dude if he'd never smoked a joint. That's a bunch of conservative propaganda bullshit. Nope. Dicky was never going to turn out right. There was something wrong with him from the start. I mean, what kid starts drinking hard liquor at age nine, trying to fuck his own eight-year-old sister at age twelve, and robbing old ladies and sucking dick for crack before his first day of high school? Dicky was fucked from the day he slid out his mom's snatch. He wasn't ever going to be right, with or without the drugs.

"Yo, chill, Dicky. This ain't heroin. I never said I had heroin. I said I had horse. This is some new shit. The government been giving this shit to soldiers to make them like super soldiers or some shit. It's supposed to make you feel like motherfucking Superman, yo!"

That's not really how I talk, but you have to know how to code switch to be a successful drug dealer. I can't walk into the hood flashing my master's degree in business management. They'd think I was a narc. Talking like a Colombia University graduate wouldn't do shit but just get my ass shot. So, I save the Queen's English for when I head back to my family in the suburbs at the end of the day.

"How'd you get this shit, and why ain't I ever heard of it?" Dicky asked.

"You ain't never heard of it because you too high all the time to watch the news. All you do is watch cartoons and porn all day. But this shit is everywhere, yo. It's the hottest shit on the streets right now."

I wasn't lying. One day, everyone was fiending for crack, meth, and heroin. The next day, the streets were ringing with people fiending for "that red shit". I don't know how it got the name horse, but it stuck. There were rumors that the CIA was pumping this shit into the ghettos, that it was some sort of genocidal plot to wipe out poor people and minorities. I don't know about all that. All I know is ever since I got laid out from the corporation I had given ten years of my life to, horse is the only thing keeping the lights on and food on the table.

"Man, I just want some heroin. I don't trust that red shit. How I know it won't make me sick?"

"How'd you know heroin wouldn't the first time you tried it? Or crack? Or even weed? You didn't. You wanted to get high, so you just gave that shit a try."

"Why you pushin' this shit so hard, yo? Just give me some regular ass heroin! You said you had some, and then you come at me with this shit!"

"Ain't nobody sellin' heroin no more. No more crack. No more meth. Don't nobody want that shit no more. Everybody be wantin' horse now. You can't get that old shit nowhere."

I wasn't lying about that either. It was like horse had done what the entire federal government and local law enforcement had been unable to do for the past sixty years, get heroin and cocaine off the streets. Hell, the local news was practically running commercials for the stuff. I first heard about it on a special news report.

"There's a new drug sweeping through the inner-city. The drug is called 'horse' and it is supposed to be stronger and more addictive than meth, with a high that last ten times longer. Oddly enough, there have been no reported cases of anyone overdosing on the drug. There does not appear to be a dosage that would be considered lethal as far as doctors can tell, however extreme paranoia and aggression caused by the drug, has led to a dramatic increase in violence all over the city..."

The very next day after that report aired on the six o'clock news, every dope fiend on the street was clamoring for that shit. And, I swear with God as my witness that I hadn't seen a drop of the shit on the street before that news report aired. Not a whisper or a rumor of it. It was like they created the demand first, and then dropped the product.

It hadn't been hard for me to find a connection for it. I asked one crackhead, who pointed me to another, who pointed me to a dealer, who pointed me to his connection. And, I'm going to tell you right now, it ain't ever that easy. You don't just walk up to a dealer on the street and say you want to by a kilo of anything and they just introduce you to their connection without vetting you and sweating you. The whole thing was just fucking weird. But the money? That shit was good. I made more in a week selling horse than I used to make in a month selling heroin. But even I could see the results. Shit was getting scary in the city, and now this shit had spread to the suburbs.

I heard a congressman's daughter shot a Muslim baker after shouting anti-Islamic insults at him. She'd known the guy for years, been going to his bakery every morning for coffee and croissants. Then one day she just snapped. Her father said it was the drugs. I laughed that shit off at first, but then I started to notice it too. People were tripping on this shit.

"Okay – well – I ain't payin' for shit unless I get a taste first."

"You know I don't work that way. Look, you don't want none? Don't buy none. But, I'm tellin' you, you ain't gonna find nothing else out here, and at least you know with me, it ain't gonna be cut with nothing crazy."

"Alright. Alright! Fuck it! Give me an ounce."

He handed me twenty dollars in crumpled ones. I handed him an ounce of horse.

"So, what do you do? You just shoot this shit up, like heroin? Sniff it? Eat it?"

"All of the above. It works the same either way. Probably hit you quicker if you shot it up, but if you snort it you ain't got to worry about catching the HIV from a dirty needle, you feel me?"

"Yeah, yeah, true dat."

Dicky opened the little ball of aluminum foil I'd sold him, looked around to make sure no one was watching, as if anyone would care, then pushed his right nostril closed with his finger, and took a deep snort of the red dust with his left nostril. As if I could already anticipate what was about to happen, I put my hand in my jacket pocket and gripped my Berretta. I clicked off the safety and put my finger on the trigger. That's when Dicky's eyes turned red.

"Whoa! This shit is intense. I feel like going on a faggot killing spree right now, killing every cocksucker in the world!"

"What the fuck did you just say, motherfucker?" I asked.

"You heard me, cocksucker. I'm going to bash your fucking brains in and then fuck you in the ass, you gay motherfucker!"

I don't know how he knew. I had always been really good at "playing straight". I even thought I had the hardcore, cis-het, gangsta image pretty well established. I guess I was wrong.

"You better watch who you talkin' to like that, cause I ain't the one."

"Oh, don't play with me, motherfucker. Everybody knows you got a boyfriend up there in the suburbs where you stay at. You ain't foolin' nobody! I'm going to ass-rape your corpse!"

"And, you don't see anything wrong with threatening to anally rape me for being gay?" I said, slowly pulling the gun from my pocket. This batch of horse was a lot stronger than the last. I hadn't seen anyone get so agro after just one hit before. I knew something about the drug seemed to bring out people's prejudices and make them act violently. But it usually took a few days of constant use to really get them riled up. I guess whoever made this shit thought that was too long, and decided to rev it up.

Dicky snatched the metal lid off a nearby trashcan and swung it at my head. I shot him in the chest seconds before his blow landed. We both fell. Everything went black for a second, and when it cleared again, I was lying on my back, in the alley, bleeding from my forehead and from the back of my head where it had struck the concrete. Dicky was lying across from me, trembling and shaking in his death throes, a gurgling and whistling sound coming from his mouth as blood bubbled up out of it. *Well, at the very least, that ought to give me a little street-cred*, I thought.

I struggled to my feet. My head ached, and I was still dizzy. Obviously a concussion. A bad one. Luckily, my car was only half a block away. I had paid one of the neighborhood junkies to watch it for me, like I always do. One dollar now, and a dollar when I come back and my car hasn't been stolen or vandalized. I wasn't positive I would even be able to drive in my present condition, but I knew I didn't want to be caught down here with a body, the murder weapon, and a fanny pack full of horse.

I wondered if maybe it was the fanny pack that had given me away, but then I dismissed that. Most straight people thought all gay men had excellent fashion sense. A gay nerd selling drugs in the hood, pretending to be a gangster was absurd enough that no one should have been able to imagine it, let alone believe it. That's what I'd told Michael, my husband, when I first let him in on my plan for our financial salvation.

"You're going to get yourself killed." Michael said.

"Well, you want me to sell drugs to our friends? How would that look? You want our neighbors knowing you're married to a drug dealer?"

"Don't be a fucking drug dealer! There are other options."

"Like what? I have been sending out ten resumes a day for over three months. No one is calling. No one is hiring. We miss another mortgage payment and we lose this house. You want us to be the cute, gay, homeless couple? You ready for life on the streets? Because I'm not."

After a few more such discussions, Michael relented. Once we got caught up on our mortgage, then paid off the house entirely, and bought two brand new SUVs, he really seemed to enjoy being married to a successful drug dealer. But Michael didn't know anything about what this drug does to people. He thought it was just a harmless party drug like Ecstasy. He hadn't seen the pure hatred that comes with the euphoria. The rage that accompanies the rush.

Old Willie, the middle-aged junkie I had paid to watch my BMW, had obviously tried his best to earn that extra dollar. My car had been destroyed, completely vandalized, but so had Willie. His entrails decorated the roof of the car with a garland of gore. His disembodied head had been placed on the dashboard with his own cock and balls crammed into his mouth, eyes gored out, nose smashed, and almost every last tooth knocked out. Various internal organs were strewn around the vehicle in pools of coagulating red ichor as if Old Willie had been a piñata filled with blood and viscera and someone had taken a bat and a hatchet to him in their eagerness to claim the goodies inside. The rest of him sat behind the wheel of the car, his chest torn open like an oyster that had been cracked, shucked, and bled all over. He had been gutted. His chest and abdominal cavities were completely empty. It almost looked like it had been licked clean.

The car hood was open, and the battery, radiator, and most of the engine, was gone. What remained had been smashed, or torn out and tossed to the ground. Loose wires and hoses dangled everywhere, dripping oil, wiper fluid, engine coolant, and blood. Willie's blood. Written in blood and oil, on the inside of the hood, and repeated on the passenger-side door were the words "Go back to Mexico!" Which was odd because I'm not Mexican. I'm not even Spanish.

I knew I was in shock. That, along with the concussion still clouding my thoughts and causing my head to pound in agony, may have explained why I stood there for so long just staring at Old Willie's corpse, trying to make sense of what I was seeing, not fully registering the horror of it, wondering how I could drive a car home with slashed tires, a shattered windshield, a missing engine, and a headless corpse in the driver's seat.

"Men! Fucking men! Rapists! Fascists! Fucking wife-beaters and baby-rapers!"

I looked across the street, tearing my eyes away from the massacre that had taken place inside my BMW. On the opposite sidewalk, a woman was stabbing a man with a kitchen knife as he batted and punched at her in a feeble effort to defend himself. The woman had her hair in rollers, some of which had fallen out, and she wore a robe over a diaphanous gown that did little to cover her massive breasts that flopped up to her chin then back down to her belly with each rise and fall of the knife. She was bleeding from her nose and her lip was swollen. I wasn't sure if the damage to her face had inspired her rampage, or if they had been wounds inflicted by her victim's fruitless attempt to fend her off.

The woman grabbed the man by the hair, then began sawing at his throat as he flopped and convulsed like a dying fish. A horrible gargling sound came from his throat while he was slowly decapitated.

"Oh, shit. What the fuck is going on?"

But I knew. It was the horse. That new red shit. It was driving people insane. And moreover, I was absolutely certain now that that's exactly what it had been created to do. The conspiracy theorists were correct. The CIA or some other government operatives had deliberately dumped that shit in the ghetto to make all the poor folks kill each other.

"I've got to get out of here," I muttered to no one. There was no one there to help me, no one to rescue me. Michael was a good thirty miles away. That was a forty-five-minute drive in traffic. I could call him, but he'd never make it in time to save me, and I'd be putting his life in danger too. Of course, I could call the cops, but I had just murdered someone in a drug deal. Even if I ditched the gun and the drugs, something I was hesitant to do with all the chaos roaring around me, there would still be gunpowder residue all over me, and I would have to explain what the fuck I was doing down here in the first place. My best bet was to make my way to the nearest bus stop and pray it came quick. Once I was somewhere less dangerous, I could call an Uber or something to get home.

Then I'd have to tell Michael what happened to the car. I'd have to tell him everything. He wouldn't be happy. He'd want me to stop. But, if I stopped selling horse, the cashflow would also end. We'd be right back where we started. None of that mattered now, though.

I was thinking too much, wasting time. I had already stood in one place too long. The woman who'd just sawed that dude's head off was walking toward me now.

"Rapist!" She screamed, pointing her blood-spattered carving knife directly at me.

"Rapist? Me? Honey, I'm gay. And, unless you've got a cock and balls under there, you ain't got nothing that interests me, girl," I said, queening it up and feeling a little ill for doing so. Just like my fake gangster voice, my "gay" voice was an amalgamation of stereotypes. I was doing the LGBTQ version of a minstrel show. But, if it kept this crazy bitch from trying to saw my head off, and me from having to make yet another body, I could finger-pop and neck roll with the best of them.

The woman paused, squinting her eyes and studying me, trying to process what I'd just told her. I put one hand on my hip, cocked that hip to the side, then lifted my other hand, wrist limp and dangling almost lifelessly, before I snapped my fingers four times making a "Z" in the air like I was a gay

Zorro. I felt as ridiculous as it sounds. My face reddened with shame, but it seemed to work. The woman lowered the blade.

"Gay? Like queer?"

Finally, it was sinking in.

"As queer as a three-dollar bill, girl," I said, adding another snap in the air for emphasis.

"Did a man do that? Did he hurt you?" She asked, pointing to the gash on my forehead. I reached up and touched the wound. It was still bleeding profusely.

I nodded. "Yes. Yes, a man did this."

"They're fucking animals. They're all fucking animals," she said. I nodded again.

"Yes. Yes, they fucking are."

She cocked her head like a dog listening to a strange sound.

"What are you doing here? You don't belong down here. You're going to get yourself killed."

"I'm just trying to get home to my husband."

"Did he do that to you?"

"No. He's a good man."

"There are no fucking good men!" She yelled, raising the knife again.

"I- I mean he's gay—like me."

She nodded.

"Yeah. Gay dudes are cool. I ain't never been hurt by no fag—I mean—a gay person."

I thought it was odd that a woman who'd just decapitated a man would be worried about offending me by accidentally using a homophobic slur. It was almost as odd as me standing in the middle of the street having a conversation with someone who'd just sawed a dude's head off in front of me.

"Okay—well—I have to get home. My husband's going to be worried to death."

"It's not safe. But I'll get you home. I'll protect you. We on the same side, right?"

"Right," I said. Who was I to argue? Besides, it wasn't like I couldn't use the help. She wrapped a belt around her blood-drenched robe, then took my hand and began leading me away.

"I need to get to a bus stop. They destroyed my car."

146

"We'll get you another car," she said. And I knew better than to ask how. I suspected I was going to be party to another felony whether I liked it or not.

"My name's Melody," the woman said, switching the kitchen knife to her left hand so she could offer me her right hand to shake. Her fingers still dripped with blood, but I shook her hand anyway. There was no sense in me being sensitive about it. We were all killers tonight.

"My name's Brandon."

"Pleased to meet you, Brandon. You just follow me. I'll get you out of here. And, I'll kill any motherfucker that tries to stop me!" Melody screamed into the night. I immediately began having second thoughts.

We hadn't walked more than a few blocks before the sounds of screams and gunfire echoed all around us. Angry shouts and curses, the smack and thud of fists against flesh, bodies falling to the pavement. I watched a gang of teenagers drag a man through the streets, chained to their lowrider. We passed an alley where a stocky middle-aged man was beating some dude to death with his bare fists, muttering "baby-raper" and "fucking pedophile" as he pulverized the frail-looking man who looked well into his late forties or early fifties. We paused for a second to watch as the big guy pulled down the other man's pants, then took a broomstick and rammed it so far up the guy's asshole that blood exploded from his mouth.

"Serve's that piece of shit right," Melody said. I didn't know if the guy had actually been guilty or not, and neither did she. He looked like a pedophile: white, balding, beady eyes, pencil neck with a bulging Adam's apple, thick glasses, pants too tight, pinstriped polo shirt buttoned all the way up to his throat. If I saw him on the street, I'd have thought he was a baby-raper too. But that didn't mean he was guilty. If he was, then he definitely deserved it, though.

"Fuck you, bitch-ass nigga!"

"Kill that white boy!"

"Goddamn spic!"

"Fuckin' stank ho!"

"Chink!"

"Wetback!"

147

"Sand nigger!"

"Jew!"

"Greasy dago!"

"Slut!"

"Whore!"

"Fag!"

"Pig!"

"Liberal commie snowflake!"

"Fascist repugnican!"

Every ounce of bigotry, prejudice, intolerance, and hatred in the entire neighborhood was bubbling to the surface. Not everyone in the neighborhood was high on horse, but enough to light the spark. After that, mass hysteria, mob mentality, a primordial, tribal groupthink had taken over. Nothing galvanizes people like hatred. Small insignificant differences and divisions became insurmountable chasms, reasons to fight, kill, or die. Anyone who didn't look like them, think like them, dress like them, worship like them, or vote like them, was now the enemy. Blood was being spilled in every direction I looked.

We reached Germantown Avenue. The Ave was an open-air drug market. Two separate gangs slung rocks, coke, and heroin with impunity. Eastsiders on the east side of the street. Westsiders on the west side. In between, dope fiends, crack heads, and tweakers wandered back and forth, bargain shopping. But not today.

Today, drug addicts attacked dealers, fighting them for more horse, killing them for it. Two tweakers who weighed less than two hundred pounds combined, were tearing open a teenaged dealer with their teeth and nails, one chewed at his face, tearing off his cheeks, nose, and eyelids, while his homeboy eviscerated the man, clawing open his stomach and pulling out his entrails in handfuls. An older man with a huge greying afro was beating a gangbanger with a cane. The gangster's skull had already caved in, but the old man continued whacking him with the cane, reducing the guy's head to a misshapen blob of red pulp and white bone.

The sound of gunshots echoed out, and I looked up to see a group of nearly twenty men carrying shotguns, semi-automatic handguns, and military style assault rifles, AK-47s,

MAC-10s, Uzis, and AR-15s. They wore sagging jeans and bandannas on their heads and wrapped around their heavily tattooed faces. The men were mowing down people indiscriminately as they strutted, swaggered, and strolled forward. Heads, torsos, and limbs blew apart in sprays of blood and meat. The men continued to advance, killing everything in their path.

Six patrol cars roared into the intersection of Washington Lane and Germantown Avenue. For a brief moment, hope swelled in my chest. I was just about to run over to them, when I felt a hand on my shoulder, pulling me back. It was Melody. Her eyes were still blood-red, but there was less madness in her eyes now. Or perhaps that was just what I wanted to see.

"Don't," she said.

"It's the cops! They can help us!" I cried out, nearly hysterical. I didn't care anymore that I was carrying enough Schedule 1 narcotics to put me away for twenty years, or that I had a murder weapon in my pocket. I just wanted out.

"Look," was her only response. She pointed to the cops exiting their vehicles in riot gear, carrying shotguns, some carried M-16 assault rifles. They were ready for war.

"They ain't here to help nobody." Melody's voice was calm and steady. Despite the narcotics firing uncut hatred through her synapses, she seemed to be thinking clearer than I was at the moment.

The police officers began opening fire, killing men, women, and children alike, marching toward the group of gangbangers, sandwiching civilians between the two small armies, cutting them to pieces with gunfire.

"They're killing everyone!" I shouted.

"No shit, Sherlock," Melody said, and just then a man stepped out of the alley behind us, carrying a revolver, aiming it at the center of Melody's chest. He had those same blood red eyes Melody had, the same look Dicky had on his face right before he tried to decapitate me with a trashcan lid.

"Cheating whore!" He yelled. I thought maybe he was her husband or boyfriend, but the confusion on Melody's face made it clear. She had no fucking idea who he was.

"Fool, I don't know you! And who the fuck are you calling a whore?"

"You, skank bitch!"

If sanity had begun to creep into Melody's eyes earlier, it was now scattered like grains of sand in a tsunami. I tried to swat the gun out of the man's hand, feeling protective of this madwoman who had vowed to protect me. Then she sank her knife deep into the man's chest, with much more force than her skinny arms should have been capable of. I heard the man's sternum crack, the knife crunch through muscle and bone before embedding itself deep in his lungs. Melody wrenched it free, and then repeated the action, this time aiming for his heart. I watched the life flee from that man's eyes like his soul had been little more than an annoying insect that Melody had casually shooed away. His carcass collapsed at our feet, an empty sack of meat. It made a wet smack on the concrete.

"Let's go," Melody said.

"Where? I don't know where to go! The bus stop is right there where those cops are killing everyone!"

"Well, then we definitely can't go there," Melody said.

"Well, no shit we can't go there!"

"Why are you yelling at me, Brandon?" I saw something dark slither across her red pupils. As if there was something in there with her, something sharing space in her body that had peeked out for a minute. She was still clutching that knife, wet with yet another man's blood.

"Nuh—uh—nothing. Nothing. Just tell me where to go. I need your help."

"Well, how the fuck should I know where to go? Why the fuck are you asking me? First you yell at me, then you want my help? Fuck you, Brandon!" Melody shouted, pointing the knife at me. She was getting crazy. My testicles crept up tight against my body, and a chill of fear raced down my spine. Melody was about to kill me. I knew it. I could feel an itch in the center of my chest, right where I knew she was intending to stick that knife.

"Can I call my husband? Please?" It was the only thing I could think to say. I knew I was going to die. I just wanted to hear his voice one more time before it all went away, before everything I was became nothing. I still had the Beretta. I probably could have shot her. Maybe. But I just didn't think I'd be fast enough. I knew I wouldn't be. If she was going to kill me, then I was going to die. It was as certain to me as the ground under my feet.

"What?"

"I—I just want to call my husband. Please. Please let me call him."

Her expression softened. A little of the madness left her eyes.

"Shh—Sure. Sure. Okay. I ain't stopping you."

I began to cry. Tears fell from my eyes, one, two, and then a river. I was sobbing uncontrollably as I fumbled my phone out of my pocket, dropping the Beretta. I called Michael. He answered on the first ring.

"Brandon! Where are you? You have to get home. I'm scared. I need you. Everything's going crazy over here! Everyone's killing each other!"

"What?"

"People are killing each other. The neighbors are going door to door killing everybody!"

It wasn't just the ghettoes. It was happening everywhere.

"Just stay inside. Keep the door locked."

"I need you here, Brandon. I need you with me. You're supposed to protect me. You're supposed to take care of me!"

He was right. I was the big bad drug dealer. I was the one who went into the worst neighborhood in the city to sell drugs every day, carrying a gun and talking bad. But I was scared too. I didn't know what to do.

"I don't think I'm going to make it Michael. I think I'm going to die here."

"You can't! No! No! No! You can't leave me! You get home right now! Do you hear me? You get your ass home!"

I shook my head, still sobbing. I could barely hear Michael's voice over the screams and gunshots.

"I can't, Michael. I love you. I love you so much. But I can't make it."

"Bullshit!" Melody snatched the phone from my hands.

"Is this Michael?"

151

"Who is this?"

"This Melody. And Brandon is my friend, and I'm gonna get him home to you, you hear? He's gonna be alright. I'm gonna get him home. Now tell him you love him too so we can get out of here."

She handed me back the phone and I just stood there with my jaw hanging open.

"Come home to me, Brandon. I love you. You do what that woman says. You come home to me."

But Michael didn't know that this crazy woman had been about to murder me with a kitchen knife two minutes ago.

"Let's go," Melody said, and grabbed me by the arm, pulling me down the alley, away from the bloodshed and slaughter taking place on the avenue. She still wore only a bathrobe and slippers and was still carrying that same knife. She hadn't bothered picking up the revolver the guy she'd murdered had been carrying, content with her bloody kitchen utensil. I had to admit, it had served her well so far. Why change what works?

We walked three blocks until we came to a grocery store. It was on fire. People were still looting the place even as it burned. The smell of burning flesh was unmistakable. There were people dying inside. The parking lot was full of cars, but not people. There were maybe a couple dozen people running out of the store with whatever they could carry that wasn't already incinerating. There must have been fifty cars in the parking lot though. Most of the people must have still been inside.

"You know how to hotwire a car?" Melody asked.

"No."

"I do," Melody said. I wondered why she had bothered to ask me at all.

Melody walked over to an oversized SUV that looked like it got about a mile a gallon. She began hammering on the driver side window with her fists, attempting to break through the glass. I looked around, scouring the parking lot for something to smash the window with. I found a hunk of concrete that had crumbled off one of the parking barricades. I picked it up, and walked back over to Melody. I considered moving her aside, and bashing the window myself, but Melody had become rather invested in breaking through that damn plexiglass, so invested she'd already beaten her hands bloody on it.

"Here," I said. "Try this." I handed her the hunk of concrete. A wicked smile tore across her face as she hefted the hunk of concrete in her hands. I knew what she was thinking. She could have easily cracked open my skull with it. Instead, she turned and smashed the window.

"Come on!" She reached through and unlocked the door, then dropped down and reached underneath the dashboard, ripping out wires. I hoped she knew what she was doing, because it looked to me like all she was doing was damage. I saw her twist a few wires together, and suddenly the big SUV engine roared to life.

"Fuck yeah!" She whooped, leaping into the air with childlike exuberance, and then her head exploded. I watched her skull rupture like a cantaloupe that had sat in the sun too long. Her grey matter and skull fragments splattered all over me. I ducked and looked around, but couldn't see anyone shooting at us. There was so much shooting going on, it was hard to tell, though. But it seemed to have just been a stray bullet. Just bad luck.

"I'm sorry, Melody," I said, looking down at the empty, shattered shell that had housed that beautiful, mad woman, as it leaked blood and brains onto the asphalt. "Thank you for helping me get home."

I heard a siren go off as I climbed behind the wheel of the SUV. I remembered hearing that same siren the previous day, right before the U.S. announced the end of the war in the Middle East. They had "won" by killing every man woman and child in Iraq and Afghanistan. I thought the siren was some sort of celebration. Then I heard it again earlier in the day, when I was on the freeway, driving down here to meet with Dicky. It sounded like an old air raid siren, but louder, coming from all directions, blotting out every other noise. When It stopped, I was already driving out of the parking lot, heading down Washington Lane, taking my ass out of this crazy neighborhood, heading toward whatever madness awaited me in my own crazy neighborhood.

The radio was on. I hadn't been able to hear it over the siren, but it was finally dying down. It was a news station. NPR, I think. They were talking about all the drug violence that had taken hold of the city.

"Reports are coming in that this is not just a local phenomenon, but a global one. The street drug called 'horse', so called because of its red color and its penchant for driving men to acts of violence, like the red horse of the apocalypse, has now spread across the globe. In cities across the world, rioting, assaults, murder, and looting has taken hold. Martial law has been declared in..."

I zoned out, stuck on three words: "across the globe". It was everywhere. There was nowhere safe. Nowhere for us to go.

I turned onto the freeway on ramp, right into bumper to bumper traffic. But it wasn't just traffic. It was mayhem. It was a slaughterhouse. On the freeway, as far as the eye could see, people were being dragged from their cars, shot, stabbed, beaten, strangled, raped. Bodies littered the road beside and between stalled vehicles, making them impossible to pass. I pulled out my cellphone and began dialing Michael again. I had to tell him the bad news.

HELL PASO

C. Derick Miller

Mankind knew nothing. For everyone on planet Earth, it was a day like any other. Morning commuters clogged the interstate highway system with hopes of landing that life-altering promotion and mothers offered sustenance to innocent babies in tidy, suburban kitchens. However, for two unfortunate Army soldiers in the epicenter of the apocalypse, it was the beginning of the end.

"Holy shit!" screamed Sergeant Cross as his feet hurried through the blood-soaked desert sand. "You just shot Jesus in the face!"

"How was I supposed to know Jesus was brown?" replied Private Daniels with labored breath, dodging mortar explosions. "Blame Caucasian society for that shit, not me! Sunday School told me he looked like bearded Ewan McGregor, not the reanimated corpse of Osama bin Laden floating through the fucking sky! I thought he was coming to get us and I panicked!"

The two soldiers ducked through the broken glass doorway of an abandoned base commissary as another explosion rocked the surroundings. So far, it was the safest place that came to mind. Peeking up through a dust stained window, Sergeant Cross watched the continued carnage that took place on the streets of Fort Bliss.

"This is bad, Daniels! This is very fucking bad!"

A last-minute decision to join the Army National Guard had saved Sergeant Tom Cross from a lifetime of mediocrity. He'd grown tired of the nine-to-five grinds at the local slave pool of his tiny hometown and wanted more. He craved excitement. Before anyone could notice his absence, Tom filed for divorce, signed the paperwork, and dedicated one weekend a month to military service. Two months' worth of basic training nightmares was a small drop in the bucket when compared to the failed suicide attempts he'd be destined to endure on a nightly basis if his current life path had continued. As of this moment, a strong strap over the shower curtain rod felt like the better option.

"Here, eat this!" Cross ordered Daniels, throwing a package of fruit pies his direction. "We don't know when we'll get another chance and we need to build our strength."

"Here, eat this, Sarge!" Daniels motioned toward his own crotch with his free hand. "I think the chain of command has flown out the window, Tom! Fuck your orders, fuck your fruit pies, and fuck the Army!"

Private Dan Daniels was born a child of privilege. Raised on a massive Texas ranch overshadowed by the family mansion, he'd barely lifted a finger in his life unless it involved an insult to his enemies or a trip into the head cheerleader's panties. His purpose of military service was to offer a black eye to his father who'd spent the duration of his early twenties as a dedicated marine. They'd turned Dan's bedroom into his mother's craft space upon departure. Cut off from the family fortune, he was on his own.

Another screeching demon buzzed by the building's window, feasting on a fallen comrade's remains. Daniels wished he'd stayed home.

"How much ammo do you have left, Daniels?"

"Enough to get back to the motor pool and boost a Hummer!" Daniels exclaimed. "I can pick up more along the way from the dead guys. I've played video games. You can be a hero if you want or stay in this store and eat candy until you get fat. I don't care. I'm getting the hell out of here!"

The book of Revelation had come true during their summer maneuvers at Operation Roving Sands. Just across the border in Juarez, a portal of sorts poured nightmares into Mexico at an alarming rate. Within hours, the residents of the Mexican city littered the ground in pieces, and the buildings burned with inextinguishable fire. It didn't take long for the apocalypse to cross into Texas.

Daniels pulled and checked his weapon's magazine for an ammunition count.

"Did you ever think this is why the president was so hell-bent on building that wall? Like, maybe he knew this shit was coming and he wanted to keep it contained in Mexico. They say that Bush knew all about 9/11…"

"That is officially the dumbest load of crap I've ever heard!" Sergeant Cross interrupted "If the president knew impending doom was coming, he would've been banging three Playboy bunnies at once live on CNN. Do you not know who our president is? He'd be grabbing them all by the…"

Sergeant Cross fell quiet as a massive shadow eclipsed the store window. Motioning to Daniels, the two of them switched their weapons from the safety setting into pulse. Daniels nodded in agreement as the two of them silently slid behind the nearest shelf for cover.

The blood-covered demonic entity peered around the corner of the building and into the glass. Steams of crimson dripped from its massive teeth as its tongue retrieved the sustenance into its own mouth. It obviously enjoyed the taste and appeared to be in search of more. A blast of burning breath fogged the already grimed window. Disappointed, it leapt into the sky with a single flap of its wings. The two soldiers exhaled in relief.

"I don't think we're going to make it to the motor pool, Daniels," Cross whispered. "Those bastards are ten feet tall and can fly. They'll see us long before we'll see them. We need a backup plan…"

"A backup plan?" Daniels laughed. "Who said I was taking you with me? To me, this appears to be an 'every man for himself' situation and, as far as I'm concerned, every man can blow me! We're easier so to see if we're in a group. I swear I'll fucking shoot you if you try to follow…"

With that, Sergeant Cross leapt to his feet in challenge, aiming his rifle directly at Daniel's head. Dan followed suit only to be slapped across the face by the butt stock of the Sergeant's weapon. Spitting blood, he landed hard somewhere in the vicinity of the bread rack and tuna fish cans. He immediately threw one into the face of his oppressor. It missed by inches and landed with a metallic thump in the next aisle.

"Fuck you, Tom!" Daniels shouted "Who the fuck do you think you are? So help me God, I'll…"

You'll what, Private? You'll throw food at me again? Is that how we're going to beat the devil? Challenge him to a food fight? Satan is *not* John Belushi, Dan!"

The men dove to the floor in terror once again as two more demons landed in the street beyond. Whatever remained of their argument was insignificant next to survival instincts. Sniffing the air frantically in the direction of the commissary, they exhibited animal-like behavior as if searching for prey. One looked at the other as an expression of distraught appeared across its red-tinted face followed by a howl interpreted as disappointment. Together, they flew into the direction of the portal, allowing what remained of the day's sunlight into the building.

"Goddammit!" Daniels cried "It's almost like those things have it in for us! Help me loot this place for a Bible!"

Sergeant Cross looked downward at the puddle of Daniels' blood as it gleamed rays of daylight near his feet. A thought echoed in his mind which caused a possible escape scenario to form if needed. The demons were tracking the humans by the scent of spilled blood and, since neither of them were wounded during the initial battle, it allowed their stealthily existence to continue. If push came to shove and all hope was surely lost, he'd bleed Daniels as a means of escape. Unfortunately, Daniels was probably pondering this same gruesome thought. He had to be on guard for anything from this point forward.

"What do you need a Bible for? Do you plan on throwing that at them, too?"

"Ha!" Daniels yelled sarcastically. "No, funny fucker, I need to see what happens next! If this is the Book of Revelation come to life, I need to know the next step in the plan."

Sergeant Cross shook his head in disgust. Placing his hand softly on Daniel's shoulder, he pulled the man in close as though a secret confession was in order. Tom moved his head slowly upward from the ground to meet Dan eye to eye. How pleasant would it be to watch this man's life drain from those same eyes? How many more men would he be willing to kill to secure his own survival? Tom's mouth began to salivate at the thought, but he sucked it back into his throat as he began a well-deserved explanation to the idiot at arm's length.

"First of all, we don't have time to read. Second? These Army base commissaries are all staffed by Korean immigrants and I doubt very seriously any of them left a Bible just lying around. They're all into Buddhas and shit. Third? Humanity went off track from the Book of Revelations when you shot Jesus Christ in the fucking face!"

Cross could almost hear the ping of realization echo in Dan's brain from the sudden realization. A sly smile slowly spread from ear to ear on the Private's face as a chuckle escaped. He soon doubled over in laughter.

"So, what you're saying is, Satan isn't the guy bringing on the apocalypse? I did it? I swear, man. You and my father. Ironic. He used to say some shit like that all the time when I wouldn't mow the yard or got an F on my report card. He always said I'd be the cause for the end of the world…"

"You are *the* cause!" Cross put an end to the reflection. "The horns blew, and Jesus came floating out of the damned sky like Magneto to save us all! How did you repay him? You shot him in the fucking face and he hit the ground! He hit that shit harder than Paul Walker driving through a Christmas tree farm! So, yes! Congratulations! You're the Antichrist and your father was a psychic!"

"Semantics," Daniels expressed convincingly. "We were all shooting at everything when the shit went down. How do you know I was the one who tagged him? It could've been anyone! Hell, it could've been you!"

"No," laughed Cross. "It was you! You said, and I quote, "Hey, Sarge, watch me tag this tan hippie with the robe in the fucking face!" You even got my attention before you did it like I was going to pat you on the back!"

Daniels broke into crazed laughter at the end of the story's recap. Hunched over, he appeared in pain caused by the hilarity of it all. He rested his weapon across his lap as he sat atop the polished tile floor, fluffing a couple of loaves of bread into a makeshift pillow.

"It was a bad ass shot, though," Daniels expressed, closing his eyes in rest.

Sergeant Tom Cross occupied the floor next to his temporary roommate and followed the example. There wasn't much else either of them could do at that moment other than run outdoors with guns blazing into the setting sun toward inevitable doom. Death was coming for certain. At least they wouldn't be sleepy when it finally arrived.

"Maybe you've got the right idea, Dan. Maybe if we're not bleeding, yelling, and throwing tuna cans at each other, they'll move away from here and give us a chance to escape. Maybe I'll write my ex-wife's address on the front window of this place in shoe polish, so they'll know where to go next. With any luck, she'll start to nag at them for walking on the lawn and they'll retreat into that portal. Problem solved."

"Nah," Daniel's assured "According to your lovely description of the lady, she'll probably let them all take turns on her and they'll slowly die of gonorrhea. Apocalypse avoided, porn style."

The two men slept as the continued screams of the dying offered a sickening lullaby of peace.

*

Cross and Daniels crept from shadow to shadow under the cover of desert darkness. The sky above, usually dotted by the pin hole glimmers of a million celestial stars, now glowed with the green hue of Hell's portal. It was temporarily interrupted from time to time with an explosive blast of orange as the fire's raged in both Juarez and El Paso. They couldn't help but wonder if the remainder of the world boasted similar destruction.

Upon waking, they monitored the streets of Fort Bliss for any signs of demonic presence. Both fortunate and unfortunate simultaneously, the screams of their fellow soldiers were no more. It either meant Sergeant Cross and Private Daniels were the last two men alive from the assault earlier in the day or the remaining soldiers discovered a way to victory. Private Daniels defeated the latter thought as he stepped into yet another pile of human remains.

"This is some straight up disgusting bullshit!" he exclaimed aloud, shaking his right foot to remove the guts from his boot. "I can't tell if it's G.I. Joe or G.I. Jane, but I'm sick of slipping in it!"

"Stop being so inconsiderate!" Cross corrected his fellow soldier. "Whoever it is, they weren't granted the lucky break we got. He or she signed the same papers and wore the same uniform as you. Show some respect!"

Sergeant Cross had grown tired of Dan's constant whining three blocks ago. It appeared as though the subordinate insisted on the two of them being discovered by a roving patrol of demons. In the grand scheme of things, would that have been so bad? Being chewed to bits and swallowed by the spawn of the underworld seemed joyful compared to the Private's babyish tantrums. Cross would've shot him between the eyes already if he had reassurance it wouldn't bring Hell upon him. No pun intended.

"Nope," Daniels continued "That is definitely a detached vagina. Hey, Tom! Have you ever seen what one of these things looks like from the inside? I can't believe I used to stick my face in that! Check it out! It's still moving! It's making little kissy noises and everything! It's enough to make me want to…"

"Oh my God, will you shut the fuck up!" Cross screamed behind his teeth for the sake of silence. "Of all the people I could get stuck with while enduring the end of days, I got stuck with Private Dan Daniels! The 'lips' of the apocalypse!"

Daniels couldn't help it. In his defense, he was attempting the make the best of a bad situation. This was indeed the most horrible situation he'd endured and even his own screwed up imagination paled in comparison to current reality. Cross didn't seem to appreciate his efforts to lighten their hopeless mood and, soon, he'd have to die for it. Dan didn't plan on spending his last moments alive being shushed and corrected. He had a mother for that. Somewhere. He hoped.

"Look!" Daniels laughed. "That one still has a tampon in it! Whoever that chick was, she had the worst bad flow day of her life! Kind of looks like a puppet smoking a cigar…"

Sergeant Cross dropped to one knee with his weapon at the ready. His closed fist shot into the air as a signal to end Dan's grotesque trip down discovery lane. The Private obeyed, joining the lead man behind a demolished LMTV transport vehicle. There were footsteps approaching their direction. Lots of them.

From the temporary safety of the vehicle's cover, both men witnessed an organized platoon of demonic soldiers marching in time to a single evil entity in the lead. Smaller than their winged counterparts from before, these beings were less fairytale-esque in appearance. Almost humanoid except for their frightening faces, they all stepped in cadence to a single, larger demon who acted as their superior. He called out rhymes in a completely unknown language. They had swords at the ready.

"I think we can take them, Tom"

"Don't be ridiculous, man," Tom responded sensibly. "There's like twenty of them and two of us! We will die!"

"Oh, ye of little faith, Sergeant Cross," Dan spoke calmly "Those bastards brought knives to a gun fight and have no idea we're even here. We can jump out, shoot them up, and get on with our lives…"

"What lives, you dumb bastard?" Cross explained with closed eyes "Our minutes are numbered as it is! I'm not trying to end it prematurely by mimicking a stupid, rich boy fantasy! We sit here, we let them pass, and we keep heading to the motor pool. It's our best chance!"

Sergeant Cross suddenly realized he was talking to a ghost when his eyes finally opened. During the instruction, Daniels obviously snuck off into the direction of Hell's troops for a suicidal delusion of grandeur. He tightened the chin strap of his Kevlar helmet for the coming battle. The only decision left to make was whether he planned on allowing the buffoon to storm the horde without assistance. Daniels hurried that decision for him half a second later.

"Hey, boys! You soldiers looking for a good time?"

The demons' heads shot to attention at the sound of the human voice and growled in unison. Daniels stood his ground fearlessly as the monster in command stared down his prey with ferocious determination. It gave one last grunt to his troops as he pointed in the direction of the visible human soldier, causing the bunch to sprint his direction with weapons raised. Daniels stood his ground with foolish bravery.

Cross couldn't believe the scene playing out before his eyes. Jumping to his feet and bracing his weapon atop the bumper of the LMTV, he aimed for the head of the demon in charge who refused to move with the advance of his troops. Tom glanced away from his gunsight momentarily to witness Dan's last stand only to have his vision blinded by the sudden flash of fire. The demonic troops collapsed into piles of unidentified flesh as the Claymore's pellets shredded their existence. Daniels was obviously not as foolish as previously conceived. Sergeant Cross smiled as he squeezed the trigger of his second hand M16-A2 rifle, dropping the commanding officer to his knees with a single shot. Silence returned to the streets as Daniels rejoined his superior in the shadows of safety.

"You son of a bitch!" Tom hollered. "Where in the hell did you get a Claymore mine and how did you set it up so damn fast?"

"Practice, baby. Practice. I've had that thing for days now stuffed into my ruck sack long before all this crazy shit started! I was going to sneak it home when maneuvers were over so I could plant it in some poor asshole's driveway for fun."

As crazy as it seemed, Sergeant Cross suddenly developed a new-found love for the idiot gloating in his own self-proclaimed genius. Whether or not it was intelligence cleverly disguised as lunacy, he believed a chance existed they'd both live to see the sun rise from the west once more. Still, Cross would have to bleed Daniels at some point to throw off the hounds but, as of this very moment, he bathed the man in envy. Trial by repetition guaranteed his feelings would be short lived.

"C'mon," Cross added. "I'm sure some of them heard that. We have to get off the streets and into some cover before they show... a Hummer!"

Tom's orders ceased as he discovered the military vehicle only two blocks away from their current position. It appeared to be intact from where he stood except for a fresh coat of blood paint provided by some poor souls formerly of Fort Bliss. That was good enough for him.

Slowly, the two soldiers crept from cover to cover once more with a goal in sight but were soon forced to halt by a heavy, recognized flap of wings. Cross and Daniels found their hiding spot just as the demon descended from the tarnished sky, landing atop the prized transportation. The beast glared angrily in all directions in hope of finding the cause of its comrades' demise. Frozen in fear, the two men dared not to move a muscle.

"Dammit, man," Cross whispered. "Check out the claws on thing! We wouldn't stand a chance if he got his hands on us."

"Yeah, he's definitely a 'He'," Daniels followed up the comment "Look at that cock swinging between his legs! He's knocking knee to knee with every turn! Lucky bastard..."

Tom slapped his face into his palm yet again.

"That's the third time you've said something that involves dicks since this chaos started! Are you obsessed?"

"I wasn't aware you were keeping score, Tom," Daniels mocked "Are you saying I should bump up the dick count? Would it make you happier if I threw a few more dicks your direction?"

Cross just shook his head hopelessly as he observed his demonic enemy from the safety of the shadows. Sniffing the air profusely, the creature began to jump up and down upon the vehicle's roof causing it to cave in more with each landing. It only took a few more bounces before the front driver's tire popped from the added weight and impact. Obviously satisfied with its actions, the demon gave a pleasured smile and ascended toward the heavens once more.

"You've got to be fucking kidding me!" Daniels exclaimed aloud "Now why would he go and do such a thing?"

"Isn't it obvious, Dan? Cross realized. "They know we're out here. They might not know exactly where we are, but they know we're not in a pile of dead soldiers on the battlefield."

"And just how in the hell do they know that, smarty pants?"

"Simple," Cross explained. "Satan was once an angel and probably best friends with the old man in the sky. You shot God's son right between the eyes and that's drawn some unwanted attention. I don't think they're looking for us at all. I think they're looking for you."

Daniels swallowed hard upon hearing the sergeant's words. What were the chances he was truly marked in some way like Cross said? It didn't matter. All he knew for certain was that it was time he got his skinny ass to the motor pool, commandeered a working vehicle, and got the fuck out of "Hell Paso" while a chance for survival still existed. With or without Tom Cross, the time for ducking in shadows and hiding was over. No guts, no glory. It was high time Daniels let the sergeant know who was really in charge of this situation.

"Okay, Tom. Here's the deal. I think I've had just about enough of you talking shit to me and acting like I still have to follow every single one of your damned orders as though the military still exists. It does, I mean. Sort of. It still exists in a festering pile of blood and guts on the far side of Fort Bliss where we started running for our lives, and something tells me that none of those soldiers have much to say regarding their current situations. They're dead and I'm not so I must be doing something right."

The sergeant looked at Daniels with stone-cold eyes but allowed him to finish his rant.

"Go on," Sergeant Cross twirled his hands in a circular motion "Get it all out of your system."

"Thank you, I will." Daniels accepted the offer. "Now, you've treated me like some kind of worthless turd since the day I was assigned to this unit. Yes, I'm aware of the fact I'm just a Private First Class when compared to the rank of Sergeant, but I'm a human being, too! Right now, we humans must stick together with no regard for military rank or social status. You need to recognize the fact I saved our asses back there when that horde from Hell showed up with the swords. I took care of that shit. That was me."

There was an extended pause in Daniels's story as though he waited for some type of praise. Cross cocked his head to one side out of curiosity, but no more words spewed from his twisted mouth. It was as though Daniels had ranted himself speechless. Obviously, for every good lecture given, a retort existed on the lips of the opposing side. Sergeant Tom Cross was indeed the opposition.

"Are you finished?" he began. "Do you have anything else to say for yourself? No? Good, then that means it's my turn!"

Sergeant Cross began to pace back and forth in visible strides of anger just as the Army had taught him. To make things worse, Daniels still stared blankly into Tom's direction but didn't thwart his planned tirade not one bit. Cross was finally going to unleash his fury upon the subordinate in a way he should've done the minute dire straits were realized back in the commissary. If he had to punch the bastard directly in the face to make his point, so be it.

"What do you want, Daniels? Do you want a pat on the back for using the Claymore mine of which you originally intended to use harmfully toward another innocent human being? Do you want me to give you a high-five for going against my orders to stay hidden and for every other order of mine you've ignored since the day we met? Do you want me to hug you from behind and give you the reach around for every time you've tried to turn the horrendous situation at hand into a moving comedy show? No, sir. All you're going to receive from me is the punch in the face you've deserved since the beginning of this freak show!"

Private Dan Daniels was frozen in fear as the sergeant reared back his fist to strike. A puff of steaming breath upon his neck caused Cross to realize all too late that the impending assault wasn't the origin of Daniels' petrification. With a minimal effort twist and tug of the demon's clawed hand, the superior non-commissioned officer's head came free from his shoulders, leaving a crumpled mess of flesh and blood at the feet of the frightened Private. Daniels responded with the most basic of human characteristics to the carnage which played out before his eyes. He ran.

Dodging the debris of war-torn vehicles and a few more collections of shredded, mangled bodies, Daniels sprinted for the motor pool at the far end of the Fort Bliss main drag, screaming every step of the way. He peeked over his shoulder just long enough to realize the winged demon was keeping up to his pace by casually walking. Hopeless, Daniels halted and spun, releasing a fury of bullets into the body of the hell spawn with no negative effect to its wellbeing. The demon expressed a face to face howl of terror into the ears of its victim as Dan realized escape was no longer an option. He made sure to faint long before the creature's teeth could have their way.

*

Private First Class Dan Daniels slowly opened his eyes to what he imagined to be the luminescent glow of the afterlife. Afraid to move out of creating unwanted attention, he lay flat upon a foreign, hardened surface which vibrated with each pulse of his still beating heart. Had he found some way to survive the encounter and escape his pursuer from the streets of the military installation, or was this indeed the gates of Heaven as suggested by the Sunday School classes he rarely attended during his youth? Dan's vision cleared with each spared breath and he soon realized his surroundings to be all too familiar.

The vibrations at his back were nothing more than the slamming of a basketball against the highly polished floor of the Fort Bliss gymnasium. Upon further inspection, Heaven's radiant glow was only that of the suspended lighting which dangled from the roof's support rafters. Confusion began to set in even more than all he'd experienced during the previous day's events as he came to his feet without pain or realized loss of limb. He was alive.

"Catch!" came the gravelly voice from the far end of the gym, but his reaction time was far too slow to prevent a face full of rubber.

Daniels fell to the floor again with a thud that seemed to echo forever between the concrete walls of the structure. A ringing between his ears caused by the impact permeated his senses as he faded in and out of consciousness. Bring his tired body to its knees, he crawled on all fours from the current location to prevent anymore projectile interception. The stomp of feet approached his direction which made him shrivel into the fetal position once more.

"Whoa, hey, man. Sorry about that! I saw you waking up, so I thought I'd see if you wanted to play a round of basketball before I got on with this crazy plan of world domination. You do play hoops, right?"

Clearing the stinging sweat from his eyes, Daniels glanced around the gymnasium to see mob upon mob of demons gathering in the bleachers on either side of his position. Bloody footprints collected while tromping through fields of fellow fallen soldiers stained the once clean floor of the out of bounds areas from their clawed feet. They sat in waiting of their master's next order with wings folded. Daniels dared not to say a word.

"Excuse the mess," the chosen officiator announced "They may be nasty but they're my kind of nasty. All I've got to do is point my finger in any direction and they lay waste to everything. It's almost like an army of trained dogs with big ass teeth and wings. Pretty cool, really! It's good to be the master sometimes."

Daniels averted his eyes from the direction of the demonic leader which he only imaged to be Satan himself. Fearful for what remained of his miserable life, he fell to his knees one last time to grovel at the feet of the being now in control of his destiny. He felt the being walk behind him in what could only be interpreted as the coming of the end.

"Are you going to kill me now?" Dan cried as the entity paused his advance.

"Kill you?" the unseen voice boomed. "Are you crazy? No way, my dear boy, I'm not going to kill you! You actually saved me from a shit storm of trouble earlier today! Jesus was about to come down here and kick my ass until you intervened with what I have to say was a clean, well placed shot atop his

168

unibrow! No sir! I'm not going to even think about killing you! You've managed to make this all possible. It's a dream come true as far as I'm concerned!"

The being began to circle Daniels as he continued his speech. His knees started to ache from all the recent running over previous hours as they popped uncomfortably against the hardwood floor. He closed his eyes tightly once again as he awaited his unsure fate.

"Do you know how hard it is to be the Father of all things evil? I've got enough stuff to deal with on a daily basis without old J.C. coming down here to scold me for destroying his Dad's creation. Have you ever done that before? Were you ever over at a friend's house when you were a kid and accidentally broke one of his Dad's Jimi Hendrix records or something? It's not the most fun feeling, man. I mean, you know the other kid's Pops isn't going to wail on you personally but you feel bad knowing your friend will get his ass kicked later after you go home. It's pretty much the same shit. God is probably kicking that ass right now. I'd love to be a little demonic fly on the wall up there."

Daniels was finding it harder and harder to keep a straight face during the satanic monologue from the being's rant. He never would've guessed the devil had such a sense of humor. Twisted much like his own, maybe it wouldn't be such a bad existence living out the remainder of his days as the right hand buddy of Beelzebub. Dan attempted to test the waters for a sign of tolerance.

"So, let me get this straight," his voice crawled with uncertainty. "I shot Jesus Christ for you and you're going to let me live, even though you've killed everyone else on Earth?"

The head demon paused in his pacing as he ran very human like fingers across Dan's military style flat top haircut. Thumping the top of the soldier's head in order from thumb to pinky, Dan could sense the being was in deep thought regarding how to answer the blunt question. He removed his hand and continued to encircle his prisoner until a band of winged demons to his right began to chuckle furiously.

"Well, that all depends on what you consider your definition of the word 'living' to be," the creature teased, raising his hand to shush his amused crowd of servants. "I'm probably going to make you do some fucked up shit all the time like you're some kind of abused pet, but I'm definitely going to let you live. You're an endangered species now, after all! Kind of like a collector's item of sorts. I'm the proud owner of the only human in the world. It makes me feel all special!"

Dan's curiosity begged the question.

"Like, what kind of fucked up shit are we talking about?"

"Oh, I see!" the master responded to the inquiry. "You're the kind of guy that likes to know the end of the book before he even gets a chance to read the first chapter! You probably went to see *The Empire Strikes Back* a second time just to blurt out who Darth Vader was to the unsuspecting theater patrons! Don't you dare speak out of turn again, human!"

Enraged by the soldier's premature inquiry, the being quickened his pace with every word. Dan's eardrums were pierced by horrible scenarios flying from the master's tongue which could only be interpreted by tone. He spoke them with blurred velocity and they seemed to worsen with every new verbal assault. The demons in attendance who understood his language erupted into fits of laughter and, this time, there was no stopping them. Daniels couldn't help but think his life span as Satan's pet would be short lived after all. The speech slowed once more into recognizable English.

"…and finally, I'm going to make my flying monkeys go scoop up your dead friend from the alley outside, so I can sit and watch you eat him one piece at a time. You better not even think of stopping until that bastard is all gone, and don't think for a second you'll be privy to any cutting utensils. No, you're going to have to start with the skinny parts and work your way up. I'm thinking his extremities! Maybe one in particular…"

Dan's mind faded away into happier places and far from the nightmarish scenarios offered by the devil's endless imagination. Thoughts of whether or not he should run head first into a bleacher full of demons to ensure his death rather than feast upon the severed cock of Sergeant Cross ran marathons in his mind. Coming to his feet, his eyes opened to the shocking sight and grinning face of his captor for the first time since waking below the lights of the gymnasium. Ultimate fear gripped him as the being's name rolled from his panic-stricken tongue. It was a name which symbolized certainty to the before mentioned fates offered from the continued rant and little chance of escape.

"John Belushi?"

CULT OF THE ANGEL EATERS

Mark Deloy

The prison psychiatrist sits across the table from me. He is twirling his pencil between his fingers and staring at me over his glasses like a school teacher. I glance over his right shoulder and smile.

"Yes, I'll tell you my story," I say, still smiling. "I'll tell you where it all began..."

*

I was serving time upstate for armed robbery and Willy was my cellmate. I thought from the get-go that he was a strange dude. He had a full beard, unruly, bushy and unkempt, and had these crazy eyes that seemed to look everywhere at once, darting around like ferrets in their sockets. I was just a kid back then, barely twenty and scared shitless. Willy kind of took me in, protected me on the yard, shit like that. In turn, I watched his back as well. It was a good agreement.

So, anyway, like I said, I always thought he was a strange guy, but when he started talking about angels and demons and "the other side", I thought he had really lost it. He told me he and I were destined to lead others in a place far from there.

I kind of laughed at him. I didn't mean to, but he was talking some crazy shit, telling me all about the astral plane and the veil between humans and ethereal beings. He told me the old myth about God and Satan being at war was just a bunch of bullshit, and the real war was between humanity and anything spiritual. He told me that angels and demons were just

172

flip sides on the same coin, all working together to bring about the downfall of humanity.

I went to sleep that night, thinking my friend had lost his mind and I'd better start sleeping with one eye open or I'd wake up with a shank sticking out of my head. But, in the end, I went to sleep anyway, figuring whatever happened happened and there was nothing I could do about it anyhow.

I woke early the next morning around four a.m. or so. Willy was sitting real close to the cell bars, his ass on the dirty floor and his eyes fixed on something just outside the bars. He was rocking back and forth, his lips were moving, but I couldn't hear what he was saying. I was a little pissed off and very weirded out. I almost said something to let him know he had woken me up, but I decided to keep quiet and see what he was up to.

All of a sudden, Willy got real still and stared out into the corridor. I couldn't see anything out there, just a bunch of shadows. I remember the air was very still, and I caught the briefest whiff of something acrid and thick, like burning tires.

Then Willy's hand shot out through the bars and grabbed a hold of something. Whatever it was put up a hell of a fight, slamming Willy against the steel bars until his nose was broken and his face was a bloody mess, but Old Willy never stopped smiling. He looked back up at me, as if he knew I'd been watching the whole time. His nose was smashed, a few of his teeth were missing, and blood trickled from his nose. He reached his other arm through the bars, braced his feet against them and pulled with all his might. I could see his back muscles straining through his shirt.

I thought about helping him. That was my natural first reaction, but I couldn't see anything on the other side of our cell, nothing at all. It was like he was struggling against the very air itself. I sat up and stared harder into the gloom beyond our cage, trying to make out what was out there, but I couldn't see a fucking thing. I almost yelled out for a guard, but something told me to be still, so I just sat up on my bunk and watched.

Whatever Willy had gotten a hold of was still fighting like a king-sized catfish. My cellmate kept grinning like a madman as his body was bashed against the steel bars over and over. Still, I had to give him credit, he wasn't letting go.

After about ten minutes, the struggle started going Willy's way. The thing beyond the bars seemed to tire and Willy started reeling it in and inch at a time. I heard the thing let out an agonized scream that echoed through my brain rather than my ears. Willy turned to me.

"You hear that?" he asked me. "You did, didn't you? There's hope for you yet, boy."

Then Willy gave one final jerk and heaved himself backwards. Whatever he had been fighting against slid through the bars and I saw it shimmer like summer heat on asphalt. Willy pounced on it, growling and cursing. He was tearing at it with his teeth and clawed hands. I sat back against the wall, amazed and horrified.

As Willy bit and clawed at the shimmering air, the thing began to materialize. I saw golden wings and a child-like body. Its eyes were black, like pools of ink and it had short fangs. It tried to bite back at Willy, but he crashed a tattooed forearm into its face. The creature was stunned and hung its head across my friend's lap like a sleeping dog. Willy ripped one of its wings off and the creature let out another ghostly howl.

Its blood spilled onto the dirty floor of our cell. The stuff looked like mercury, silver and wet. Willy licked some of it off his fingers as if it were chicken grease.

Willy turned toward me. His eyes were now the same quicksilver as the creature's blood. I could see my reflection in them.

The creature never stopped struggling, never stopped moving until Willy tore its head from its body, lifted its head and stared into its beautiful face.

"W... Willy. What is that?" I asked, although I already knew.

"An angel. Just a small one though. It'll serve though. Good enough to get us out of this shithole."

Then Willy began to eat. He tore chunks out of the angel's shoulders, thighs and arms. Silvery blood coated Willy's face, shirt and the cell floor. I watched Willy consume the creature as if it were a Thanksgiving turkey, eating everything. Then he began breaking the creature's bones and sucked out the marrow.

"Waste not, want not," he said, grinning through the silvery gore.

He threw the bones and the wings into the corner where they rattled like castanets on clouds. Then he wiped the silvery blood that smeared his mouth onto his sleeve and began gathering up his possessions. He wrapped everything in a sheet from his bunk and slung it over his shoulder.

"You comin' or not?" he asked me. His eyes still shined, and I felt a shiver go through me. I couldn't answer his question, couldn't speak at all. He might have just killed and ate an angel, but we were still surrounded by concrete, steel and barbed wire. We weren't going anywhere.

Willy shrugged, and then turned toward the cell door. He waved a hand like a magician. The locking mechanism began to smoke. I heard a soft click and the door swung open. Willy stepped out onto the catwalk and looked both ways before deciding to go right toward the guard house at the end of our cellblock.

I cautiously poked my head out of our cell and watched as Willy fearlessly walked into the guardhouse. I watched through the large picture window. The uniformed men inside seemed stunned at first and quickly scrambled to their feet, grabbing their aerosol cans of pepper spray.

Willy took his time, gave them a Jedi mind trick with that same wave of his hand that he had used to open out cell. The guards just stood there like apes, slack jawed with glazed eyes and hunched shoulders. He gave one of them a command and the guard retrieved his keys and handed them over. That was when I decided to follow him, wherever he was going.

*

Our destination turned out to be the desert. Eventually Willy's power faded, but before it did, he'd gotten us a new corvette, a sack full of cash and more pussy than a rock star could ever hope for.

175

Eventually, Willy said it was time to get back to business. He told me we had a mission and we had to go to Arizona. He had a plan, and that was good enough for me. I'd seen what he could do, and I was with him all the way. Turned out, he was planning on starting a family and he wanted me to be the first member.

We settled twenty miles south of Sedona. Willy used some of our cash to buy an old horse ranch. There was plenty of room in the main house as well as bunk houses for everyone who Willy said would follow us.

We spent the next few weeks preparing for the others. I didn't argue; I woke every morning to the smell of fresh air and saguaro instead of shit, sweat and pain.

Willy explained that angels were all around us, but they were fast. The bigger ones had the most power but were harder to catch. You had to be patient, and when the time came, you couldn't hesitate because once you threaten an angel, they turned on you like a cobra.

The fallen angels, what most people called demons, were another story altogether. They were the most dangerous but held more power. Willy told me he'd once caught a demon and stayed high from its blood for a full year. When Willy was high, he could do all kinds of things. He could push people's minds, move objects without touching them, and even levitate over short distances. He promised to show me how to spot the ethereal beings and eventually capture them. He told me he would show us all.

*

The others came, one by one. Men and women lost to the world, eager to learn, eager for power. We gave them food and a place to stay and in return, they joined our family. The Final Observers, he called us. We were to watch for the end. He said we were supposed to fight God's angels and Satan's demons, and that they were all the same.

"All cut from the same ethereal cloth," he'd say. "Only difference is the demons are a hot meal." Then he'd start laughing.

First we were two members, then six, then twenty, then sixty. I took several wives and so did Willy. He led us in meditation and exercise, honed our minds and our bodies. We bought guns and trained for the coming war, not with men, but with the angels or demons, or whoever came for us first. We dug tunnels under the house and set traps along the walls. Willy taught us that when they came, they would come in human form, cased in flesh and bone to protect them from our hunger.

And we were hungry. I led hunting parties into town every month. Like a pride of lions, we roamed the desert cities searching for Seraphim and Nephilim. Most of the time, we caught nothing, but occasionally we would spot a lone, minor angel who had strayed away from its host, or a lesser demon on its own trying to corrupt one weak mind among many.

We would track the creatures following the angels glowing footprints on cracked sidewalks or the demon's black, slime trails along the sugary Arizona sand.

When we caught them, we pounced and fed, always saving the head for Willy who said he could sometimes see the future in their dark shimmering eyes.

Life was good for a while. The power was good, but the sense of family, of belonging was better. All that ended when they finally came for us, just as Willy said they would.

*

The battle began on a windy day in May. We'd prepared for it for almost a year, but none of us were ready when it came. We never imagined they would come with such force, angels and demons fighting side by side against a common enemy. Willy said they had teamed up, just this once just to destroy us.

The morning guard spotted them at seven a.m. coming up the long dirt road that led to the compound. ATF and FBI advancing on our home like locusts. Black SUVs and armored personnel carriers surrounded the ranch, blocked off the only road in. They looked ready for a fight.

We saw them; saw through them, a mighty mass of angelic warriors and demonic hoards. They wore their human hosts like clothing.

177

They gave no warning, no ultimatums. They just came, and came, and kept coming, wave after wave of expendable human bodies hiding the divine and the corrupt.

We gunned down the bodies, but the spirits kept coming, pulling themselves out of the skin, bone and Kevlar like butterflies from steel cocoons.

We dropped our weapons, knowing they would do no good once the parasites left their physical hosts. We stood at the ready. Willy began chanting and speaking a guttural mantra. I felt my arm begin to tingle then get hot. As I looked down, I saw a blue blade materialize as part of my hand. It extended like a short sword and I could feel its power through my whole body.

The massive hoard flowed through the walls of our compound like water, snatching our children up first, eating them in front of us as if they were Christmas lambs.

Then they came for us. We fought well, feeding as we killed, gaining strength. But in the end, their numbers were too great, and they had billions more in reserve. Family members were torn apart one after another until only Willy and I were left. We ran down into the basement and hid in the tunnels. A legion of demons followed, armed with spears and teeth.

"You've got to survive," Willy said as we cowered in the darkness, waiting to die. "You've got to rebuild it all."

I just stared at him, seeing only his outline in the gloom. The demons were right behind us, screaming for our blood, moving toward us through the tunnels like wolves.

"Take this tunnel," Willy said. "It'll lead you to the surface. I'll keep them off your trail."

"Thank you, Father," I said and hugged him tightly. As I ran down the alternate tunnel, I heard the demons tear Willy apart. They growled and snarled as they ripped flesh from bone. Willy never screamed, not once.

The tunnel came to an end just outside the compound walls. The local Sheriff's department apparently. They must have been asked to provide perimeter security. I sniffed one as they handcuffed me. They hadn't been possessed. I gladly went with them, spared to fight another day.

That was ten years ago.

"So you expect me to recommend that you be transferred from general population and be placed in psychiatric care?" the psychiatrist says.

"No. I know you don't believe me, but your disbelief doesn't change anything. You will never see what I've seen."

I glance over the doctor's shoulder again. The angel had entered with him and now after hearing my story, looked eager to leave. It was, however, a guardian and thus linked to the man by a silvery umbilical cord.

I stood up and clamped a hand over the man's mouth before he could cry out for a guard, but it wasn't him I was after.

The cord felt wet and slippery in my calloused hands as I reeled in my fish. The angel struggled, but my mouth was watering now, and I would not be denied.

SIX DEGREES OF SEPARATION

Delphine Quinn

"I can't," she screamed, agony etched across her face into road maps of wrinkles forming paths for the dripping sweat to make its way in rivulets down the brilliant red skin of her once slim face. "John, I can't do it! Please! Make it stop!"

"It's okay, honey. You're doing great. You're doing fine," her husband responded, softly brushing a drenched strand of chestnut hair from her eyes. He looked up at the nurses and doctors who surrounded his wife's lower half, trying to sense any complications they might not be conveying. Everything seemed normal.

"Just one more push, Mrs. Kennedy. One good push and your little girl will be here; she can't wait to see you," the nurse murmured to John's exhausted wife.

"No more pushes! Get her out of me! This is *your* fault, Jonathan!"

The doctor chuckled softly. "One more, and we're done, Jessica. You can do this. I can see your little girl's head, hair as bright as the sun," Doctor Mitchell said, comforting his patient.

Jessica pushed as hard as she could, feeling her insides tearing wide open, raw, visceral sensation of her muscles straining, resisting the path being forged by her child, as Jessica's fragile skin, paper thin, gave way to a healthy seven pound, eight ounce little girl.

The pain was immense, but as soon as Jessica heard the deep and strong cry from her firstborn, the excruciating forty hours of labor vanished from her memory. She was instantly

180

more in love than she had ever been the second the doctor handed her this tiny little being, a little baby made of love by Jessica and her husband of five years, Jonathan. The wrinkles of fury and weariness faded from her face, sweat turned to a glow, and a smile that could have illuminated half the city graced her lips.

"My God, John, she's perfect."

"Yes, she is," John replied, leaning forward and kissing first his wife's forehead and then his daughter's. Pride swelled in his chest, tears in his eyes, and all at once he knew this little girl was his everything. "And so are you, Mrs. Kennedy. So are you."

"I love you, Mr. Kennedy. I'm so glad I married you," Jessica leaned up and kissed her husband more deeply.

"You'll be wanting to cut the cord, and then of course there are the medical procedures to see to," the nurse interjected, a clipboard in hand.

"Of course," John responded quickly. "Just standard, right? I counted fingers and toes; she seems perfectly healthy."

"She is. We just need to check her over, and of course, you'll be wanting the implant?"

Looking down at her newborn, Mrs. Kennedy cooed, "Yes, of course we want the implant. Our little girl deserves everything we can give her."

"I agree," the nurse answered, filling out forms, "The Grand Counselor and Six Degrees of Separation has changed the world, if you ask me. But we still ask, more of as a formality."

"Of course. We'd like the implant," John confirmed. He tenderly picked up his minutes old daughter and handed her to the nurse. "Thank you."

*

Baby Rachel, thirty minutes old, had passed all medical tests. A perfectly healthy child, beautiful, even, the nurses mused. Nurse Grace wheeled her into the sterile Six Degrees of Separation Department of the hospital, filled out the forms, and handed them to Dennis, the technician in charge of implantation and marking.

"Another cog in the machine," he said to Grace.

"Don't be like that," Grace chastised, giving him a little pat on his arm. "We all know how much better life is since the Grand Counselor brought together the civilized nations and helped us to be connected and responsible to each other with Six Degrees."

"Christ, Grace, why don't you marry him?" Dennis joked, as he entered Baby Rachel's social security number, birth date, full name, blood type, parents' names and information into his computer. Hitting ENTER, he turned his chair to the 3D printer that was working tirelessly to create a minuscule implant made of a mixture of metals and computer chips. When the printer stopped its work, Dennis opened the glass enclosure and removed the implant with tweezers.

Turning to the baby before him, he placed the implant into an implantation device, similar to a syringe and needle, that Nurse Grace was holding, as she had thousands of times before. Grace leaned forward, whispering nonsense to the baby in the carriage, and quickly injected the metal object into her wrist. The baby made no reaction, just stared up at the strange woman before her with a look of confusion.

Dennis took a small tattoo gun and etched a single six around each side of the triangular implant, finishing three. The baby fussed, but Nurse Grace held her hand steady. This was an integral part of the process. The three sixes represented the Six Degrees of Separation everyone from the UK to America to Canada to Japan lived under since the uprising of the Grand Counselor, the tips of the sixes uniting as one, as the civilized world had, and the Period of Peace that followed.

The baby was now at a social merit score of 650, completely neutral. But over time, her score would fluctuate, all based on her interactions with others, her online activity, even her thoughts, as the implant could detect hate speech, even in the mind. By the age of fourteen, citizens were expected to always maintain a merit score of over 550. If someone fell below a merit score of 550, you were given a warning. If it did not improve in the allotted time, you were sent to reinstitutionalization training. If it still did not improve, you were banished. Many people had lost their family members and friends to the New East, never to be seen again.

"Hopefully she is as sweet as she is beautiful," Nurse Grace commented.

"Doesn't hurt she's a chick," Dennis replied.

"Dennis, honestly, if anyone had heard that, you'd be getting a reprimand and your score would lower. You'll be lucky if it doesn't anyway. You know the chip can sense it. That was deeply misogynistic."

"Right. You're right. I'm sure she'll do wonderfully. She seems like a nice kid."

"That's better." Grace patted him again. If his score wasn't so dismal, she would have definitely considered going out with him, but associations could deeply affect one's own standing. Grace preferred to be in the good graces of Tthe Grand Counselor and his police. "Now let me get this little angel back to her mom and dad. Have a good day, Dennis."

"You too, Grace," Dennis said, logging into his Six Degrees of Separation account to see how badly his "misogynistic" comment had set him back this time.

*

Rachel skipped up the steps to her two-story, Victorian home. As she passed the mailbox, she grabbed its contents, as she often did when her mom and dad were too busy with work. She flipped through the small stack of envelopes. Bill, bill, a report from school she had been expecting, a pamphlet from the Grand Counselor that came every week, filled with information about which words were to be used or avoided under penalty of one's social merit being lowered, and finally an envelope to remind Rachel that her college test was in two weeks and that she should not let her family or her people down by failing.

Rachel sighed as she opened the front door, dropped the stack of mail on the side table, and called out for her mom.

"In here, honey," her mom called back from the kitchen.

Rachel made her way through the spotless living room where the flat screen was on medium volume and some old man was arguing with another old man: *"It's inevitable, really. We cannot allow minorities or women to be marginalized in any society; it's barbaric."*

Rachel ignored the two crotchety old guys going back and forth about nonsense that never happened and would never happen. She entered the kitchen to find her mom rolling out dough on the kitchen island, her graying, brunette locks pinned up into a messy bun, white smudges across her face, red lips shining: her visage a clown having a bad night. Her apron was covered in flour, but still she wiped her hands on it and came around the island to give her daughter a warm embrace.

"*Another pie,* Mom?" Rachel snarked.

"How was school?" Mrs. Kennedy asked, ignoring her daughter's dirty look.

"It was fine. I'm still at a steady 700, but that kid Jeff from my math class went below a 550 today because he called Elisa a whale. Security came and got him from my period."

"Well, calling a woman a whale is disgusting and wrong. He needs to be reinstitutionalized, clearly. Shameful that his parents haven't taught him better," Mrs. Kennedy replied, sneering at the thought of *anyone* going below a 550.

"Yeah, I guess you're right. but Elisa was being kind of mean first," Rachel half-heartedly responded, dipping her finger into the burgundy pie filling her mother was making.

"It doesn't matter, Rachel. You know that. We never think or speak ill of people, especially those who aren't privileged. That poor girl is female, *and* she's overweight. You can't make fun of overweight women. Actually, I read a study recently that said the more oppressed you are, the higher your social merit. Why do you think I keep making all these pies? If you gained some weight, I'd bet your merit goes up 20 points," Mrs. Kennedy said matter of factly in that sing song voice that said, *I'm being nice but I can stop anytime, young lady.*

"You're right. Sorry. Anyway, there's a kick back happening at Ashley's tonight. No drinking or drugs. Just a few of us hanging out, talking, playing video games. Can I go?"

"Are these people above a 650?"

"Yes, Mom. In fact, two are above a 725."

"Well then, I'd say you have to go! Being close to a 725 would boost your merit, and with college acceptances looming, the higher your merit, the better. You go and have fun, dear," Mrs. Kennedy leaned down and kissed her daughter's cheek before turning back to the cutting board that resembled a cocaine war zone, humming happily to herself.

*

"It's your turn, Rach," Ashley said, prodding her friend with her frail, ebony elbow, and holding out the controller.

"I think I'm going to pass on this game. I need a drink," Rachel replied, much to her friend's disapproval. But Rachel wasn't paying Ashley any attention. In fact, ever since a guy she'd never met had shown up at the party, she only had eyes for him. Not that she was making it obvious; at least, she hoped not.

She had seen him go into the kitchen alone, and Rachel seized the opportunity, following him in shortly thereafter. Rachel didn't think he'd noticed her. The radio was on softly in the background and she could just make out heated voices, *"The Grand Counselor's word is law, and we obviously must respect that. Whatever his solution, it is the correct one."*

"Oh, hey," the tanned teenager with soft blonde hair and strikingly blue eyes said as he turned from the cooler and saw Rachel behind him, his voice covering the radio easily. "Sorry, um, am I in your way?"

"No. Take your time. It's fine," Rachel stammered. *This was a stupid idea. You look stupid. Oh God.*

"Well cool. Here, can I grab you something to drink? Uh, my name's Tobin," he reached out his hand to shake hers, then realized it was covered in ice cold water. Sheepishly, he wiped his hand on his jeans and made the motion again. "I actually noticed you when I came in and wanted to talk to you, but I wasn't really sure how to approach you."

Rachel laughed, shaking his hand. "I noticed you too, and I'm very happy to meet you."

"Would you like to take our drinks outside, maybe? Talk?"

*

They talked for hours as the rest of the party carried on indoors, their soft voices mixing with the crescendo of crickets and the soft rustling of the leaves beginning to fall, creating a kind of symphony, making their already strong connection even deeper, more magical.

Finally, inevitably, the topic of scores and the Grand Counselor came up. Rachel was surprised at how long it had taken. Usually that was one of the first topics of conversation between two people first meeting, like some yardstick measurement of who was better or worse, a way to compensate for other shortcomings, or secretly take pleasure in your own successes.

But with Tobin, they'd talked about home, family, school, their beliefs and books they'd read. It was entirely new to her, but it didn't seem to be for him. He seemed completely at ease, like a man from an era long left behind, just sitting on a deck, taking in the sweet jasmine smell of the evening, looking from her to the stars... until the topic of scores came up.

"Merits," Tobin spat. "Six Degrees of Separation, no comment."

"What do you mean 'No comment'?' You can't just no comment about Six Degrees," Rachel said cautiously, warning him of an infraction she wasn't even sure *was* an infraction but felt it must be, *right*?

"Look, Rachel, you're really nice, but I don't need someone to lessen my score for anything. I'm dancing pretty closely to a 570, and my mind gets me in enough shit as it is."

"I wouldn't report you," Rachel said softly, knowing it was true. She liked Tobin. He wasn't like everyone else, and though it felt dangerous, she wanted to know why she'd felt so comfortable *not* caring about his score and why she wanted to know his views, illegal or not.

Tobin examined Rachel's face for what felt like an eternity, evaluating her, studying her every line and expression, looking for any telltale signs of a snitch. He didn't see any, and he'd become very good at finding a snitch. He paused for a bit, took a breath, and whispered to Rachel.

"I don't think I want to be a part of Six Degrees. It's this prison I feel trapped inside. I can't think what I want. I can't do what I want. I can't say what I want. I can't say that someone is wrong because I am a *privileged* member of our society. It's considered bullying to have a discussion or disagree. I've almost dropped below a 560 at least twice a year since I turned seven. I'm not made for this kind of a society. I just want to be able to sit down, like we're doing now, and decide whether we even *like* the Grand Counselor without being taken in the night and murdered."

Rachel gasped. She'd never heard anyone speak like this, ever. Not anyone. Sure Tobin was going to be scooped up by the police any moment, Rachel tried to take in everything he'd said, memorize his face before he was taken from her for reinstitutionalization...or wait: *murdered?*

He'd said murdered. *Surely that can't be right,* she thought. But her mind was racing and she realized every single person who'd ever been taken for reinstitutionalization had never come back. Everyone agreed they'd been banished, sent somewhere like the New East, or that their families had moved away out of shame. *But every single one?* To Rachel that suddenly seemed unlikely.

"I've scared you," Tobin said, eyes shifting from her face to his shoes, staring down like a scolded puppy. "I'm sorry."

As he said that, his watch dinged, and he looked at it absently. Rachel caught a glimpse of the number, 570. Suddenly Rachel realized that she didn't really like the whole system either. She'd gone along to get along, especially because of her mother. But Tobin seemed like a good person, and he was rated a 570? And not just that, he'd risked going to a 550 or less to tell her the most dangerous and deepest secret she'd ever been told.

To say that she loved him in that moment would've been an understatement. That teenage, first love—I can't imagine my life without you in it, hormones spinning like ballerinas performing a dance that stirred every piece of her—took over and wouldn't let go.

"Yes," she admitted, "you did scare me. But you also made me realize a lot of things. And you put yourself at risk to tell me how you felt. No one's ever done that for me. Not even my parents."

"Well, hopefully we can keep hanging out, and maybe you'll even bring my score up." He winked at her with a grin creeping over his face.

"Oh so that was your plan all along then, was it?" Rachel softly punched his shoulder, laughing for the first time in a long time, her voice rising up deep from her belly, not forced. After she pulled her fist from his shoulder, she allowed it to hover for just a moment above his forearm.

Tobin casually took her hand without even looking back at her, his gaze now back on the stars. Their hands entwined, he pointed up at the stars and told her about different planets and constellations until the early hours of the morning. Only stopping as the sun began to crest the horizon, turning the once dark sky into a cascading waterfall of sherbet, and the new day had begun.

*

That school day moved slow, minutes feeling like hours, hours stretching on like days lost in the desert. All Rachel wanted to do was meet up with Tobin after school and talk again. She wanted to feel his hand in hers, to sense the danger of their relationship rushing through her like methamphetamine.

In her final class, *Misogyny in Classic Literature*, she received an update to her merit. She glanced down at her watch, which read 1:57 p.m., swiped to the left, and found her score had gone from a 720 to a 590 in a matter of seconds. Panic consumed her.

A 590 was abysmal! She couldn't get into college with that score. Nobody would want to be friends with her. And her mom. *Oh God, my mom.* Rachel looked around, knowing she hadn't said or done anything. She didn't think she'd thought anything either that would make such a drastic change. *What if it was thinking about Tobin?* she wondered. But no, she'd not lost any merit when they sat together last night.

A glitch because of the update. That's got to be it. Rachel looked around and saw a few others absently checking their watches. Maybe they had a glitch too. Rachel tried to calm herself, and focused on the rest of the lesson until school let out at 2:15. By 2:25, she'd met up with Tobin at a park bench.

She sat down, tucking her purple skirt beneath her legs which brushed up against Tobin's jeans.

"How was school?" Tobin asked first, looking her dead in the eye, as it seemed his habit to do.

"It was okay. The strangest thing, though. My score dropped from 720 to a 590, for no reason. Damned if I know why," Rachel said, picking at her opal nail polish, releasing her concern and anxiety with each pearly shard she tore off and cast aside.

"Probably a glitch," Tobin replied. "Or maybe you shouldn't be hanging out with me."

His solemn reply took Rachel aback. *How could he say that?* "I don't want to stop hanging out with you. I want to hang out with you more, actually. And besides, if it was you, I'd have gotten lowered last night for sure."

"That's true," Tobin's face rose, and it screamed relief. "You know, you wouldn't have to worry about this Six Degrees merit shit if we just left it all behind."

"Left it all behind? There *is* no leaving it all behind unless you're banished to the New East," Rachel said, and shivered. She'd heard about the New East. There, women, people of color, overweight people, and even LGBTQ people were disagreed with and oppressed. You could get into deep arguments and discussions about the rightness of things, as if the Grand Counselor hadn't already told everyone what *was* and *wasn't* right. Heathens.

"No. There are compounds. I've heard of one in the Appalachians, not more than 500 miles from here. People live there in isolation, but they have their own food, animals, shelter, homes, and they can talk and learn and read whatever they want. It sounds kind of amazing. I've always thought about going," Tobin spoke as if telling a fairytale, weaving his

189

passion and hope into every word, his eyes gleaming and a hint of a smile lifted his lips.

"That can't be. The Grand Counselor would shut them down, or send them away. Wouldn't he?"

"Why? Nobody believes they exist, even the few who have heard of the compounds. The Grand Counselor says it doesn't exist, so it doesn't," Tobin said with certainty. "But what if it *did*? I could go. *We* could go."

"Oh, Tobin. I don't know. It could be rumors, or a trap set by the Grand Counselor to find people defecting. And even if it *was* real, what would happen to my parents? My mom can be obnoxious but she loves me, and my dad is the best dad you've ever seen. He can always make Mom laugh. Sometimes I walk past the kitchen and see them dancing slowly, arm in arm, to music that isn't there, except for my dad's soft humming.

"When my mom worries about our merits, Dad always calms her down and tells her how beautiful she is, 'even when she frets'. They love each other so much, and they love me too. If I left, I'd destroy them. Their merits, their hard work, their love for me, destroyed by my selfishness in chasing a dream that might not even exist.

"I'm sorry. I know I'm rambling, but you don't know my family like I do. My mom and dad are soulmates; they got married right after school and five years later, they had me. They can't have any other children. I'm all they've got besides each other." Tears poured from Rachel's eyes.

She realized she did want to go with Tobin, but she knew she couldn't because of her family. She also realized that Tobin might be the only person with whom *she* could find a love like her parents', and she was about to throw it all away. Her sense of duty clashed with her affection for Tobin and her desire to be free, a desire she didn't even know she had until yesterday. She felt like a whirlwind of emotions had enveloped her, spinning her from side to side, stay or go, Tobin or her family, her own love or her parents'.

"I understand," Tobin replied, his hand squeezing hers softly. "It's not like I'm leaving tomorrow. You have time to think about it. And if you can't leave your family, I understand.

My parents split when I was a baby, and I haven't seen my dad since. My mom works all the time, and my merit is always bringing hers down. She might actually be relieved if I was gone. But I know it's not the same for you."

"Thank you for being so understa..." Rachel began to say, interrupted by a notification to her watch again. It was 4:12 when she swiped left for the second time that day and found her merit score listed as a 775. Her face crumpled into confusion.

"What's wrong? Your merit didn't lower, did it?" Tobin asked, genuinely concerned, peering toward the screen. "775! Holy shit! How did you do that?"

"I, I have no idea. Another glitch, maybe? I haven't done anything. Maybe I should have my mom call and find out if something is malfunctioning. Now I don't even know my own merit score," Rachel said, feeling like she was at sea, swaying wave to wave, high to low, with no stability and no way to ground herself, or feel safe. *This is how much you depend on this damned score,* she thought. *Tobin's right.* But no matter how right he was, she couldn't betray her parents by leaving. She was stuck.

"Well, we should probably get going anyway. My mom gets home early on Wednesdays and I usually make something to eat," Tobin said, squeezing Rachel's hand again and casually lifting her from the bench beside him. They looked at each other for a moment and then kissed.

It was blissful, and Rachel imagined Tobin sweeping her into his arms, swaying along to music he could hum softly forever. Maybe she could convince him to stay.

"That was... nice," she said awkwardly.

"Yes it was," Tobin's wide grin appeared again, and he laughed to himself. "You're something special, Rachel. Call me and we can meet again when you have time. Hopefully soon." he winked his wink again and turned to walk away.

"Okay! See ya," Rachel called over her back as she walked the opposite direction to her neighborhood. As she walked the half mile, she kept swiping her watch back and forth, unable to believe she somehow had a merit score of 775. It had to be a glitch.

Rachel dropped the mail on the table in the living room. The flat screen was, as always, on in the background.

"The Grand Counselor knows best. There are always casualties in any movement, be they economic or otherwise. If the New East cannot abide by the law then they must be sanctioned, dealt with…"

She walked past, calling out for her mother like always, and unsurprisingly hearing Mrs. Kennedy call back from the kitchen. Rachel pushed through the doorway and saw a familiar sight.

Her mother stood behind the island, face covered in white dust and crimson filling. Her apron was an abstract painting of reds, creams and the tans of dough. The rolling pin was covered in scarlet, the liquid seeping slowly toward the cutting board, where the crust lay.

"Hello, darling!" her mother called, a brilliant white smile on her face, her skin practically beaming through the flour and filling. Her eyes danced, bright cerulean encircled by a sea of white so wide, she almost looked surprised. "How are you? How was school?"

"I'm fine, Mom. School was fine," Rachel felt uneasy. Her mom was loving, but this was a crazed and manic kind of love with which Rachel was entirely unfamiliar. "Another pie?"

"Well, of *course* another pie! What else would it be, dear?" She looked at Rachel, eyes like a deer's in headlights, hair askew.

"Okay…" Rachel was beginning to feel nauseous. This wasn't her mother. "Why don't I help then?"

Rachel moved around the island slowly, afraid her mom might be having a mental break. *She saw the merit score go down and panicked*, Rachel realized. *Of course!*

"You know, Mom, about the merit scores today…" Rachel stepped closer to the side of the island.

"Oh so you saw it too! What a *disaster*! What a *disgrace*! A 530! Can you even imagine it? *Me! A 530,"* Mrs. Kennedy spat on the floor beside her.

"Mom it was probably just a glitch. Mine fixed, I think. It even ros—" At that moment, Rachel reached the corner of the island, faced her mother, and felt her foot come to an involuntary stop. She'd run her toes into something hard. Rachel looked down and suddenly, her entire world collapsed around her. Acrid vomit made its way up her throat with no resistance, the bile burned her nose and her tongue as it sprayed across the floor, mixing with her father's pooling blood, and landing on his barely recognizable body.

Rachel's eyes rose from her dad's bludgeoned corpse, his face a mash of cartilage and viscera, craters where there were once high cheek bones, mounds of lymph and flesh where his eyes and teeth should have been. Unable to look straight at her mother, her gaze fell on the crimson drenched rolling pin, where she saw minute pieces of bright alabaster bone mingled with clumps of silvered strands of hair splaying out from the wooden instrument at haphazard angles, like the spines of a porcupine.

She retched again, her stomach convulsing as if trying to expel her insides in hopes that the memory of her dead father would somehow be dislodged along with them. Wiping the remaining fragments of bread and mucus from her paling chin, Rachel finally brought her mother into her vision, suddenly terrified Mrs. Kennedy might raise the once lovingly cared for implement up as a weapon against her own daughter.

Mrs. Kennedy was still steadily kneading the dough before her by hand, her body relaxed and natural, as if it was just a normal Wednesday afternoon. Her mother didn't even spare a glance for Rachel or her dead spouse of twenty-two years as of July.

"Mom…" Rachel's voice trembled, fear coalescing with shock, uniting Rachel's heart in a harrowing state of terrified numbness: "What have you done?"

"What I had to do, Rachel," Mrs. Kennedy responded sharply. Resetting her face as she pounded the batter, her voice came out softer, more maternal, with a hint of pride behind the words that followed. "Your father decided that he was going to publicly challenge the Grand Counselor today at work. Whatever got into him, I'll never know. I asked him when he got home early after they'd let him go. He came in just before 4 p.m., and his boss had already called to tell me what happened. But your dad was insane, out of his mind; he made no sense.

"He just kept saying that the Grand Counselor was going to doom us all. That we should never have opted into Six Degrees. He said merit scores were a farce. *A farce,* he said. As if our lives and society haven't been brought to something beautiful and Utopian, as if we'd somehow wronged not only ourselves but *you* by getting our chips when they were optional.

"He was dangerous, Rachel. His outburst had cost us all hundreds of merits. *Hundreds.* Your life would've been over. *Mine* would have been over. The police would have come and taken him, taken us, and we'd have been sent to the New East." Her mother stopped kneading and took a deep breath, turning to face her daughter, as if to drive the point home with her eyes.

"I couldn't let that happen. So I did what I had to do. And someday you'll thank me for it. Someday, if your husband, God forbid, has some kind of psychotic break like your father, you'll do the same, of that I have no doubt. And that's all I'll say of the matter. You have homework, I presume. Go get started. Exams are in a few days."

Mrs. Kennedy faced the island again, her stylish pumps drowning in a lagoon of her recently deceased husband's coagulating gore. The discussion was closed, and Rachel backed away slowly, her feet shuffling inch by inch, carrying her body away from her mother without making any sudden movements. Her trachea clenched so tightly, Rachel wasn't even sure she was drawing breath. Abject terror and revulsion clouded her vision, as did the silent tears falling down her face. When she felt the door brush against her back, Rachel leaned into it and turned swiftly, bounding into the living room, her legs sprinting, vaulting the steps in front of the Victorian building she'd once thought of as safe, as home, in one leap. She ran as quickly as she could, turning the way she'd just come, headed to Tobin's neighborhood.

*

When Tobin answered the door, Rachel could clearly see he was surprised to find her standing there on his doorstep, shaking, mascara running down her face, looking like a rabid raccoon. Before he could say a word, everything poured out of her. She told him about the pies, the merits, what they thought was a glitch, and coming home to find her dad, her best friend, lying across the white linoleum he'd installed himself as a gift to her mother, his body disfigured and discarded on the ground like a piece of trash.

Tobin let her speak. He stepped from the doorway, closed the front door behind him, and led her to the porch steps where they sat, her quaking hand in his. Rachel couldn't stop the tears from cascading down her face. She couldn't think about anything but how calm her mother had seemed standing over a dead body, and how proud she'd been that *her daughter* would do the same someday.

"Tobin," Rachel began, her voice quaking and a thin line of snot tracing its way down her face, "we have to leave. We have to fucking get out of here. Now."

Tobin didn't hide his surprise. He looked down at this emotionally destroyed girl he'd come to care so much for in a matter of days and wanted only to protect her from everything. Tobin wished he could take the memories and the pain from her, but all he could do was take *her* from the memories and pain. And in that instant, he decided that's exactly what he would do.

"Okay," he said calmly.

"What about your mom?"

"She didn't even come home for dinner tonight. An extra shift or a date, I don't even remember. She made sure to lecture me about my merit and then rushed off the phone. We can go. She'll be better off, and I can't stay in this fucked up city anymore. What your mother did…" Tobin stopped himself, not wanting to tear open that wound again. Rachel had just stopped crying. "Look, let me grab a few things, and we'll go. We'll get the hell out of here and go to the compound. If it's not there, we'll fuckin' start our own. Do you have anything with you?"

"No. I just ran." The realization suddenly dawned on Rachel that she'd left in one outfit, without clothes or a jacket, only her watch and phone in her pocket.

"It's fine. I'll pack extra. Why don't you grab us some food from the kitchen, whatever you want. There's a cooler on the fridge." Tobin turned and opened the door, running up the stairs to his room as Rachel went to the kitchen.

They made quick work. He packed two duffels of clothes and toiletries and she filled the cooler with the dinner Tobin had made and the fixings for sandwiches and loads of snacks. It would be like the road trips Rachel's dad used to reminisce about.

Within fifteen minutes, Tobin was turning on the hybrid car and reversing out of the driveway. As they turned onto the highway, neither looked back. The radio droned on softly, men saying the New East had crossed some line. Neither Tobin nor Rachel listened. They rode silently, nervously, his hand in hers for a couple of hours down the mostly empty highway.

As they passed a sign telling them they had another 200 miles to go until they reached the area of Tobin's rumored outpost, a rumbling sound echoed out from behind them, slowly crawling into their hearing, and then picking up speed. A crashing boom of steel on steel and the tearing of rocks from the ground surrounded the car, invading the enclosed space where they'd been cocooned, feeling safe, as Rachel was forced to shield her eyes from the brightest light she'd ever seen, stronger than a thousand suns, forcing its way into her vision even after she'd closed her eyes and covered them with her hands.

The car jolted from side to side as Tobin pulled off the road blindly. As quickly as it had come over them, the brightness faded, and Rachel turned to face the city they'd left hundreds of miles behind. It was a ruin, of that she was sure. The massive cloud of dust and debris and split atoms that rose miles into the sky was proof of that.

"Oh my God," Rachel said, shock overtaking her again.

"We have to get our chips out, now," Tobin said, frantic, reaching for a hunting knife he'd stowed in his pants.

"What? Why?"

"Rachel someone just blew up our entire city. We could have been there. We *should* have been there," he said, as he dug the knife into his arm, wiggling it around as blood spewed from the wound. "If we get our chips out now and we destroy them, everyone will think we *were* there. They'll think we're dead. Nobody will come looking for us." As he said this, he pulled the chip from his arm. He opened the car door, threw the chip on the ground and smashed it with his foot.

"Now you," he said, handing her the knife.

"You do it. I can't," Rachel replied, pushing the knife back toward Tobin. Without saying a word, he softly sliced where her chip remained. She faced away and tried not to think about the blood, or about her now dead mother, and all her friends... everyone she'd ever known.

"Okay," Tobin said, his fingers removing her chip. He tossed it beside his and stamped on it as well. He exited the vehicle and stomped and crunched both chips until nothing remained. He sat back in the driver's seat and a smile came over his face. "Rachel, we're free. Nobody knows we left. The city is destroyed. Our chips will be registered as destroyed along with the blast. Nobody will ever take us back there. We are free!"

"Thank God," Rachel laughed. "I can't believe it! We're free! We're free!

"We're fucking free! Now let's get out of here and to the compound. Let's start a new life, one together," Tobin kissed Rachel strongly and pulled the car back onto the road. The radio was silent as they drove the next 200 miles in blissful, hopeful excited silence. They were going to make it, and they'd never be a part of Six Degrees again.

*

As they pulled off the highway and onto a gravel back road, Tobin and Rachel's smiles still hadn't left their faces. The car moved forward at a slower pace, the rocks jostling them from side to side, when the radio suddenly produced static. Tobin and Rachel jumped in surprise and looked at the station readout in the center console. A voice soon spilled forth from it.

"Citizens of the United States, we have been attacked by the New East. Rest assured, we will respond with force the likes of which they have never seen. We have suffered many casualties, and we are aware that many of your chips are malfunctioning. Do not panic. As your all-seeing Grand Counselor, I have made accommodations for such an event. As I am speaking to you now, your back-up chips, connected to your Vagus Nerve at the back of your neck are being activated. You will be reconnected to Six Degrees of Separation momentarily.

"Those of you with malfunctioning chips will find yourselves back to normal. Those of you foolish enough to have removed your original chips at any time will also be reconnected and found. We are one great unit, and all citizens must rise to meet this challenge. You may return of your own accord, as I am a forgiving leader, or you may be found and brought in. I would recommend you return.

"Have faith, my people. For this struggle has just begun, and we will be victorious as we are the righteous."

As their vehicle slowly came to a halt, the vibration of crunching gravel suddenly mingled with the sound of two familiar pings echoing from the watches Tobin and Rachel still wore.

THE UNVEILING

Cody Higgins

The unveiling came in forms, as most such things do, that she could not possibly have imagined: like a serpent in the night, resting in the darkness of the dusk of an otherwise festive day; though, of course, who ever said snake bites aren't festive? Both champions and tragedies being reason enough to celebrate. And, in fact, many of our most cherished moments stem in the darkness of pain and suffering, same as the birth of our children, through the pain and suffering of their exact ability to exist.

There was a deep, heavy silence that soaked up the sounds of the telephone ringing next to her bed, sounds smothered as they took breath like flames erupting and instantly quenched by water, its purity laughing with the affluence lingering off clean white teeth. The ring, like a choked gasp, startled her senses as it dragged her immediately from sleep, sleep left waiting, like death, like it always is, while she nearly frantically grasped and fumbled with the receiver.

"Hello?"

And that's all it took. Sometimes it is all it takes. Something so simply seductive shackling the rest of our lives as a seemingly serendipitous salutation: *hello*. Life being like that. Taking its toll in ways spawned from moments we wouldn't even notice. Every now and then seeing while looking back. Mary could see while looking back. She knew that moment she answered the phone it would change her life, but only knew such because she had already begun living it.

199

Maybe that wasn't enough to stop from saying "hello" again some other day. Letting life take yet another turn.

That night, in the specific type of dark where those types of rings screamingly jingle from ringers... the voice on the other end of the receiver mumbled words Mary could hardly understand. Or, looking back, maybe the voice had enunciated every syllable perfectly, and it was only her understanding that became mumbled.

"I'm sorry," she crooked out through more forced than tired voice, "come again?"

"There's been an accident."

They carried on, in that voice on the other end sort of way, telling Mary that her husband, John, had very likely been killed in a car wreck, only less than two hours ago. Eighty-eight minutes to be precise. A number that for some reason burned itself into her consciousness. Maybe we grip onto spaces of logic inside the moments of chaos. The trivialities through our tragedies become the narrative. Because though we can't make sense of them still, they pretend at being concrete for us, like a path below our shaky feet.

Mary told the voice she would have to find a sitter for their daughter (oh God their daughter) before she could come down to identify the body. And hesitantly ended the call. Even then, a sense of finality. Not wanting to put the receiver down, she sat there in the dark, on the edge of her bed, of their bed, hers and John's, holding the phone in silence but for the *beep. beep. beep. beep.* of the dial tone. Not wanting to hang up. Wishing she had never said hello.

Beserel lay sleeping in her bed as Mary looked on from the open doorway, having eventually hung up the phone, having eventually got up off the bed. Grandma would come and watch her. While Mary... killed the cat in the box. She imagined holding the box. Maybe there was movement in it. But maybe that was just her mind playing tricks on her. Seemed hard to argue that reality was anything beyond that. Human consciousness getting its dirty little fingers so deeply into the pie. And it's all just our minds playing tricks. What does that make of the pie? So she tossed the box into a wood chipper. Cardboard mangled and spit out in a blood red mist. But if she never went down to the hospital. If she never answered that phone. If she had never said hello.

But, she had said hello. And the rest, we all know, is inevitable at that point. So the box goes into the wood chipper. Cat and all.

The doors to the waiting room opened with a gliding ease. No wonder why healthcare was so damn expensive, Mary thought as she walked into the brightly lit box. Made her feel like a cat with expensive luxuries waiting for someone to verify her existence. She was there to verify that John had seemingly driven off the side of the road (how could he have been so careless? John? her John?). But who was there to verify whether or not Mary had lived through the news? Maybe this was Beserel's story after all. How she found her mother dead in the bathroom sopping wet from slit wrists and tears. Maybe all of us are just waiting for someone else to tell us we're dead; cats in a box waiting to be let out.

Mary was slightly more than slightly disappointed that the hospital waiting room for the mortuary was so... normal. Comfortable seating. Carpet that was designed more intricately than it had to be. There were no strange noises or hushed screams from dimly lit hallways with endless corridors. No flickering lights or attendees with blood-stained lab coats shuffling around. It was as mundane as any medical building she'd ever been in. Which under normal circumstances was maybe appropriate. But this wasn't normal circumstances. This wasn't mundane. Was it?

Was the death of our love mundane? Was coming to verify that, "Yes, doctor, that's him," mundane? Maybe it was meant to be. Maybe we all died and it didn't matter. Just another day at work. Just another cup of burnt coffee, the fumes seeping through the doors that slide open too often. Just another waiting room. Maybe that's what made it beautiful, having to imagine the flickering lights, having to pretend there's monsters behind the doors.

He lived his life like a tourist of his own existence; always only passing through. John had begun to feel that way even with Mary. That slow aching disconnect that you can't put a finger on. It taunts round the spine, making muscles and joints heavy with the weight of being alone. Alone in a crowded room. He laughed. The sound instantly eaten up by the silence of his car interior, like injured rabbits in a fox den. More evidence of loneliness isolated.

There was something in John that knew he was only passing through with Mary, or would be, from the moment they met. Still silenced. Still alone. She'd pretend to listen, and she would do so well for some time, but eventually it would become obvious, just like all pretense. And that isolation would creep in. Did creep in.

Sometimes he felt like a stranger to everyone he knew. Sometimes, even, he felt like a stranger to his own skin. Someone seen across a crowded room. And we fall in love. We move in together. Have children.

We build romances and tragedies. Betray them only seconds before or after they've already lain their cards out showing their own rotten hand. We break each other's hearts, in that casual glancing instant across the room, when we realize what strangers we are, and that the beautiful lassie drawing us through the crowd towards our tragic nature is really only a stranger herself, living inside a mirror skin reflecting ourselves back at us.

"If we're all mirrors," John tried to laugh again but the car wouldn't let him as it bolted down the highway, "why do I have such a hard time being seen?"

He felt silly for feeling the way he did. Which didn't change at all even under such examination. Which in turn made him feel even worse: most of the time. Surely he was too old to be so terrified of how everyone else seemed to look right through him. Wasn't he?

Or was it reversed? Maybe our age is little more than a compounding of all the life we failed to live, failed to be heard, failed to be seen. With age we learn what John always knew; no one is paying attention.

The car subtly pulled John ever so slightly towards the yellow center-line, dividing worlds as he thought of the last conversation he and Mary had had.

"It's hard cause it feels so important to me." His voice was so defeated. Something that was sadness a long long time ago, and now only sounded like sadness grown tired.

"It is important." She meant it. But it was still hard to believe her. "It's important to you. And it's important to me. Others will come around."

"Is there time for that? Is there time for them to come around?" He watched her eyes, knowing she didn't have the answer, knowing there may not be one. "You know what scares me most?" he whispered out to her as though the devil himself were listening in, "I used to be scared of monsters and murderers, of the dark, you know, of the closet and under the bed. Even as a grown man. Standing in the bathroom with the lights out was difficult on my nerves. That tingling on your skin when your foot is dangling over the edge of the bed late at night. But now… now I stand in the dark and dare things to come out of the shadows for me… because," voice quivering in that way she both loved and hated, "…because I'm fucking terrified that *this* is it for me. The beginning and the end."

"It's never the end John."

"For who? For them? Maybe the world can be saved. But what about me?"

He could almost feel her hand reaching out for his as fingers tightened around the steering wheel, same as sitting at the kitchen table. Same as comfort that we all know is a lie but still absolutely need. More lies we needed than not. Though truth was what got all the glory.

It was all the same.

It was all the same and so he let go of the wheel.

It was all the same.

Mary cried when they showed her the photograph. It was John. Of course it was. They knew it was. This was just a formality you see. A fitting end for life. The formality of paperwork. She sobbed. Sobbed for John and sobbed for Beserel. Sobbed for herself. And some part of her was sobbing, she knew, for the world. It couldn't have known what transpired that night as tire lost grip on gravel and John's car careened off the road, not for cleaning, though… maybe in a way.

The photo was pushed back across the table; its particles dragged against the smooth surface. Mary could see in their eyes that they had expected she might keep it. She watched them. Maybe she was supposed to share it on social media with friends and family. How they'd pay attention to that, she thought, and fell once again into a pool of tears that felt like razor blades.

"This is what desperation looks like," she managed out through guffaw like yelps of sadness to no one in particular.

They acted like they knew; like they had heard it all before. And that was why her John lay dead on a cold steel tray somewhere in the bowels of this place. Though that was something they couldn't possibly understand.

Beserel was upset, tears filling large brown eyes, before her mother even got the words out. A heavy sadness fills the air of such spaces for everyone. Her being seven made things no less obvious. Mom was sad, very sad. And Dad wasn't here. This alone was enough to set her young nerves on edge.

The words tumbled fast from Mom's mouth as though they had to be rushed. Maybe if Mom didn't let the words tumble out like that, she wouldn't have been able to say them at all. "Like a band-aid," she cooed out.

"What honey?"

"Daddy's gone quick," heavy tears for such a small thing, "like a band-aid," she said again, this time loud, though trembling for it so much more, and both Beserel and Mary collapsed into sadness.

That night Beserel dreamt awful things for her strained, grieving mind. Terrible... awful things.

Darkness twisted and turned through her room that night. It played games with whispered screams and creeks under the bed, and while seeping out from below the edge of her closet door. There *are* monsters under the bed, demons in the closet, always, for all of us. Their forms take whatever shape you need them to be. For Beserel, that night, it was her father.

The shadows of the night grew a deep red out of the darkness, pulling meat from the earth below and through the grain of the wooden floor. John, or what can be called John, would form from this mist, as it brightened up its hue from dark slowly to brighter and brighter red. Guts and viscera dragged across the floor through the small room as the darkness continued to play its games, spreading John a bit here, a bit there, a bit everywhere, as he transformed back into life.

Beserel stirred from the sounds of blood covered bones dancing along the floor carried in a rustling bustling symphony of shadow and darkness games of tag. She rubbed her eyes, tired and sore from all the crying just hours before. How many hours she couldn't be sure. Floating in that space where it could have been minutes, though it could have been years, and either way one wouldn't be surprised. And as she rubbed her tired eyes, it seemed as though she had rubbed some sort of tinted glasses onto her face. Because surely something was making her room glow with such brilliance.

Something danced around, leaving more of the illuminated trail behind it while moving to and fro. An energized waltz it seemed to be. Though just as Beserel began to feel the swing of the music of bones she realized what the illumination was; the gore dripping in delicately violently oafish patterns all along every surface in her room. She looked down at her hands, seeing the very same brilliant brightly lit red, and began to scream.

The dancing shape scurried into Beserel's closet, the door swinging partway shut behind it, but not completely, and silenced immediately. Though the little girl's screams continued for a bit. The after-effect of the life that happens to us, not lived, but pressed down upon by some other force. Her screams were a metaphor for the fear that controlled her in that moment, same as the actions of our very existence in everyday life. That desperate plea. The requirement that we analyze our lives. That was Beserel's screams: the analysis of the life she just lived through. And as she quieted, and understood, the bleeding waltzing shape crawled its way along the floor and out of the closet, glowing bright red like the kaleidoscope patterns in the room, and headed straight towards Beserel in her bed. It felt horrible, but comforting, all in one. She couldn't have screamed even if she wanted to, which she wasn't sure of.

It got closer quickly, and in a flash it grabbed her tightly by wrists, squeezing like vices. Tension trying tenaciously to bust bones. But not just so. The waltzing shape whispered to her as it sprouted heavy thick threads of blood from would be fingertips into her veins, and pumped something into her tracks, "He that overcometh shall not be hurt of the second death." She felt as though a bucket filling up with the gore of a slaughterhouse as this waltzing shape lifted her up with it and, continuing to pump her veins full of the second death, danced around the room together. He told her he was her father, "It's me Beserel," but something in that felt like more blood growing from the mist rising up through the floorboards.

Mary heard screams coming from Beserel's room with bright tonalities as though she were lying in bed right next to her. The chaos of such terror always happening in exactly the same way; all of a sudden. She shot up like an arrow and rushed into her daughter's room. Her body jerked backwards as... she could have sworn... there was bright red blood splattered all over the room, but in the same jerking movement she reached terrified hand out to flip light switch, and the room was... the room.

Only thing out of the ordinary being Beserel sitting up on her bed crying, her little body rocking back and forth, as she mumbled out over and over, "I know thy works, and where thou dwellest; I know thy works, and where thou dwellest; I know thy works, and where thou dwellest;" Mary rushed to her daughter and pulled her in close, wishing she could pull her right out of this cruel world.

"You're okay sweetheart... You're okay."

Beserel cried into her mother, "I wet myself," she croaked out, "I'm sorry."

The two got cleaned up, had some hot tea and toast thick with butter, and let the settled calm of the night ease both their fears before laying down together in Mary's bed. Like the hours after a good acid trip: a normal quiet night felt soothingly familiar compared to what they both had just been through, each knowing it had only been temporary, and a reality of the unreality variety. Right?

Though Mary didn't sleep for even a moment the rest of that night. An unease, even in the calming now quiet, that tumbled in her belly, keeping her eyes wide open as the minutes ticked by one by one. There was something in the world she could no longer recognize. Death had washed away the veil that she lived behind. And it wasn't what was behind it that unsettled her world. It was the idea of what was behind *that*, itself, which now terrified her.

That night had been so long ago. Mary remembered it distinctly. The day after was when she found out she was pregnant with Manny. Everything changed over that one night, now almost four years ago. How could it not stick to her gums like maggots looking for bits of damp food? How could it not stick in her brain like steam screaming from teapot? She searched her memories in the sunshine of that day after, trying desperately to remember when she and John had last slept together. And then, same as now, she could not remember. Couldn't remember his skin touching against hers. Couldn't hear his breath caressing her neck as he held her close, voice but sneaking out, a prisoner in the night. Too often passion caged up even while running wild. Tamed madness. Tamed us.

She tried to shake it from her head as eyes fell instinctively on Manny playing with toys in the center of the living room rug. The designs on the rug always seemed to move to Mary's eyes. Subtly tempting her to believe it. Maybe that's what all belief was, just a dare between cursory glances of the universe as it was, only passing through; a dare for us to believe. Manny was directly dead center of the rug. How did he manage to do that? His eyes purposely drifting up to meet hers, long enough for the both to pull their faces into a smile, before looking back down to what he was doing. He always managed to be the center point of things.

Manny's hair was a light brown. The type of brown that would fall as nearly black when he was grown, and that would blacken, even, till he was a man. When did babies become men? Mary wondered. Wondered with the nostalgia of a mom who already knew the answers to such questions, though who would never speak out loud. Not all truths were meant to be. Some may argue more aren't than are. Same who'd argue more aren't than are for people as well. More of us are not. Which begs the question who of us is? Who of us are?

John was. Mary squinted into the memory of the thought of his name, and Manny felt her skin quiver beneath the expression from across the room. Sometimes we quit thinking our thoughts and only remember them; feel them like a day smelled in the air from long ago when our loves weren't yet dead. Or at least they hadn't yet told us. Manny liked something about the way Mom missed moments manipulated morphologically by memories mauling emotions that no longer had a progressing narrative perpetuating her own grasp of existence. But only because he didn't believe in progressive reality. As a three-year-old, the idea wouldn't have made any sense. Children allowed to live inside of the moment they exist in.

What future did Manny have to die through? What regrets had he fallen in love with? What did he think *yesterday* meant?

What *did* yesterday mean (Mary tried to smile at her baby boy as he turned gaze back towards her), except no more tomorrows?

Just then Beserel came out from her room. Hair bounced behind her like a symphony conductor. She rushed over and elegantly scooped (or tried, he had grown so much) up Manny into a hug, his legs working instantaneously to wrap round her waist and help hold his toddler-sized weight snug against his big sister's frame. They looked like each other. Mary always thought so. Though not at all like her, or John, for that matter.

Beserel could always feel Manny searching her heart when she had him tightly in her arms. What was he looking for? When was he looking for? And, more importantly, what was it he found there? Were our hearts the metaphorical hub of what we were at our core? Like portrayed in all the romantic words we'd scrawled all over the universe? The heart. The self. Or was it only the hunk of meat as motor that pumped us along when nightmare fathers were too absent to fill our veins with fuel for fragmented figments of finality flailing under children's frowns?

She remembered best, of her father, that waltzing bleedy shape. But surely he was part of what kept her heart beating.

And maybe that was what Immanuel had always been searching for; his father in Beserel's heart. Sometimes what he might find in his searchings scared her. Though his eyes, when she looked down to him, reassured her of any of those fears. Manny giggled up at his big sister, and she almost forgot to be afraid that the memories of her father, held deep in her blood red heart, might frighten her invigilating baby brother, making him believe things that were not real.

All, that which was our lives, believing in things that were not real. An individual reality that mandated no universal. Except that of the fear that always seemed to creep back in, no matter how comforted away in the temporary. Was there any comforts that weren't temporary? Should there be?

Late that night Mary sat up in bed reading under the gentle gaze of her side table light. There was a mystery about how different lights could change the entire atmosphere of a room. The core self of what it felt like in that space could be controlled completely. Our perspective in the world the same. Like a light on; we illuminate the world in our own very specific ways, changing not just how but also what we see.

Noises like rustling hands through the silverware drawer subtly subverted Mary's attention from the narrative she was attempting to follow. Existence just a hodgepodge of intersecting narratives vying for attention. It continued, and Mary lowered the book while raising her eyes in the direction of the gently ajar door to her bedroom. The light she read by cast a dim red hue over the scene that danced in rhythm with the raindrops carelessly falling outside. Everything lining up together. Maybe what she heard was just some part of that symphony. So many instruments. But yet, it made her worry about Manny. He was such an odd little boy. His gaze made her uncomfortable. The gaze not of a child, a little boy, but something so much more than that. Eyes that soaked into her as though daring her defend herself. Nothing in particular. Just self. Just Mary. Though she imagined all who met his sight felt the same. It was just the looking of her little boy. This embarrassed her when out in public. The guilt rising up in her, inevitably, afterwards, at being embarrassed by her precious son simply looking at other people.

But surely they felt it too?

Mary swung her legs over the edge of the bed, thinking of John and his used to be fears of what was hiding underneath, in the dark, quietly breathing in cobwebs waiting for tired flesh to give way to its hungry claws. Her weight shifted and she stood up, feet welcomed by the soft touch of freshly cut grass. The nature of her world both surprising and calming. A certain tension floated into Mary's blood flowing through her body, up into feet from grass on floor, circulating through the rest of her. She felt an ineffable fear overcoming her senses, and though she wanted to jump back into bed, pull up the covers, and force eyes to sleep through the night; she began walking towards the hallway as if controlled by an unseen puppeteer hovering over the rain clouds above her in the sky. If Mary concentrated hard enough, she could even feel the bits of rain falling on her bare skin, splashing, in other spots, against nightgown that lovingly hugged the curvature of her body.

What was happening here? Where was she? Surely she hadn't left her bedroom, her house, her home… but… but this place was so recently unfamiliar.

Attention twisted round right as she reached the door ajar. A groan eked out from underneath bed. Mary turned to see. She didn't want to, but want had little to do with anything here, if it had ever before. Our desires nothing more than distractions so we don't have to need to be. Life was a choice, like a carnival ride. Crawling out from beneath the bed, a sweet trail of blood dripping down grass tips, each like bristles on a brush painting a canvas to redefine the world, Mary could see John's hand. She knew it was him as she let out a suffocated scream at his goreish shape. It was more than senses could handle, and, turning quickly like dream state fast forward, she rushed out of the room.

Behind her she could her the door click closed and muffle the anguished screams that John, or the shape passing itself off as John, continuously let loose from its rotten lips. A barrier of paper thin once upon a time skin. But Mary had bigger concerns than what surely was a guilt-ridden hallucination.

The clatter she heard was now so much more distinct. Definitely coming from down the hall, round the corner, and out of the bathroom. Feet carried Mary along the same soft grass as met her touch as she stepped away from her bed only moments ago. Green but for the trails of blood. Mary didn't pay them any mind.

When she came to the end of the hallway, there was a certain conclusion in her skin. The door was closed. Music seemed to play happily from behind the cheap wood as Mary reached out shaking hand to turn the knob.

The inside of the bathroom was barely lit. Dimmer, and darker than the hues thus far; the shadowed darkness fell down on more grass covered floor. Such consistency forced Mary to think of it as the ground more so than the floor. And standing there, in the slightly higher than the rest grass, back facing her, was little Manny.

"Manny, honey, you scared Mommy." Her voice trembled with fear. She could see into the mirror, just over Manny's shoulder in the darkness of the bathroom. Manny made no motion. A low rumbling trumpeting pulsating from where he stood. "Immanuel, did you hear me?" Such subtle anger under her fear.

He began to turn round. Slowly. Mechanically. Inhuman. His neck rose up, his face pulled forward into the shape of a trumpet, skin stretched tightly over the instrumentation, and from the mouth of the horn came a great and terrible booming voice, a trumpeting of eons, **"and I will kill her children with death,"** it burst into the atmosphere, **"I am Alpha and Omega, the beginning and the end. I know thy works, and where thou dwellest."**

She had heard those words before, hadn't she? So hard to concentrate on anything outside the trumpeting. Her baby boy a mutated, sickly darkened mass of skin that became brighter as it reached over his horn as face, till its cup shone brightly like golden rays reflecting off glass. "Manny please," Mary screamed out as she stepped backwards away from the scene. But nothing could be heard over the rumbling of clarity.

The overwhelming nature of brushing away the façade. She could see the future.

Legs gave way and Mary's body collapsed into the still soft grass that lay below her, almost as though it anticipated her fall all along. She let it caress her skin as trumpeting fell to a hush. The gentle pit-pat of Manny's feet replacing the madness, and just as she thought her blood would catch fire from anticipation inside her veins, the boy stepped out from the bathroom doorway.

His face had gone back to a form she recognized. Grass having burned away leaving cold wood floor below her. He walked up to her, same as he had done thousands of times, drenching little arms around his mother's neck. But she had seen. She knew what he was.

Write the things which thou hast seen, and the things which are, and the things which shall be hereafter.

Mary sat at the edge of Manny's bed, having, reluctantly, conceded to his wishes to be tucked in after she managed to calm her breathing there in the bathroom hallway. He was such a sweet boy. Always smiling. But there was always that... that... something else. Something below. And now, now he was something else entirely.

What about the world? What about, oh God, what about her Beserel? Hers and John's Beserel? It all had to be ended. Did it? The moment of judgement come. But what about when it's come and gone? And what right did He have anyway? What right did He have at all?

"My Manny," Mary so quietly sobbed out, tears thudding against her face and chest the loudest part of the drama. It had to be quiet. She knew that as she looked over to Beserel sleeping soundly in her bed. Though Beserel was in her own room, Mary felt as though she could see her there, on the other side of Manny's. A sleeping innocence that begged to be saved. It all begged to be saved. Like bits of memories from our childhood, and how those bits shift to new spaces as we age further and further, ourselves, in turn, being of the beggars. "I'm sorry," words like sounds in the rain, "but I can't let you."

The pillow felt so coldly familiar in Mary's hands. She had held it so many times before. Something so simple, that carried with it so many memories of its own. It always seemed like you couldn't suffocate someone with a pillow, the way they do in the movies. And at first that seemed true here, for Mary. Manny's little body made no hint at change. No resistance. But

212

then, like a lazy electrical charge waking up early Monday morning, there was a jolt through her baby boy. Subtle but there. Followed by another. Followed by another.

Then like prepubescent fire in a dry field; Manny exploded with violent resistance. He squirmed and fought, hands grabbing at any of his mother he could reach. Already so short of breath as to keep silent; nothing could be heard but legs kicking against bed and hands hitting body. Well that and Mary's sobbed pleas for forgiveness.

Manny was so much stronger than she could ever have imagined. But eventually, sooner rather than later, his body gave in and went limp. Mary held down firmly on him for some time longer. It felt like an eternity. Maybe that's what she deserved for her act, for her decision. It's all a choice... like a carnival ride.

Door creaked open only stopping against its own hinge as Beserel stood just inside her little brother's room. Mom was stooped over the boy's cold form, holding a pillow wet with tears tightly over his face. Neither moved. Mary slowly looked up to meet her daughter's gaze. It had been such a hard life. Maybe Mary could have done this better. She could have taken her time with the decision. Could have planned out her choice. Avoided this confrontation of reality for Beserel. That was what all our moments were. It was the pleasure and the pain we experienced in this world. It was all our happiness and each of our sadnesses.

A confrontation of reality.

It made us bleed and made us cum. And everything in-between. Though, if we are being most honest; people had no interest in the in-between. A place we barely even knew. A place we pretended wasn't there far more than not. Once in a while it forced itself upon us. But those were memories we easily forgot.

This was not a memory Beserel would easily forget. And maybe she shouldn't. The extremes of our sacrifices in giving birth. Sometimes life looked a whole lot like death. Sometimes we have to do terrible things to save the world. Mary smiled. It was like the death of new life. Like being a parent for the first time. Though she frowned at the loss. And knew she could never live with it. Having lost John. And now her Manny. And in a different, and maybe worst way of all, Beserel. Each of them living their own apocalypse. Each of them dying it as well.

Mary never took her eyes away. "He said," she pleaded with her sweet Beserel, "he said he was the end."

MARK OF THE BEAST

Richard Raven

Brother David Samples, pastor at Antioch Baptist Church, was deeply puzzled as he stood in a small storage room directly behind the altar. The source of his puzzlement was a door set in the back wall of the storage room. A door he had always known about but could never open. He had always assumed it was either locked or frozen shut in its frame and had never given it or what lay beyond it much thought in the year he had been pastor.

Now he was wondering about it; the door was cracked open.

How very odd.

To his further surprise he discovered the door provided access to a set of old and wooden steps that led down to a cellar directly beneath the floor of the chapel. There was nothing to see except raw dirt at his feet, several support beams spaced at even intervals, and what looked like a pile of discarded lumber at the far end of the chamber opposite the stairs. The lumber, no doubt, left over from some work that had been done. Possibly by one of the previous pastors, which puzzled Brother Samples even more.

What work was done? Why had this work not involved the steps, which were in dire need of repair or replacement? More to the point, what was the purpose of the cellar and why was there nothing about it in the records left by his predecessors?

Since no one had ever mentioned it to him, he believed none of his flock knew of the cellar; he vowed to keep it that way. This was soon after the one and only time he explored the

215

dark and dank chamber by flashlight. The steps were clearly dangerous to anyone who dared to tread upon them. Especially mischievous children in search of adventure. It was a genuine concern... but Brother Samples had another reason for keeping the steps and cellar off limits. A reason he would never divulge to any of his flock for fear he would appear as a man of God who had lost his faith. Something he would often question himself during the second and last year of his service as pastor.

The reason was that the cellar frightened him badly.

While there was no outward sign of anything sinister... something about that cellar was so threatening and oppressive that it left him feeling as if he was in the presence of evil itself. Even after he had fled back up the steps, even after the construction crew he hired had sealed off the door and paneled over it so that it blended with the rest of the wall, the feeling never left him. It preyed on his mind to the point that he would often remain at the church, sometimes well into the night, praying for strength and guidance. It quickly became a burden that began to exact a terrible toll on the man and his health, which wasn't the best to begin with.

Yet the feeling and crushing weight remained, his prayers unanswered.

It was in the last days of his tenure that he began hearing noises: soft and furtive echoes; faint and stealthy sounds of scratching and clawing. It all seemed to emanate from down in the old cellar. Only he heard these sounds and only at night when he was alone in the church. It became a nightly occurrence; each of those nights he prayed with renewed vigor and conviction... but still there was no answer.

Had his God, the God he had served to the best of his abilities, forsaken him?

It was on a Wednesday night, long after the end of the evening's service as he prayed on his knees at the altar, that he felt the floor beneath him moving slightly as if the chapel, perhaps the entire church was... shifting? This stopped after only a few seconds; then there was a loud and reverberating crash of splintering wood, followed immediately by an unholy shriek that froze the breath in his lungs. It had all come from the storage room.

"My God and Savior," he croaked, hurrying as best he could on weak and trembling legs out of the chapel and down a short corridor to the storage room. There was a heaviness in his chest, his breathing more labored than it should have been.

He drew up at the door to the storage room, suddenly and keenly aware of the malevolence awaiting him on the other side of it. The urge seized him to flee, but he couldn't do that. This was his church and his flock; he had to face the evil. Whatever it turned out to be.

Lord, I pray to thee to forgive me of my sins…

He pushed open the door and fumbled for the light switch.

…and to protect me in this, my darkest hour of need.

Where the old door had been walled over was a gaping hole… and standing amid the wreckage, it's body heaving…

The second demon that will rise from the earth! Brother Samples, paralyzed by fear and the first stirrings of pain, could only stand there and watch as the abomination moved with deliberate purpose toward him.

"Where is thy God… holy man?"

Piercing pain erupted in his chest. Brother Samples collapsed to his knees, grasping his chest and gasping for breath as gnarled hands reached for him.

*

About twenty minutes after clocking out for the day, Mary Younger exited the office complex where she worked. She pushed through the double-glass doors, her cell pressed to her ear. Usually, she was in a rush to leave the office and get home, but not today. She was approaching her car, fumbling in her purse for her key fob to unlock the door, when she noticed, off in the distance toward downtown, four separate plumes of dense black smoke rising into the sky. Then she noticed the sky itself.

The forecasters had said it would be sunny and cool with a light breeze and it was a pleasant morning when she first arrived at work. So what had happened? There wasn't a breath of air stirring, the afternoon unseasonably warm, and the sky

217

had scudded over with a heavy overcast the color of an old battleship.

They certainly missed it today.

"So, how are you enjoying your newfound freedom?"

The question drew her attention back to her call; she had to laugh at the words from Meg Tyler, one of her closest friends. "Well, I would hardly call it freedom," she replied, though she had wondered, even dreaded what it would be like when the last of her two fledglings left the nest several days before to start college. "I still have my job—not to mention Charles, who can be quite the handful."

"A little time to yourselves for a change will be good for both of you," Meg said.

Mary agreed that it would be good for her and her husband of twenty-plus years. A chance for them to slow down a bit and, hopefully, reconnect again. Not that there were simmering problems lurking within the marriage. It was just that they had raised two kids, both led busy lives, and Mary had felt for a while that they were drifting apart. Charles had agreed and declared he was as anxious as she to rekindle the spark.

"Maybe now you and Charles will be able to attend church more often," Meg added.

She made it sound like a casual observation, but to Mary it sounded more like her friend was broaching a subject very much on her mind, and Mary believed she knew why.

In truth, neither Mary or Charles had ever been regular church attendees. The day before was the first Sunday morning worship service they had attended in weeks and they could never make time for the Wednesday night service. It was Charles, about six months ago when he met and developed a friendship with Brother David Samples, who suggested they start attending Antioch Baptist. "A way for us to at least spend part of one day out of the week together," he had said. Mary had agreed it sound like an idea worth trying and had never regretted her decision.

Not until now.

"Perhaps," Mary replied. She got into her car and asked, slowly and carefully, "Meg, what do you think of the new pastor?"

A long pause, and Mary knew she had been right. Finally, "Between you and me," Meg said, "I don't care much for the man. He's certainly no Brother Samples."

"No, he's not," Mary agreed. Brother Samples was a soft-spoken man, who had sprinkled his religious messages with equal amounts of common sense and practical ideas that Mary found inspiring without feeling brow-beaten.

"I'm going to miss Brother Samples," Meg was saying. "Strange, though, that there was no warning that he was leaving. Then again, with the way he was going down there at the end, maybe not so strange at all. I do hope he's doing okay."

Mary shared her friend's concern and was equally puzzled by his abrupt departure. It was even more puzzling to her how the new pastor had just shown up, offering little in the way of explanation beyond that Brother Samples had decided to take some much-needed time off and had selected him to serve in the interim.

"But this new man," Meg was saying. "I mean, even his name—Lucien Tombs?—is eerie when you think about it."

Mary, herself, had found the man's name rather strange—and that was only one thing she had found disconcerting about the man. "Was I the only one to think the way he has of looking you straight in the eye was a little creepy?"

"No, you weren't the only one. Several times I left like he was singling me out and chastising me with his eyes right in front of everyone. I heard several women, including Judy and Dawn, whispering about it."

Judy Haines was a mutual friend, but Mary didn't know Dawn Mitchell as well as Meg did. One of the youngest women in the congregation at twenty-three, Dawn Mitchell was pregnant—very close to the end of her term—and unmarried, her spineless boyfriend having run out on her when he heard the news. The young woman was clearly nervous the day she showed up at her first service with Meg and her husband, but Brother Samples had welcomed her with open arms.

Brother Tombs, on the other hand, given the fiery fervor with which he approached his religion, wasn't as welcoming. Mary had seen the way the man had stared down from the pulpit at the unwed mother-to-be with clear and undisguised contempt.

"To be honest," Mary said, "if Lucien Tombs is confirmed as the new pastor, then Charles and me will likely be looking for another church."

"Can't say I blame you. Frankly, I doubt he'll be confirmed, but if he is, me and Jim will likely be looking for another place ourselves. If I can convince Jim to do it, that is. For some reason, he seems to think a lot of this new man."

So did Charles, Mary reflected. While it was all she could do not to squirm on the pew under the man's withering stare, Charles had seemed completely mesmerized by the man. Even after the service, as everyone mingled and visited outside the church, Charles and Meg's husband and several of the men were grouped around Brother Tombs, each of them clearly hanging on the man's every word.

"In fact," Meg was saying, "Jim's supposed to be on his way over to the church to help with some moving and lifting the man needed done."

"So is Charles," Mary said. "He said he would likely be late getting home, so that means I'll have the house all to myself for a time." While not a prospect that displeased Mary, she was puzzled by the summons for help with moving and lifting. It was like Lucien Tombs was moving right in and making himself at home before being confirmed as pastor.

"And just how are you going to spend this free time?" Meg asked, her voice teasing.

"As soon as I get home, get these clothes and these heels off, I'm going to give this body of mine a long, hot soak." *How long has it been since I had the time or the chance to do something like that for myself?*

"That does sound nice, and I may do the same thing later on tonight. Right now, I think I'll head over to Dawn's apartment and check on her. She's so close to her time and all and, frankly, she's scared to death."

The call ended shortly after that. Mary started the car's engine and pulled out of the parking lot. She expected to catch the worst of the evening rush… but traffic was strangely light. A quick check of her watch and the private and expectant smile playing on her lips gave way to a puzzled frown. *Surely, everyone hasn't made it home already.* Then her expression changed again to one of faint worry when she stopped at a red light and glanced at the sky through the windshield.

Definitely looks like we're in for some nasty weather.

Then she noticed that there was at least two more plumes of black, each in a different part of town and far removed from the other four that were still belching smoke into the sky.

Six fires at the same time? That's certainly odd.

The light turned green, and she thought no more about it.

Only seconds after she cleared the intersection, the green light blinked several times, then went out.

*

By the time she reached home, her smile had returned and there was nothing on her mind beyond a tub of hot water. She hurried inside without so much as a glance at the sky, stripped off her clothes in the master bedroom, then padded naked into the bathroom. Her few remaining cares melted away and she lost herself and all track of time as she lowered herself into the steaming and scented water's embrace.

She was still reclined luxuriously in the tub, her eyes closed and a contented smile on her face, when she heard the chirp of her cell in her purse in the bedroom. But it didn't compel her to leave the almost sinful pleasure of the tub. Probably only Charles, calling to say he was on his way home. *So I better enjoy this as long as I can.*

It wasn't until the ground line started ringing in the kitchen, and only seconds after her cell had stopped, that Mary opened her eyes. No one ever called the ground line unless it was something important and the caller couldn't reach either she or Charles on their cells. *Charles? One of the kids?*

Mary had climbed out of the tub and was reaching for a towel, when the phone stopped ringing as the message service answered the call.

Only seconds later the phone began ringing again. Concern now blooming in her belly, and not even bothering to wrap herself in the towel, Mary hurried into the kitchen.

"*Mary?*" Meg greeted, her voice a fearful hiss in Mary's ear.

Mary remembered that Meg was going over to Dawn Mitchell's apartment. *Has she gone into labor?* "Meg, what is it? Is it Dawn?"

"They took her!" was the reply, her friend now sounding near the point of panic.

"Dawn? Who took her? Where are you?" Alarmed, Mary fired off the questions with barely a pause between them.

"At Dawn's apartment, locked in the bathroom!"

Oh, my God. "Meg, who took her?" Mary could now barely control her own voice.

"Jim and Judy's husband and a couple of others! They busted down the door and two of them grabbed Dawn before either of us could even scream!"

What? "Are you sure Jim was one of them?" To say nothing of Judy Haines' man.

"*Yes*, I'm sure! Jim and Alfred Haines grabbed for me as the other two dragged Dawn out the door!" There was a choking sob from Meg, then she added, "It scared me so badly that all I could think of was to get away from them. So, I locked myself in here."

It was then that Mary heard a dull pounding sound in her ear... a sound that hadn't been there before. "Is that them beating on the door?"

"*Yes!* I can't hear Dawn screaming anymore—and now they've come back for me!" Meg was now sobbing uncontrollably. "There's something wrong with them... they're all bloody... and their eyes... my God!"

"Meg, call 911!" *What in the name of God is going on over there?* "Do it now."

"I tried, but the call wouldn't go through!" There was a loud crash in Mary's ear, then Meg screamed, a sound that chilled Mary to the bone. Then, "Jim, *No!*" Meg wailed in a voice beyond hysterical. "What are you doing? Jim, please, don't—"

Then there was only silence in Mary's ear. She yelled Meg's name several times, but there was no sound or reply. So

222

frightened now that she could hardly breathe, she tried to get the dial tone back so she could call 911.

But the dial tone never returned, the receiver dead in her hand.

Mary simply dropped the receiver without hanging it up and ran for the bedroom. Now verging on panic herself, she quickly found clothes to put on. She pulled on panties and was reaching for her bra on the bed when…

…there was a smashing crash from the living room that seemed to shake the entire house. The front door? Mary managed to stifle the scream that rose up from her throat. She had yet to recover from the jarring surprise when she heard the pound of running feet.

Seconds later, Charles burst into the bedroom… and a hideous sight he was. Again, it was all Mary could do to keep from screaming.

"Jesus, are you okay?" she blurted. There were splatters of blood all over him, his face and white button-down shirt covered with it. On his blood smeared lips was a twisted and leering kind of smirk, and his eyes…

…they're all bloody…and their eyes…my God!

…as black and lifeless as the eyes of a corpse. Instead of going to him, Mary backed warily away from her husband. He followed her slowly, step for step.

"I believe you said something about reconnecting?" he growled in a way Mary had never heard from him. She backed into the bed, her feet suddenly going out from under her and her legs splaying open as she sprawled flat on her back. She barely had time to blink before he was on her, his body wedged between her spread legs, his weight pinning her to the bed; one hand clamped around her throat. She gasped as he twisted one of her nipples painfully with his free hand. "If you mean some good old nasty fucking, like we used to do before the heathens came, then count me in." He rose up from her just enough to get his free hand between her legs.

"What is wrong with you?" she screeched, not quite able to suppress the doubt that this blood splattered man, who was roughly fondling and pinching her through her panties in a way

223

Charles never had, was really the man she had married. "Stop that, damn you, you're hurting me!"

He laughed, and it was an ugly sound. "Woman, you ain't felt nothing yet," he said, his hand now under her panties and moving even more sadistically. "Always wanted to fuck you in the ass, so guess what's coming?"

She was squirming, trying to get away from him as he leaned his bloody and dead-eyed face closer to hers... and it was then that she saw his forehead clearly. Despite the brutal way he was thrusting his fingers into both her orifices, her struggles ceased under him, her mouth hung open in shock.

The numbers 666 were crudely cut into the flesh of his forehead and still seeping blood. A spark of what might have been life appeared in his otherwise dead eyes and he withdrew his hand from under her panties.

"See the mark, do you?" he said in that awful hissing voice that wasn't his. "That reminds me that I must give you the mark." A hideous grin spread across his bloody face as his free hand reached for a pocket and withdrew a small knife, the blade extended. "Right hand or forehead? Your choice... then we can have some real fun."

"Get that away from me!" Mary screamed, again struggling beneath him as tears of fear and confusion streamed down her face.

"You refuse the mark?" he growled.

"I refuse to let you cut me with that!"

His hideous grin vanished, the expression now fixed on her one of wrath and pure hatred. "Then, bitch, you'll suffer like the rest who refuse the mark and like you've never suffered in your life."

With that he pushed up and away from her. She tried to roll away from him, still trying to fight him, but he was possessed with such incredible strength that she was no match for him. With relative ease he subdued and bound her with ripped pieces of her clothing from the bed. Then, still clad in nothing but her panties, he hoisted her up on one shoulder and carried her out of the house and toward his SUV parked in the driveway.

He strapped Mary into the passenger seat and drove with one hand, the other with the knife pressed to her bare thigh. She feared the slightest tremble from her or bump in the road would mean her leg and femoral artery would be sliced wide open. Yet even that couldn't prevent her from staring in horror at all the sights that met her eyes within minutes after leaving the house.

My God...what is happening? Did all this *begin while I was in the tub?*

The sky had been angry and threatening when she left the office; now it was as black as a nightmare. Almost as dark as night itself and from the blackness it was raining fire. It was impossible to count all the homes and buildings and wrecked or abandoned vehicles that were burning. Impossible to look away from the bodies or pieces of bodies that littered the streets and sidewalks. At times the black and acrid smoke from all the fires was so thick that she wondered how Charles could even see how to drive through the carnage.

Yet not everything was in flames. A few of the vehicles and structures remained untouched. There were even live people. A lot of them, in fact, and mostly all naked and bloody and all of them killing and butchering and fornicating in a grisly tableau that both horrified and sickened Mary. One naked woman was laughing hysterically as she pounded the face of another naked woman to bloody pulp with a baseball bat, the fire falling all around them like drops of napalm. On a street corner, in plain view, two men and a woman were rutting like wild animals on top of a pile of severed arms and legs.

Charles never said a word to her as he steered around burning vehicles and piles of the dead and hordes of those still alive and in the throes of mindless savagery or writhing in obscene ecstasy.

Armageddon. The very thing Lucien Tombs had preached so emphatically only the morning before. But what had sparked all this?

A question Mary could only ponder helplessly as she wondered what fate awaited her. She wondered about her children; about Dawn Mitchell and her unborn child… Meg Tyler and Judy Haines. She silently prayed they were all safe, but she feared the worst for them. She feared it because she had seen the worst.

Or so she believed at the time…

*

She felt she had endured an eternity of the obscene and grotesque when she finally spied the towering steeple of Antioch Baptist Church. Miraculously, the church looked intact and unmarked by the flaming rain that continued to fall. Even as Charles pulled off the street and into the church's parking lot, Mary wondered why he had brought her here, to a house of worship. Then she wondered about the number of vehicles already there, many of which she easily recognized, and all of them untouched by the flaming rain.

Still without saying a word, Charles pulled her struggling and screaming out of the passenger seat, across the console and out through the driver's side door. Again, he hoisted her up on his shoulder and started toward the church. More frightened than she had ever been, her hands and feet having long since gone numb, she could do little more than scream in terror.

The only light inside the church was from what seemed like hundreds of candles. Once beyond the chapel, she realized that Charles was heading for a storage room located behind the back wall of the altar. He entered the room and carried her toward a gaping hole in the wall opposite the entrance. She realized the hole had once been a doorway that had been covered over. She could now hear many voices; they all seemed to come from beyond the hole in the wall and from down below. Another room? A cellar? Through the hole in the wall she could now see more flickers of dancing candlelight.

Charles carried her down a set of old and groaning wooden steps she never knew existed. Once they were down the steps, he simply heaved her off his shoulder and flung her to the ground. The candle flames and press of bodies made it hot in the cellar, the dirt cool against her skin. It took her a long moment to get her breath back from the jarring impact with the ground and to take in the many and horrible sights and sounds that greeted her.

Not the least of which was an ungodly figure surrounded by a group of men and women, many of them naked, who all knelt before it. Looking at the curved horns sprouting from the goat-like head and its blazing red eyes, Mary could only assume it was some kind of demon. The figure moved away from those kneeling on the ground and toward her and Charles, who had dropped to his knees as soon as the red eyes rested on him.

"Without the mark, I see," the demon said in a grating voice that, strangely, struck a familiar chord with Mary. Where had she heard it before?

"No, she refused it," Charles murmured, head bowed.

"Shame," the horned beast intoned. "Watching her yesterday, playing with the hem of her dress, I could think of little else beyond ripping that dress off her and fucking her where she sat and hearing her scream."

It was then that Mary placed the voice. *Lucien Tombs... my God.* Or, rather, what had been Lucien Tombs only yesterday. Now he was naked, his body covered with tuffs of fur in places and what looked like scales in others. A massive penis swung like a pendulum between thick and muscled legs when the demon moved.

"She's not worthy," Charles said, head still bowed. "I beg you, just throw her ass in the pit with the so-called man of God and let them both roast in the flames."

It was then that Mary saw the pit Charles referred to at the far end of the cellar and the crudely built wooden cross that thrust up out of the hole.

And the bloody and naked man nailed to it. Mary gasped.

Brother Samples. Mary was trembling uncontrollably, tears streaming down her cheeks; unable to tear her eyes away the crucified man.

"An excellent suggestion," said the red-eyed demon that was Lucien Tombs. "But first, she's going to witness what I've brought you all here to see."

With that, he moved back toward the group of kneeling men and women, some of whom were already scrambling out of his path. Mary saw several faces in the candlelight; many of the faces she knew, including Judy Haines and her husband, their foreheads and those of all gathered with them bloody in the candlelight from the mark carved into their flesh. When enough had moved aside, Mary saw what the press of bodies had concealed.

Dawn Mitchell lay gagged and naked and spread-eagle on the ground, several of the men holding her down. Blood dripping from the men covered her body; her own sweat gave her distended belly a faint shimmer in the candlelight. Her eyes were wild with terror.

My God... what are they going to do to her?

The demon stepped between the hapless woman's legs. In one gnarled hand it held a long and gleaming dagger. The demon was grinning down at Dawn.

"The Fallen Angel, as so many call him, was denied this and cast down here to earth as punishment. But I will not be denied this chance to honor and serve Him."

There was a blinding flash of light and a blast of searing heat. Mary had to avert her face as the roar of flames filled her ears. Through squinted eyes, she glanced toward the source of light and heat.

She screamed, the wooden cross and the crucified body of Brother Samples engulfed in flames. The stench of burning flesh that hit her nose made her gag.

Good Lord, this place is going to burn to the ground!

Then a glint caught in the corner of her eye and she looked back at the struggling figure of Dawn Mitchell; at the men holding her and the demon brandishing the dagger. The flames glinted on the shiny steel of the blade as the demon lowered the razor-tip to Dawn's swollen belly.

"Lord, *No*!" she screamed. "Not that!" She was bound so tightly that she could do little more than roll in the dirt like a turtle on its back.

The knife in the hoary hand dipped, pierced and sliced savagely.

Dawn Mitchell screamed; even through the gag in her mouth it was the worst thing Mary had ever heard, and it only grew worse when the demon reached with its free hand inside the gaping slash in the writhing woman's belly. Even as the demon's hand rooted around, as if searching for what it sought, Mary noticed Judy Haines.

Her friend looked enraptured as she gazed at the slaughter taking place, one hand stroking her erect nipples, the other working feverishly between her legs. A few of the men in the group, including her husband, were watching her, clearing enjoying what she was doing. Most, however, were staring transfixed at the demon.

It was standing at its full height now and holding by one leg a bloody baby still attached to the umbilical cord. The baby was still and silent. The demon slashed at cord, cutting it, then raised the baby high into the air, as if brandishing a trophy.

"Gather close, children of the beast, and partake of the flesh," the demon intoned, bringing the child to its mouth. It bit into one of the tiny arms, twisting it free with a shake of its head. Then it passed what remained of the child to eagerly reaching hands.

Mary, her stomach churning and feeling faint, realized that the flames had reached the floor of the chapel above their heads. She could feel the heat. She could also feel the eyes of the demon. It still had the child's arm in its hand, its mouth working as it chewed.

Finally, it swallowed and said, "Deal with her," to her husband, pointing at the burning cross and body with the child's arm. "And as you suggested."

Mary had barely registered the demon's decree when Charles and another man were dragging her toward the burning cross. Mary writhed and twisted to no avail. The two men halted some distance from the flaming pit; the fire was so intense that Mary could already feel her skin starting to blister. The two men seemed not to feel the heat at all.

"Would have loved to fuck that ass," her husband drawled. "But too late now."

Then the two men heaved her toward the licking flames as if she was no heavier than a pillow. Mary screamed as the flames and heat enveloped her.

Then she was falling, tumbling head over heels, through what seemed like a sea of flames. The heat quickly seared her lungs, and she could no longer scream. There was a blackness gathering in her mind, her agony receding. Receding. Then...

*

...as if an unseen hand had grabbed her, she no longer had the sense of falling; no longer felt she was burning. In a blur of movement and sudden flashes of light, she felt as if she was being pulled up. And up. Then...

"The pain is no more, child, so open your eyes."

Trembling violently, Mary realized she was sitting on what felt like the ground, and she recognized the soft, soothing voice. Her eyes cracked open and she stared up into the solemn face of Brother Samples. He was holding a hand out to her. Mary stared at his hand, not sure what to make of this. All she was sure about was that she was sitting there in nothing but her panties, and the man before her was completely naked.

"No need to look ashamed, for we all come into this world naked," the figure of Brother Samples said. "Come now, we must hurry and escape this place."

Mary got to her feet with the help of the offered hand. Hopelessly bewildered, she stared, first at Brother Samples, then at all the others gathered with him. There seemed to be hundreds of men, women and children, and of all colors. None of them that she could see bore the bloody mark on their foreheads or their right hands. She saw her friend, Meg Tyler... and there was Dawn Mitchell, sobbing quietly.

Mary could only shake her head. "I-I...d-don't understand."

"You didn't survive," Brother Samples said. "None of us survived. But God has not forsaken us, and He will not let this pass. We must hurry to a place of safety and await the Seven Angels, each of whom will have one of the Bowls of His Wrath. Once the Angels have done the Father's bidding, He will welcome us home... of this He has assured me. So, come, we must go and gather other lost souls we encounter along the way."

"But," Mary began, hesitated, then said, "My children."

"They will be fine. This conflagration will not reach them. They will mourn the loss of their parents, but they will survive."

With that, still clutching Mary's hand, the former pastor of Antioch Baptist Church started walking toward a distant stand of trees. He led his new flock away from the smoke and flames. Away from the screams of agony, the peals of insane laughter, and the obscene cries of depraved rapture.

No one among the group looked back, their eyes all focused on the line of trees.

OUTPOURING

Jeff Strand

"What's that on your back?" asked Sophie.

"I don't know," said Caleb. "Be more specific."

"It's gross. I'm not going to spoon you unless you put on a shirt."

"So tell me what it is. I can't see my own back."

"Can't you feel it?"

"If I could feel it, I'd know what the hell you were talking about. Is it back hair? Is it a mole? Did I roll over on the wet spot?"

"Don't be crude."

"You're the one saying I've got something disgusting on my back. Why are you making me play a guessing game? Is it a zit? Is it a rash? Is it a patch of mold?"

Sophie had many positive qualities that balanced out her unpleasant pre-coffee demeanor. Few of them were personality-based, but she was fantastic in bed and considerate enough not to sleep at his place on nights when she didn't want to have sex. Caleb wasn't going to marry her and there was no evidence that she'd ask them to move in together, so it had overall been a very pleasant couple of months.

"It's a sore."

"Okay. I've got a sore on my back. Sorry to make you want to puke."

"I don't want to *puke*," said Sophie. "I just don't want that nasty thing pressing against my stomach. I can't believe you can't feel it."

232

Caleb sat up and reached behind his back. He couldn't feel anything. "Where is it?"

"Higher. To the left. My left. Lower."

"So in that spot on my back I can't reach?"

"Yeah."

"I'll go look in the mirror."

"Do you want me to take a picture?" Sophie asked.

"Are you going to post it on Instagram?"

"Yes. With a funny filter. No, of course not. It'll be easier than you trying to look at your back in the mirror of your medicine cabinet."

Sophie had made it clear that she was unimpressed by the size and quantity of mirrors in his apartment. When you looked like her, he supposed you wanted as many mirrors available as possible. If she was secretly having thoughts about moving in with him, he hoped the mirror situation was one extra bit of disincentive. He didn't want anybody sharing his apartment except his goldfish.

She picked her cell phone up off the bed stand and took a picture. A moment later Caleb's cell phone buzzed. He grabbed it and looked at the picture she'd sent him.

Yeah, it was a sore. And yeah, it was pretty gross—red with yellow around the edge. The picture didn't have any scale, so he couldn't tell how big it was.

"Ugh," he said. "I can see why you didn't want to press your boobs against it."

"Stomach."

"Whatever."

"How did you get that?"

"I don't know. How do people get sores?"

Sophie raised an eyebrow.

"I mean, how do people get sores on their backs? I must've chafed it or something. It's no big deal. I'll put some cream on it and it'll go away." He reached behind his back again. "Of course, I can't reach it, so I guess you'll have to put the cream on it."

"Ugh," said Sophie. "Where do you keep it?"

"I was kidding. I wouldn't ask you to smear anything on my deformity."

"No, no, I'm your girlfriend, I'll do it." She got out of bed and walked toward the bathroom. "Is it in the medicine cabinet?"

"I don't know if I actually have any," Caleb said. He didn't like how quickly—if reluctantly—she'd offered to perform this task. When you were comfortable enough as a couple to apply topical creams to each other's sores, you were getting too close.

"I'll look." Sophie walked into the bathroom. Caleb also didn't like that she was comfortable enough to go through the contents of his medicine cabinet. What if he had embarrassing prescriptions in there? At least he had, in fact, thrown away the box of condoms after they decided they trusted each other enough to go without using them. He'd dumped many girlfriends, but he'd never cheated on one.

He hoped she didn't find anything. The more he thought about it, the less he wanted her to touch his sore. Disregarding the "getting too comfortable" part, there was the "ick" factor, where the beautiful naked woman in his apartment would be thinking about that unsavory duty when it was time to get frisky.

She emerged from the bathroom a couple of minutes later. "All I could find was Vaseline," she said. "You'll have to get some today."

"I'll pick some up on my way to work," Caleb said. "You won't have to rub it on."

"Thank you."

He glanced over at the clock. They had about fifteen minutes before they had to start getting ready, but this didn't seem like a good time to initiate anything romantic. They showered, got dressed, gave each other a kiss, fed the fish, and left.

*

Caleb didn't think it was a good idea to ask a co-worker to put cream on his back, even in jest. So he got a plastic spoon from the break room, went into the bathroom, took off his shirt in a stall, squeezed a generous amount of cream onto the convex side of the spoon, and awkwardly applied it that way. He also used the spoon to help get a bandage over it. If he could get an extra eight hours of healing time in, he'd be eight hours closer to not grossing out his girlfriend.

By mid-morning, the sore started to hurt.

By late morning, the sore started to *really* hurt.

By lunchtime, it hurt so much that he wanted to tell his boss he was sick and go home for the day. But the office had a PTO program, which meant that his sick days came out of the same pool as his vacation days, and he didn't want to squander a precious vacation day by sitting at home whining about how much his back hurt. So he toughed it out, even though it was hard to focus, and he'd have to review his numbers when he came in tomorrow morning.

As he drove home, he wondered if he should go to the doctor.

Nah. Not for a sore on his back. It was probably just being chaffed by the bandage and his shirt. After he got home, took a shower, and left it uncovered for a while it would be fine.

As soon as he walked into his apartment, he carefully removed his shirt and the bandage. It really wasn't difficult to see in his bathroom mirror: the sore was about the size of a quarter, and deep red with yellow streaks. And it smelled awful. He'd never smelled a limb covered with gangrene, but this was the kind of scent he imagined it would have.

He turned on the shower and took off the rest of his clothes. No need to panic. He'd sleep on his stomach tonight, and if he needed to call in sick tomorrow to give it more time to heal uncovered, he would. He'd be fine.

Caleb stepped into the shower. The warm water against his back created such an intense sting of pain that he cried out. He shut off the water and just stood in the bathtub, trying not to cry. It took several minutes for the sting to fade from excruciating agony to the normal agony from before.

"Hello!" Sophie called out from the living room as she walked into the apartment. He'd been privately reluctant to give her a key but now he was glad to see her.

"I'm in here!"

She walked into the bathroom and looked surprised to see him standing naked and wet in the bathtub. "You okay?"

Caleb shook his head. "The thing on my back is worse. You wouldn't believe how much it hurts."

"Let me see."

Caleb turned around.

"Oh," said Sophie. "Oh, shit. That's... that's... that's not pretty."

"It's way worse, isn't it?"

"Yeah. It needs to be popped."

"I don't want you to pop it."

"And I don't want to pop it. But unless you can get at it yourself, it's either have me do it or I take you to the emergency room. What kind of cream did you put on it?"

"Just normal stuff."

"It smells awful."

"I think that's the sore, not the cream."

"Okay, if that smell is coming from something on your body, then yeah, you should probably go to the hospital."

One thing that Caleb feared more than long-term commitment was the hospital. He didn't want doctors hacking at him with scalpels. "All right. You can pop it."

"I wasn't asking to do that."

"What I mean is that I'd like you to pop it."

Sophie took a deep breath, as if gathering her courage. "Lie face down on the bed. Do you have rubber gloves?"

"No. Should I go out and get some?"

"That's okay, I'll just... touch it."

Caleb lay naked on the bed. Sophie sat next to him. Caleb no longer cared about her being repulsed—he just wanted the pain to stop.

"You probably want to push your face into a pillow," Sophie suggested.

Caleb pulled his pillow over and shoved his face tightly against it. He braced himself for the pain, but the sore hurt so much already that the process of having it popped might not add much additional discomfort.

This theory was incorrect.

The pillow had been an excellent idea, although the pain was so extreme that Caleb thought he might pass out, which would cut down on his screaming.

Sophie kept squeezing for about ten seconds. Finally she stopped.

"Are you done?" Caleb asked, the words muffled through the pillow.

"No," she said. "There's so much pus you wouldn't even believe it."

Caleb began to weep.

And then he screamed again as she resumed the process.

This time it felt like it went on for eleven or twelve seconds before Sophie stopped.

"It just won't quit squirting out!" she said. "I don't even know where it's all coming from! It's like there's this unlimited reservoir of pus underneath it!" She made a gagging sound. "Are you doing okay?"

"No."

"I'll keep going. This is *horrible*, Caleb. If I put it on YouTube people would think it was CGI."

"Please don't record it."

"I'm not. Are you ready?"

"No."

"Should I stop?"

"No."

Sophie squeezed again. Caleb was not getting used to the pain. He almost suggested that she make things easier for both of them and simply smother him with his pillow, but no, he wasn't quite suicidal yet. Waves of pain went through his arms and legs. He could feel this in his frickin' *teeth*.

"I swear, this is a portal to an alternate dimension that's nothing but pus!" said Sophie. "How can there be this much? When does it stop?"

Caleb had no answers to these questions and wasn't sure he still had the ability to form words with which to provide answers even if he had them.

This time he was pretty sure she squeezed for six or seven hours, even though the reasonable part of his brain—which was shrinking by the moment—knew it was probably the same ten-to-twelve seconds as before.

"I think I finally got it all," she said.

"Are you sure?"

"Not completely sure, but it seems to just be blood now. Back in a second. Don't move."

Caleb just lay there, feeling drained and miserable. He thought he could hear water running in the bathroom, although his ears were ringing so loudly that he might've been mistaken. At least the pain did indeed seem to be fading.

Sophie returned and ran a wet rag across his back.

"Stay where you are," she said. "I need to rinse it off and wipe some more."

She repeated the process. Caleb was definitely feeling better. Enough that he was able to consider that Sophie would probably never have sexual intercourse with him again, although not enough for him to care.

"All done," she said.

Caleb rolled over and sat up. "Thank you."

"That was truly horrific."

"I'm sorry. I appreciate you going through that for me."

"I'd strongly recommend going to the doctor. That wasn't normal."

Caleb nodded. "I'll do that." Then he grimaced as he became aware of the smell. It was even worse than before, like he'd been rotting from the inside. "I'm going to spray some Lysol and then take a shower. Did you want to stay for dinner?"

"I don't think I'll be eating anything tonight."

"That's reasonable."

"I'll stick around to make sure you're okay, though."

Caleb thanked her and went into the bathroom. He decided not to look at the sore in the mirror. The shower felt fantastic, even when he turned around and let the water spray directly on his back, and after he dried off and got dressed he felt like a functional human being again. He hoped the memory of this event wasn't burned into Sophie's mind.

He frowned as they walked into the living room. "What the hell...?"

All of his goldfish were floating at the top of the aquarium. The water was pink.

He took a closer look. Lefty, Righty, Northy, Southy, Easty, and Westy were all dead. They'd been fine this morning. What could possibly have happened?

"Why's the water bloody?" Sophie asked.

"I don't know." Caleb didn't see any chunks missing from any of the fish. Somehow the water had gotten contaminated. Yeah, the sore on his back stunk, but that wasn't anything that could impact water inside of an aquarium. It was just a strange, disturbing coincidence.

Sophie slapped her hand over her mouth and plopped down onto his couch.

"You okay?" Caleb asked.

Sophie shook her head.

"I know it's bizarre," said Caleb, "but there has to be a logical explanation."

"There is," said Sophie. "I understand what's going on now."

"What?"

"How familiar are you with the Book of Revelation?"

"Is that a Bible thing?"

"Yes."

"Then not very."

"Seven angels had seven bowls of God's wrath. They poured them out on the wicked."

"So you're saying that an angel poured a bowl of God's wrath into the aquarium and killed my fish?"

"No. I'm saying that when the angels poured out the bowls, terrible things happened. *So the first angel went and poured out his bowl on the earth, and harmful and painful sores came upon the people who bore the mark of the beast and worshiped its image.*"

"You can quote Bible verses?" Caleb asked.

"Some of them, yeah."

"I didn't know that."

"I didn't want to scare you away."

"The second angel poured out his bowl into the sea, and it became like the blood of a corpse, and every living thing died that was in the sea."

"The Book of Revelation is kind of morbid," Caleb noted.

"You're not taking this seriously."

"I shouldn't be, right? I mean, I assume you're joking, even though I guess I can suddenly tell from your expression that you aren't joking at all. You have to admit that this connection is a bit of a stretch. I don't bear the mark of the beast."

"I wouldn't know. I haven't looked."

"I assure you that I do not have '666' on my head, sweetie."

"We'd have to shave your head to know for sure."

"Well, we aren't going to shave my head. And I don't worship the beast's image."

"What about that?" asked Sophie, pointing to one of the posters on the wall.

"Alice Cooper? He's not the beast."

"You don't know that."

"He's a born-again Christian!"

"He's wearing scary makeup and he's got a boa constrictor around his neck. Looks more like Satan than Jesus to me."

"I don't worship him."

"Have you ever danced to his music?"

"Yeah."

"Maybe dance is a form of worship."

"Look, Sophie, I get that you're traumatized from all the pus. But the sore on my back was not because of some rerun of Bible stuff."

Sophie got up, strode across the room, and tapped on the aquarium glass. "How do you explain this?"

"I don't know. But it's not like the blood of a corpse. It's just a little pink. What was the quote again?"

"The second angel poured out his bowl into the sea, and it became like the blood of a corpse, and every living thing died that was in the sea."

"So can we at least agree that the scope here is a bit smaller? Every living thing in the sea isn't quite the same as six goldfish."

Sophie nodded. "It's a smaller scale apocalypse. I didn't say it was across the entire world. Unless..." She hurried to the coffee table, picked up the remote control, and turned on the television. She began to flip through the stations.

"What are you looking for?" Caleb asked.

"What do you think I'm looking for? A report that the seas have turned to blood and killed everything in them."

"That would certainly be the top news story."

Sophie glared at him. "Fuck you."

"Whoa!" They'd had arguments, sure, but Sophie had never cursed at him like that before. "There was no reason for that."

Sophie stopped on CNN, which was not discussing the seas of the world transforming into blood. Nor were MSNBC, Fox News, or the BBC. It was safe enough to assume that this phenomenon was limited to Caleb's aquarium. Sophie shut off the television and placed the remote control back on the coffee table.

"I apologize for my language," she said. "But you shouldn't make fun of me. This is serious business. There are seven bowls."

"What happens if the angels pour out the others?"

"*The third angel poured out his bowl into the rivers and the springs of water, and they became blood.*"

"Okay, so more bloody water. That's definitely a problem for people who don't like to drink blood. And then?"

"*The fourth angel poured out his bowl on the sun, and it was allowed to scorch people with fire.*"

"Something else we'd want to avoid for sure," Caleb admitted.

"*The fifth angel poured out his bowl on the throne of the beast, and its kingdom was plunged into darkness.* This one goes on to say that *people gnawed their tongues in anguish.*"

"We definitely don't want everybody chewing off their tongues," said Caleb. Sophie gave him a grim nod, apparently so frightened that she was unaware that he was still kind of making fun of her.

"The sixth angel poured out his bowl on the great river Euphrates, and its water was dried up, to prepare the way for the kings from the east. And I saw, coming out of the mouth of the dragon and out of the mouth of the beast and out of the mouth of the false prophet, three unclean spirits like frogs. For they are demonic spirits, performing signs, who go abroad to the kings of the whole world, to assemble them for battle on the great day of God the Almighty. "Behold, I am coming like a thief! Blessed is the one who stays awake, keeping his garments on, that he may not go about naked and be seen exposed!" And they assembled them at the place that in Hebrew is called Armageddon."

"Say what?" asked Caleb.

"The sixth angel poured—"

"No, I heard you. That one's just kind of baffling. Is the Euphrates River still around? I'm not sure if I should be concerned about it drying up or not. Demon frogs probably aren't something we want around, if I'm interpreting that right. I guess I shouldn't have let you see me naked when you were squeezing my sore. I've got to admit, this one doesn't sound as bad as everybody chewing off their tongues."

Sophie's eyes were wide and she spoke as if not really hearing what she was saying. *"The seventh angel poured out his bowl into the air, and a loud voice came out of the temple, from the throne, saying, 'It is done!' And there were flashes of lightning, rumblings, peals of thunder, and a great earthquake such as there had never been since man was on the earth, so great was that earthquake."*

"Sophie, you're getting kind of creepy. Time to let this go."

"The great city was split into three parts, and the cities of the nations fell, and God remembered Babylon the great, to make her drain the cup of the wine of the fury of his wrath."

"We're done with the revelations now, sweetie. You're freaking me out."

"And every island fled away, and no mountains were to be found. And great hailstones, about one hundred pounds each,

fell from heaven on people; and they cursed God for the plague of the hail, because the plague was so severe."

"I said stop!" Caleb shouted. He hadn't meant to shout. But he needed her to stop talking.

Sophie blinked. "I'm done now. That's all seven."

"What are you saying? You think hundred-pound hailstones are going to start falling in my apartment?"

"Not if everything is scaled down. But what if you got hit in the head by a ten-pound hailstone? That would still crack open your skull. Even a one-pound hailstone could do some serious damage, especially if you got hit by a few of them."

"Okay, well, I appreciate your concern, but hailstones are not going to start falling in my living room. I'm not worried about any of this. You're looking for an apocalypse where one doesn't exist."

"How do you explain what has happened so far?" Sophie asked.

"I got a sore on my back! People get sores on their backs all the time. If I went on social media right now and did a survey, I'm guessing that just about everybody who follows me on Twitter has gotten a sore on their body at some time in their life."

"But the—"

"Yes, it was a deep well of pus. That doesn't prove anything. How much pus is in the human body at any one time? I don't know. Do you know? You can't tell me you've researched that. It was a gross sore and once again I apologize for you having to interact with it, but we're not reenacting the Book of Revelation!"

"How do you explain the pink water? You can't, can you? Admit it! You can't explain the pink water! Look me in the eyes and tell me that you can explain the pink water!"

"A fish bled! Fish have blood in them! Just because none of them are ripped in half doesn't mean they couldn't have bled into the water."

"Fine," said Sophie. "Believe whatever you want."

"I will. Trust me, I will. What I think is that we should each get some alone time while we sort ourselves out. Because I'm not gonna lie; you still have a creepy expression on your face, and I feel like you could do something upsetting."

"Like what?"

"I don't know. But do you agree that we should call it a night and see each other tomorrow?"

Sophie stood up. "If you say so."

"Go back to your place, order a pizza, relax, and get a good night's sleep. In the morning you'll see how ridiculous this whole thing is."

"All right," said Sophie, walking across the living room.

"Why are you going into the kitchen?" Caleb asked.

"No reason."

"That's not the way out."

"I'm getting a drink. We've been together long enough that I think I can help myself to a drink from your refrigerator."

"Yeah, I mean, obviously that's okay."

Sophie walked into the kitchen.

"Why did you open a drawer?" asked Caleb.

"I didn't."

"I heard it slide open."

"You're mistaken."

"You're by the counter instead of the refrigerator."

Caleb heard the drawer slide closed.

"Please tell me you didn't get a knife," he said.

"I didn't get a knife."

"Say it convincingly."

"Okay, I got a knife," said Sophie, stepping back into the living room. She held a butcher knife. "You get it, right? If I see the beginnings of an apocalypse in the making, it would be irresponsible for me not to try to stop it."

"By stabbing me to death?"

She nodded. "You're the beast worshipper with the sores."

"I need you to calm down," Caleb told her.

"I am calm. Eerily so."

"If you kill me, I promise that you'll decide later that you shouldn't have done it. That's a guarantee. You won't be able to enjoy the world not being in an apocalypse if you're locked away in prison."

"It's not about me."

244

"Right. And your generous, selfless nature is only one of the reasons I fell in love with you. I've told you that I'm in love with you, right?"

"You've said you love me. You haven't said you're in love with me."

"Well, I am. A lot. So there's no reason to keep holding that butcher knife."

"What if the angels are pouring out bowls and killing you is the only way to stop the apocalypse?"

"I really don't think they are," said Caleb. "What I think is that if we sit down and discuss what's happening, we'll find that there's a straightforward, completely logical explanation that satisfies both of us and makes you realize that there's no reason to stab me to death. Also, and I promise I don't mean this in a sexist way, I'm bigger and stronger, so it's entirely possible that I'll be able to take the knife away from you, which leaves us in the awkward position of what to do after you've tried and failed to kill me."

"I could be saving humanity," said Sophie.

"You could also be stabbing an innocent boyfriend."

Sophie looked at him, looked at the aquarium, looked at the butcher knife, looked at him again, and then dropped the knife onto the floor.

"I'm so sorry," she said.

"It's okay," Caleb said, not really meaning it but deciding that now was not the time to be antagonistic.

Sophie picked up the knife and walked back into the kitchen. "That was wrong of me. I don't expect you to forgive me. Honestly, it doesn't matter anyway, because I don't think I could ever get over the sight of all that pus spewing out of your back. It was never going to work out."

"Fair enough."

She went over to the sink, turned on the faucet, and rinsed off the knife.

The water ran red.

"That's... that's not a river," said Caleb. "It said river, right? River!"

Sophie ran at him.

Caleb's comment about being able to get the knife away from her turned out to be incorrect, though he might have been more successful if he'd faced her head-on instead of immediately fleeing. He didn't know if she was specifically aiming for the sore, but that's where she got him, and he fell to the floor.

Getting stabbed there didn't hurt as bad as when Sophie had squeezed it, so that was something, at least.

Also, as she stabbed him in the back over and over, Caleb was surprised to discover that his final thought was a rather selfless *I sure hope she's saving humanity.*

This is only the beginning.

Made in the USA
Monee, IL
01 March 2020

22566299R00148